NEIGHBORS
AND OTHER STORIES

Mrs Caliban
Palace of the Peacock
They
Maud Martha
The Glass Pearls
A Wreath for Udomo
The Shutter of Snow
Termush
The Mountain Lion
Hackenfeller's Ape

NEIGHBORS
AND OTHER STORIES

Diane Oliver

faber

This edition first published in 2024
by Faber & Faber Ltd.
The Bindery, 51 Hatton Garden
London EC1N 8HN

Oliver published four stories in her lifetime and two more posthumously:
"Key to the City" and "Neighbors" first appeared in the *Sewanee Review*
in 1966; "Health Service," "Traffic Jam," and "Mint Juleps Not Served
Here," first appeared in *Negro Digest* in 1965, 1966 and 1967. "The Closet
on the Top Floor" was published in *Southern Writing in the Sixties* in 1966.
"No Brown Sugar in Anybody's Milk," first appeared in the *Paris Review*,
No. 244, Summer 2023.

Typeset by Typo•glyphix, Burton-on-Trent, DE14 3HE
Printed and bound in the UK by CPI Group (UK) Ltd, Croydon, CR0 4YY

A CIP record for this book
is available from the British Library

ISBN 978-0-571-38608-6

MIX
Paper | Supporting
responsible forestry
FSC® C171272

Printed and bound in the UK on FSC® certified paper in line with our continuing
commitment to ethical business practices, sustainability and the environment.

4 6 8 10 9 7 5 3

CONTENTS

FOREWORD
by Tayari Jones

A year ago, I had never heard of the astounding short-story artist Diane Oliver. This admission is embarrassing, as I am a novelist and professor. Furthermore, Oliver and I have a number of shared characteristics. We both are Black, Southern, daughters of educators, graduates of women's colleges, and we both attended the University of Iowa. Born in 1943—the same year as my mother—she was a generation ahead of me, paving the way. Yet, somehow, I had never come across her work, not even at Spelman College where Black women's writing is the core of the English major. Initially, I blamed myself. Why had I not been more diligent as a graduate student? Oliver published four stories in her lifetime, and two posthumously. Her work appeared in *Negro Digest*, *Sewanee Review*, and was reprinted in *Right On!: An Anthology of Black Literature*. In other words, *Neighbors* was hiding in plain sight. After more thinking, I faulted the gatekeepers—whoever they may be—for not including Oliver in the anthologies that form the curriculum of writing programs. But after a while I grew tired of wondering why and chose to celebrate the discovery.

I encountered *Neighbors* in a most unusual manner. I received a copy printed on plain paper, no intriguing cover, no laudatory blurbs from great writers, not even a paragraph from the publisher providing context or summary. I knew only that the author was a Black woman and the manuscript was slated for publication. The bound stack was simply labeled "Neighbors." I could have asked for more information or done a quick Google search. Instead, I recognized the opportunity for what it was: a chance to let the words introduce me to the work of Diane Oliver.

This breathtaking collection of short stories is a marvel. When I was a young writer, I remember receiving this advice from one of my peers: "Imagine that the world as we know it is over. Now imagine the people of the future trying to sort out the wreckage. Well, that's what books are for—to let the new people know what the hell happened." I had almost forgotten that scrap of undergraduate wisdom until I read the first few pages of this book. *Neighbors* evokes the feeling of sorting through a time capsule sealed and buried in the yard of a Southern African Methodist Episcopal church in the early 1960s. The political issues of the day—namely racial integration—permeate the narratives, as this is this most significant social shift since emancipation. Oliver explores the changing America while beautifully documenting the culture of Black Americans living in the South. She remembers the domestic workers who leave their own children home alone to keep house for rich white folks. Boy coats with racoon collars were all the rage for the wealthy, while poor folks took pride that their simple clothes were cleaned and ironed. "Up North" and "Chicago" are both shorthand for a promised land where a person could earn a decent wage and send her children to college. This is Oliver's world, and she shines a light in every corner.

The title story, "Neighbors," stands in stark contrast to the iconic image of six-year-old Ruby Bridges, precious in braids and a pinafore, bravely integrating her elementary school. The little girl is surrounded by federal marshals. The famous photo doesn't show the jeering crowd of adults, nor does it show the child sitting alone in her classroom, since the other parents removed their children in protest. Norman Rockwell recreated the moment in his painting *The Problem We All Live With*, but portrayed the girl against a backdrop of thrown garbage and painted slurs. In her best-known story, Oliver takes us where the news cameras will never go. This is the story of a family the night before their first grader is set to integrate his new school, alone.

When we are able to see the dynamics inside the family's home, the correct path is not obvious. Despite the triumph of *Brown v. Board of Education*, is it morally right to send a child where, at best, he is not wanted? A neighbor muses, "Hope he don't mind being spit on, though." After a sleepless night, the mother says to the father, "He's our child. Whatever we do, we're going to be the cause." And in that moment, the issue at hand is more personal than political. Is there a true distinction between what is best for the race and what is best for their little boy? Whatever decision they make, there is no way that the reader can judge them because Oliver has taken us for an uphill walk in their shoes.

She revisits the subject in "The Closet on the Top Floor." Winifred, a college freshman, is "tired of being the Experiment." Her first day of college marks the thirteenth year of integrating educational institutions. "Her father had worked hard, petitioning the trustees and threatening a court suit to get her into this college, and she had felt ashamed for not wanting to go." Although her parents have the means to keep her in the latest fashions, she never fits in on the campus of the Southern women's college. Isolated, homesick, and racially marginalized, Winifred's mental health begins to deteriorate. As she leaves college, shattered, it is tempting to read this story as a coda to the one begun in "Neighbors," affirming the family's decision not to send little Tommy to the white school. Yet an honest reading causes one to wonder if Winifred is driven mad by the racism of the school or her parents who think civil rights is just a game.

Although *Brown v. Board* was a seismic decision, hobbling "separate but equal," there were many Black folks to whom Winifred's college experience would seem like a high-class problem. These are the women who clean houses, the children who sleep on pallets on the floor, and babies born "afraid to breathe." Oliver's storytelling would be incomplete without their rich emotional landscapes.

"Traffic Jam" centers on Libby, a young mother who works for Mrs. Nelson. Her husband, Hal, is who knows where. In many ways, this story is a retelling, or perhaps an *untelling*, of the Black maid who loves her employer's family as her own. Although the bulk of the story takes place in Mrs. Nelson's kitchen, it is clear that domestic work is a *job* for Libby, not a *calling*. As she prepares breakfast for the Nelsons, she worries about her own baby left in a laundry basket on a babysitter's porch at 6:30 a.m. When she heats soup for their lunch, she thinks of her daughter scavenging for fallen fruits. And overlaying all thoughts is her longing,

anger, and concern for her husband, Hal. She yearns for
him as a lover and partner, but she also desires the security
and respectability of having a husband at home. When she
is reunited with him, the Nelsons could not be further from
her mind.

> She was almost upon him now . . . She wondered for a
> minute what she would say; she had imagined him coming
> home but not at a crazy time like this. Yet, she felt strangely
> sure of herself . . . She kept walking toward him, and even
> this far away she could see the high cheekbones that marked
> all of their children as belonging to him.

When they finally touch, the meeting is sensual, but with
Libby's anger streaking through at his long absence. She is
exhausted and embarrassed at having been driven to steal
slices of ham from a white woman's kitchen to feed her
children. Her husband announces that he bought a car, blue
with new seat covers. Frustrated that he would squander
his savings, she understands that "if she wanted him, she
had to want the car." They go home to resume their marriage. Except for the paper bag of stolen food, the Nelsons
are all but forgotten.

Oliver demonstrates a gorgeously layered understanding
of the range of Black life in the South. She understands the
life of a poor woman traveling miles on foot to take her children to the doctor. She empathizes with a couple who are
driven by racism to live in the forest, and are then gripped
by homicidal rage. She knows why destitute families would
sell everything they own to buy train tickets to the north,

having no idea what awaits them. Yet she can also write the inner life of a doctor's wife, forced to entertain a sullen step-daughter, just as these lives are impacted by the changing racial and social mores.

If Black lives are changing in the wake of segregation, then so are white lives, and Oliver turns her eye to them as well. "Spiders Cry Without Tears" explores an interracial romance in the wake of *Loving v. Virginia*. The heroine, Meg, is a "Kelham lady. All the girls in her family marched in the annual Daughters of the Confederacy Parade, smiling at the groups of Negro children who waved them to the cemetery." Meg, now divorced, falls in love with Walter Davison Carter, a wealthy doctor. Although he may be mistaken for Portuguese or some other tan foreigner, he is definitely Black. Furthermore, he is married to a woman who is terminally ill. Despite the fact that she should be dis-graced only "for her grandmother's sake," the relationship blossoms and endures for years. For Meg, there is a cost for loving across the color line. Learning of the affair, her friends distance themselves due to the mere possibility that "he looks like he's trying, well you know, to pass."

Eventually, Walt's wife passes away, and the couple marry. Meg is completely alienated from her old life, but finds that being Walt's mistress was much more satisfying than being his wife. Oliver chooses not to make their marital conflict a matter of race. "He owned her exactly as he did the house, the cars, and those poor people who thought their hearts would collapse if her husband retreated from medicine."

Oliver shrewdly allows race to dominate Meg's under-standing of the relationship during their courtship. There is even a moment just before their marriage when she berates herself for thinking of him as "colored" after so many years of intimacy. But once they are married, gender becomes a more significant factor than race. She is his wife, who happens to be white. This is what is known as *intersectionality*.

Neighbors is the rare work of fiction that is somehow of its time, yet before it as well.

Recently, an interviewer asked me who did I consider to be my literary foremothers. I listed all of the greats—Zora Neale Hurston, Toni Morrison, Ann Petry—but then I added Diane Oliver. Her name surprised me as much as it surprised the reporter. I have only recently been made aware of Oliver's work, but I feel that her thinking somehow influenced mine. There is a part of me that says that this is impossible, but the part of me that feels the presence of spirits knows that it is possible.

Writing fiction can be an otherworldly experience. Is it not magical and inexplicable that we transform imagination into marks on a page, legible and lasting? I believe that twenty-two-year-old Diane Oliver released these stories into our common air, water, and soil as she inked them onto the pages. Just as we all have ancestors whom we never had the pleasure to meet, we carry their legacies in our bodies. Their memories nest within our own. Their words are our words, whether we know it or not.

Tayari Jones
Atlanta, Georgia, 2023

NEIGHBORS
AND OTHER STORIES

NEIGHBORS

The bus turning the corner of Patterson and Talford Avenue was dull this time of evening. Of the four passengers standing in the rear, she did not recognize any of her friends. Most of the people tucked neatly in the double seats were women, maids and cooks on their way from work or secretaries who had worked late and were riding from the office building at the mill. The cotton mill was out from town, near the house where she worked. She noticed that a few men were riding too. They were obviously just working men, except for one gentleman dressed very neatly in a dark gray suit and carrying what she imagined was a push-button umbrella.

He looked to her as though he usually drove a car to work. She immediately decided that the car probably wouldn't start this morning so he had to catch the bus to and from work. She was standing in the rear of the bus, peering at the passengers, her arms barely reaching the overhead railing, trying not to wobble with every lurch. But every corner the bus turned pushed her head toward a window. And her hair was coming down too, wisps of black curls swung between her eyes. She looked at the people around her. Some of them were white, but most of them were her color. Looking at the passengers at least kept her from thinking of tomorrow. But really she would be glad when it came, then everything would be over.

She took a firmer grip on the green leather seat and wished she had on her glasses. The man with the umbrella was two people ahead of her on the other side of the bus, so she could see him between other people very clearly. She watched as he unfolded the evening newspaper, craning her neck to see what was on the front page. She stood, impatiently trying to read the headlines, when she realized he was staring up at her rather curiously. Biting her lips, she turned her head and stared out of the window until the downtown section was in sight.

She would have to wait until she was home to see if they were in the newspaper again. Sometimes she felt that if another person snapped a picture of them she would burst out screaming. Last Monday reporters were already inside the preschool clinic when she took Tommy for his last polio shot. She didn't understand how anybody could be so heartless to a child. The flashbulb went off right when the needle went in and all the picture showed was Tommy's open mouth.

The bus pulling up to the curb jerked to a stop, startling her and confusing her thoughts. Clutching in her hand the paper bag that contained her uniform, she pushed her way toward the door. By standing in the back of the bus, she was one of the first people to step to the ground. Outside the bus, the evening air felt humid and uncomfortable and her dress kept sticking to her. She looked up and remembered that the weatherman had forecast rain. Just their luck—why, she wondered, would it have to rain on top of everything else?

As she walked along, the main street seemed unnaturally quiet but she decided her imagination was merely

4

playing tricks. Besides, most of the stores had been closed since five o'clock.

She stopped to look at a reversible raincoat in Ivey's window, but although she had a full-time job now, she couldn't keep her mind on clothes. She was about to continue walking when she heard a horn blowing. Looking around, half-scared but also curious, she saw a man beckoning to her in a gray car. He was nobody she knew but since a nicely dressed woman was with him in the front seat, she walked to the car.

"You're Jim Mitchell's girl, aren't you?" he questioned. "You Ellie or the other one?"

She nodded yes, wondering who he was and how much he had been drinking.

"Now honey," he said, leaning over the woman, "you don't know me but your father does and you tell him that if anything happens to that boy of his tomorrow we're ready to set things straight." He looked her straight in the eye and she promised to take home the message.

Just as the man was about to step on the gas, the woman reached out and touched her arm. "You hurry up home, honey, it's about dark out here."

Before she could find out their names, the Chevrolet had disappeared around a corner. Ellie wished someone would magically appear and tell her everything that had happened since August. Then maybe she could figure out what was real and what she had been imagining for the past couple of days.

She walked past the main shopping district up to Tanner's, where Saraline was standing in the window peeling oranges.

Everything in the shop was painted orange and green and Ellie couldn't help thinking that poor Saraline looked out of place. She stopped to wave to her friend, who pointed the knife to her watch and then to her boyfriend standing in the rear of the shop. Ellie nodded that she understood. She knew Sara wanted her to tell her grandfather that she had to work late again. Neither one of them could figure out why he didn't like Charlie. Saraline had finished high school three years ahead of her and it was time for her to be getting married. Ellie watched as her friend stopped peeling the orange long enough to cross her fingers. She nodded again but she was afraid all the crossed fingers in the world wouldn't stop the trouble tomorrow.

She stopped at the traffic light and spoke to a shriveled woman hunched against the side of a building. Scuffing the bottom of her sneakers on the curb she waited for the woman to open her mouth and grin as she usually did. The kids used to bait her to talk, and since she didn't have but one tooth in her whole head they called her Doughnut Puncher. But the woman was still, the way everything else had been all week.

From where Ellie stood, across the street from the Sears and Roebuck parking lot, she could see their house, all of the houses on the single street white people called Welfare Row. Those newspaper men always made her angry. All of their articles showed how rough the people were on their street. And the reporters never said her family wasn't on welfare, the papers always said the family lived on that street. She paused to look across the street at a group of kids pouncing on one rubber ball. There were always

6

white kids around their neighborhood mixed up in the games, but playing with them was almost an unwritten rule. When everybody started going to school nobody played together anymore.

She crossed at the corner, ignoring the cars at the stoplight, and the closer she got to her street the more she realized that the newspaper was right. The houses were ugly, there were not even any trees, just patches of scraggly bushes and grasses. As she cut across the sticky asphalt pavement covered with cars she was conscious of the parking lot floodlights casting a strange glow on her street. She stared from habit at the house on the end of the block and except for the way the paint was peeling they all looked alike to her. Now at twilight the flaking gray paint had a luminous glow and as she walked down the dirt sidewalk she noticed Mr. Paul's pipe smoke added to the hazy atmosphere. Mr. Paul would be sitting in that same spot waiting until Saraline came home. Ellie slowed her pace to speak to the elderly man sitting on the porch.

"Evening, Mr. Paul," she said. Her voice sounded clear and out of place on the vacant street.

"Eh, who's that?" Mr. Paul leaned over the rail. "What you say, girl?"

"How are you?" she hollered louder. "Sara said she'd be late tonight, she has to work." She waited for the words to sink in.

His head had dropped and his eyes were facing his lap. She could see that he was disappointed. "Couldn't help it," he said finally. "Reckon they needed her again." Then as if he suddenly remembered he turned toward her.

"You people be ready down there? Still gonna let him go tomorrow?"

She looked at Mr. Paul between the missing rails on his porch, seeing how his rolled-up trousers seemed to fit exactly in the vacant banister space.

"Last I heard this morning we're still letting him go," she said.

Mr. Paul had shifted his weight back to the chair. "Don't reckon they'll hurt him," he mumbled, scratching the side of his face. "Hope he don't mind being spit on though. Spitting ain't like cutting. They can spit on him and nobody'll ever know who did it," he said, ending his words with a quiet chuckle.

Ellie stood on the sidewalk, grinding her heel in the dirt, waiting for the old man to finish talking. She was glad somebody found something funny to laugh at. Finally he shut up.

"Goodbye, Mr. Paul," she waved. Her voice sounded loud to her own ears. But she knew the way her head ached intensified noises. She walked home faster, hoping they had some aspirin in the house and that those men would leave earlier tonight.

From the front of her house she could tell that the men were still there. The living room light shone behind the yellow shades, coming through brighter in the patched places. She thought about moving the geranium pot from the porch to catch the rain but changed her mind. She kicked a beer can under a car parked in the street and stopped to look at her reflection on the car door. The tiny flowers of her printed dress made her look as if she had a strange tropical disease.

She spotted another can and kicked it out of the way of the car, thinking that one of these days some kid was going to fall and hurt himself. What she wanted to do, she knew, was kick the car out of the way. Both the station wagon and the Ford had been parked in front of her house all week, waiting. Everybody was just sitting around waiting.

Suddenly she laughed aloud. Reverend Davis's car was big and black and shiny just like, but no, the smile disappeared from her face, her mother didn't like for them to say things about other people's color. She looked around to see who else came, and saw Mr. Moore's old beat-up blue car. Somebody had torn away half of his NAACP sign. Sometimes she really felt sorry for the man. No matter how hard he glued on his stickers somebody always yanked them off again.

Ellie didn't recognize the third car but it had an Alabama license plate. She turned around and looked up and down the street, hating to go inside. There were no lights on their street, but in the distance she could see the bright lights of the parking lot. Slowly she did an about-face and climbed the steps.

She wondered when her mama was going to remember to get a yellow bulb for the porch. Although the lights hadn't been turned on, usually June bugs and mosquitoes swarmed all around the porch. By the time she was inside the house she always felt like they were crawling in her hair. She pulled on the screen and saw that Mama finally had made Hezekiah patch up the holes. The globs of white adhesive tape scattered over the screen door looked just like misshapen butterflies.

She listened to her father's voice and could tell by the tone that the men were discussing something important again. She rattled the door once more but nobody came.

"Will somebody please let me in?" Her voice carried through the screen to the knot of men sitting in the corner.

"The door's open," her father yelled. "Come on in."

"The door is not open," she said evenly. "You know we stopped leaving it open." She was feeling tired again and her voice had fallen an octave lower.

"Yeah, I forgot, I forgot," he mumbled, walking to the door.

She watched her father almost stumble across a chair to let her in. He was shorter than the lightbulb and the light seemed to beam down on him, emphasizing the wrinkles around his eyes. She could tell from the way he pushed open the screen that he hadn't had much sleep either. She'd overheard him telling Mama that the people down at the shop seemed to be piling on the work harder just because of this thing. And he couldn't do anything or say anything to his boss because they probably wanted to fire him.

"Where's Mama?" she whispered. He nodded toward the back.

"Good evening, everybody," she said, looking at the three men who had not looked up since she entered the room. One of the men half stood, but his attention was geared back to something another man was saying. They were sitting on the sofa in their shirtsleeves and there was a pitcher of ice water on the windowsill.

"Your mother probably needs some help," her father said. She looked past him, trying to figure out who the white man was sitting on the end. His face looked familiar and she tried to remember where she had seen him before. The men were paying no attention to her. She bent to see what they were studying and saw a large sheet of white drawing paper. She could see blocks and lines and the man sitting in the middle was marking a trail with the eraser edge of the pencil.

The quiet stillness of the room was making her head ache more. She pushed her way through the red embroidered curtains that led to the kitchen.

"I'm home, Mama," she said, standing in front of the back door facing the big yellow sun Hezekiah and Tommy had painted on the wall above the iron stove. Immediately she felt a warmth permeating her skin. "Where is everybody?" she asked, sitting at the table where her mother was peeling potatoes.

"Mrs. McAllister is keeping Helen and Teenie," her mother said. "Your brother is staying over with Harry tonight." With each name she uttered, a slice of potato peeling tumbled to the newspaper on the table. "Tommy's in the bedroom reading that Uncle Wiggily book."

Ellie looked up at her mother but her eyes were straight ahead. She knew that Tommy only read the Uncle Wiggily book by himself when he was unhappy. She got up and walked to the kitchen cabinet.

"The other knives dirty?" she asked.

"No," her mother said, "look in the next drawer."

Ellie pulled open the drawer, flicking scraps of white paint with her fingernail. She reached for the knife and at the same time a pile of envelopes caught her eye.

"Any more come today?" she asked, pulling out the knife and slipping the envelopes under the dish towels.

"Yes, seven more came today." Her mother accentuated each word carefully. "Your father has them with him in the other room."

"Same thing?" she asked, picking up a potato and wishing she could think of some way to change the subject.

The white people had been threatening them for the past three weeks. Some of the letters were aimed at the family, but most of them were directed to Tommy himself. About once a week in the same handwriting somebody wrote that he'd better not eat lunch at school because they were going to poison him.

They had been getting those letters ever since the school board made Tommy's name public. She sliced the potato and dropped the pieces in the pan of cold water. Out of all those people he had been the only one the board had accepted for transfer to the elementary school. The other children, the members said, didn't live in the district. As she cut the eyes out of another potato she thought about the first letter they had received and how her father just set fire to it in the ashtray. But then Mr. Bell said they'd better save the rest, in case anything happened, they might need the evidence for court.

She peeped up again at her mother. "Who's that white man in there with Daddy?"

"One of Lawyer Belk's friends," she answered. "He's pastor of the church that's always on television Sunday morning. Mr. Belk seems to think that having him around will do some good." Ellie saw that her voice was shaking just like her hand as she reached for the last potato. Both of them could hear Tommy in the next room mumbling to himself. She was afraid to look at her mother.

Suddenly Ellie was aware that her mother's hands were trembling violently. "He's so little," she whispered and suddenly the knife slipped out of her hands and she was crying and breathing at the same time.

Ellie didn't know what to do but after a few seconds she cleared away the peelings and put the knives in the sink. "Why don't you lie down?" she suggested. "I'll clean up and get Tommy in bed." Without saying anything her mother rose and walked to her bedroom.

Ellie wiped off the table and draped the dishcloth over the sink. She stood back and looked at the rusting pipes powdered with a whitish film. One of these days they would have to paint the place. She tiptoed past her mother, who looked as if she had fallen asleep from exhaustion.

"Tommy," she called softly, "come on and get ready for bed."

Tommy, sitting in the middle of the floor, did not answer. He was sitting the way she imagined he would be, cross-legged, pulling his ear lobe as he turned the ragged pages of *Uncle Wiggily at the Zoo*.

"What you doing, Tommy?" she said, squatting on the floor beside him. He smiled and pointed at the picture of the ducks.

"School starts tomorrow," she said, turning a page with him. "Don't you think it's time to go to bed?"

"Oh, Ellie, do I have to go now?" She looked down at the serious brown eyes and the closely cropped hair. For a

13

minute she wondered if he questioned having to go to bed now or to school tomorrow.

"Well," she said, "aren't you about through with the book?" He shook his head. "Come on," she pulled him up, "you're a sleepyhead." Still he shook his head.

"When Helen and Teenie coming home?"

"Tomorrow after you come home from school they'll be here."

She lifted him from the floor, thinking how small he looked to be facing all those people tomorrow.

"Look," he said, breaking away from her hand and pointing to a blue shirt and pair of cotton twill pants. "Mama got them for me to wear tomorrow."

While she ran water in the tub, she heard him crawl on top of the bed. He was quiet and she knew he was untying his sneakers.

"Put your shoes out," she called through the door, "and maybe Daddy will polish them."

"Is Daddy still in there with those men? Mama made me be quiet so I wouldn't bother them."

He padded into the bathroom with bare feet and crawled into the water. As she scrubbed him they played Ask Me a Question, their own version of Twenty Questions. She had just dried him and was about to have him step into his pajamas when he asked: "Are they gonna get me tomorrow?"

"Who's going to get you?" She looked into his eyes and began rubbing him furiously with the towel.

"I don't know," he answered. "Somebody I guess."

"Nobody's going to get you," she said, "who wants a little boy who gets bubblegum in his hair anyway—but us?" He grinned but as she hugged him she thought how much he looked like his father. They walked to the bed to say his prayers and while they were kneeling she heard the first drops of rain. By the time she covered him up and tucked the spread off the floor the rain had changed to a steady downpour.

When Tommy had gone to bed her mother got up again and began ironing clothes in the kitchen. Something, she said, to keep her thoughts busy. While her mother folded and sorted the clothes Ellie drew up a chair from the kitchen table. They sat in the kitchen for a while listening to the voices of the men in the next room. Her mother's quiet speech broke the stillness in the room.

"I'd rather," she said, making sweeping motions with the iron, "that you stayed home from work tomorrow and went with your father to take Tommy. I don't think I'll be up to those people."

Ellie nodded. "I don't mind," she said, tracing circles on the oilcloth-covered table.

"Your father's going," her mother continued. "Belk and Reverend Davis are too. I think that white man in there will probably go."

"They may not need me," Ellie answered.

"Tommy will," her mother said, folding the last dish towel and storing it in the cabinet.

"Mama, I think he's scared." The girl turned toward the woman. "He was so quiet while I was washing him."

"I know," she answered, sitting down heavily. "He's been that way all day." Her brown wavy hair glowed in the dim lighting of the kitchen. "I told him he wasn't going to school with Jakie and Bob anymore but I said he was going to meet some other children just as nice."

Ellie saw that her mother was twisting her wedding band around and around on her finger.

"I've already told Mrs. Ingraham that I wouldn't be able to come out tomorrow." Ellie paused. "She didn't say very much. She didn't even say anything about his pictures in the newspaper. Mr. Ingraham said we were getting right crazy but even he didn't say anything else."

She stopped to look at the clock sitting near the sink. "It's almost time for the cruise cars to begin," she said. Her mother followed Ellie's eyes to the sink. The policemen circling their block every twenty minutes was supposed to make them feel safe, but hearing the cars come so regularly and that light flashing through the shade above her bed only made her nervous.

She stopped talking to push a wrinkle out of the shiny red cloth, dragging her finger along the table edges. "How long before those men going to leave?" she asked her mother. Just as she spoke she heard one of the men say something about getting some sleep. "I didn't mean to run them away," she said, smiling. Her mother half smiled too. They listened for the sound of motors and tires and waited for her father to shut the front door.

In a few seconds her father's head pushed through the curtain. "Want me to turn down your bed now, Ellie?" She felt uncomfortable staring up at him, the whole family looked drained of all energy.

"That's all right," she answered. "I'll sleep in Helen and Teenie's bed tonight."

"How's Tommy?" he asked, looking toward the bedroom. He came in and sat down at the table with them.

They were silent before he spoke. "I keep wondering if we should send him." He lit a match and watched the flame disappear into the ashtray, then he looked into his wife's eyes. "There's no telling what these fool white folks will do."

Her mother reached over and patted his hand. "We're doing what we have to do, I guess," she said. "Sometimes though I wish the others weren't so much older than him."

"But it seems so unfair," Ellie broke in, "sending him there all by himself like that. Everybody keeps asking me why the MacAdams didn't apply for their children."

"Eloise." Her father's voice sounded curt. "We aren't answering for the MacAdams, we're trying to do what's right for your brother. He's not old enough to have his own say-so. You and the others could decide for yourselves, but we're the ones that have to do for him."

She didn't say anything but watched him pull a handful of envelopes out of his pocket and tuck them in the cabinet drawer. She knew that if anyone had told him in August that Tommy would be the only one going to Jefferson Davis they would not have let him go.

"Those the new ones?" she asked. "What they say?"

"Let's not talk about the letters," her father said. "Let's go to bed."

Outside they heard the rain become heavier. Since early evening she had become accustomed to the sound. Now it blended in with the rest of the noises that had accumulated in the back of her mind since the whole thing began.

As her mother folded the ironing board they heard the quiet wheels of the police car. Ellie noticed that the clock said twelve-ten and she wondered why they were early. Her mother pulled the iron cord from the switch and they stood silently waiting for the police car to turn around and pass the house again, as if the car's passing were a final blessing for the night.

Suddenly she was aware of a noise that sounded as if everything had broken loose in her head at once, a loudness that almost shook the foundation of the house. At the same time the lights went out and instinctively her father knocked them to the floor. They could hear the tinkling of glass near the front of the house and Tommy began screaming.

"Tommy, get down," her father yelled.

She hoped he would remember to roll under the bed the way they had practiced. She was aware of objects falling and breaking as she lay perfectly still. Her breath was coming in jerks and then there was a second noise, a smaller explosion but still drowning out Tommy's cries.

"Stay still," her father commanded. "I'm going to check on Tommy. They may throw another one."

She watched him crawl across the floor, pushing a broken flower vase and an iron skillet out of his way. All of the sounds, Tommy's crying, the breaking glass, everything was echoing in her ears. She felt as if they had been crouching on the floor for hours but when she heard the police car door slam, the luminous hands of the clock said only twelve-fifteen.

She heard other cars drive up and pairs of heavy feet trample on the porch. "You folks all right in there?"

She could visualize the hands pulling open the door, because she knew the voice. Sergeant Kearns had been responsible for patrolling the house during the past three weeks. She heard him click the light switch in the living room but the darkness remained intense.

Her father deposited Tommy in his wife's lap and went to what was left of the door. In the next fifteen minutes policemen were everywhere. While she rummaged around underneath the cabinet for a candle, her mother tried to hush up Tommy. His cheek was cut where he had scratched himself on the springs of the bed. Her mother motioned for her to dampen a cloth and put some petroleum jelly on it to keep him quiet. She tried to put him to bed again but he would not go, even when she promised to stay with him for the rest of the night. And so she sat in the kitchen rocking the little boy back and forth on her lap.

Ellie wandered around the kitchen but the light from the single candle put an eerie glow on the walls, making her nervous. She began picking up pans, stepping over pieces of broken crockery and glassware. She did not want to go into the living room yet, but if she listened closely, snatches of the policemen's conversation came through the curtain.

She heard one man say that the bomb landed near the edge of the yard, that was why it had only gotten the front porch. She knew from their talk that the living room window was shattered completely. Suddenly Ellie sat down. The picture of the living room window kept flashing in her mind and a wave of feeling invaded her body, making her shake as if she had lost all muscular control. She slept on the couch, right under that window.

She looked at her mother to see if she too had realized, but her mother was looking down at Tommy and trying to get him to close his eyes. Ellie stood up and crept toward the living room, trying to prepare herself for what she would see. Even that minute of determination could not make her control the horror that she felt. There were jagged holes all along the front of the house and the sofa was covered with glass and paint. She started to pick up the picture that had toppled from the bookshelf, then she just stepped over the broken frame.

Outside her father was talking and, curious to see who else was with him, she walked across the splinters to the yard. She could see pieces of the geranium pot and the red blossoms turned facedown. There were no lights in the other houses on the street. Across from their house she could see forms standing in the door and shadows being pushed back and forth. "I guess the MacAdams are glad they just didn't get involved." No one heard her speak, and no one came over to see if they could help; she knew why and did not really blame them. They were afraid their house could be next.

Most of the policemen had gone now and only one car was left to flash the revolving red light in the rain. She heard the tall skinny man tell her father they would be parked outside for the rest of the night. As she watched the reflection of the police cars returning to the station, feeling sick in her stomach, she wondered now why they bothered.

Ellie went back inside the house and closed the curtain behind her. There was nothing anyone could do now, not even to the house. Everything was scattered all over the floor and poor Tommy still would not go to sleep. She wondered what would happen when the news spread through their section of town, and at once remembered the man in the gray Chevrolet. It would serve them right if her father's friends got one of them.

Ellie pulled up an overturned chair and sat down across from her mother, who was crooning to Tommy. What Mr. Paul said was right, white people just couldn't be trusted. Her family had expected anything but even though they had practiced ducking, they didn't really expect anybody to try tearing down the house. But the funny thing was the house belonged to one of them. Maybe it was a good thing her family were just renters.

Exhausted, Ellie put her head down on the table. She didn't know what they were going to do about tomorrow, in the daytime they didn't need electricity. She was too tired to think any more about Tommy, yet she could not go to sleep. So, she sat at the table trying to sit still, but every few minutes she would involuntarily twitch. She tried to steady her hands, all the time listening to her mother's sing-songy voice and waiting for her father to come back inside the house.

She didn't know how long she lay hunched against the kitchen table, but when she looked up, her wrists bore the imprints of her hair. She unfolded her arms gingerly, feeling the blood rush to her fingertips. Her father sat in the chair opposite her, staring at the vacant space between them. She heard her mother creep away from the table, taking Tommy to his room.

Ellie looked out the window. The darkness was turning to gray and the hurt feeling was disappearing. As she sat there she could begin to look at the kitchen matter-of-factly. Although the hands of the clock were just a little past five-thirty, she knew somebody was going to have to start clearing up and cook breakfast.

She stood and tipped across the kitchen to her parents' bedroom. "Mama," she whispered, standing near the door of Tommy's room. At the sound of her voice, Tommy made a funny throaty noise in his sleep. Her mother motioned for her to go out and be quiet. Ellie knew then that Tommy had just fallen asleep. She crept back to the kitchen and began picking up the dishes that could be salvaged, being careful not to go into the living room.

She walked around her father, leaving the broken glass underneath the kitchen table. "You want some coffee?" she asked.

He nodded silently, in strange contrast she thought to the water faucet that turned on with a loud gurgling noise. While she let the water run to get hot she measured out the instant coffee in one of the plastic cups. Next door she could hear people moving around in the Williamses' kitchen, but they too seemed much quieter than usual.

"You reckon everybody knows by now?" she asked, stirring the coffee and putting the saucer in front of him.

"Everybody will know by the time the city paper comes out," he said. "Somebody was here last night from the *Observer*. Guess it'll make front page."

She leaned against the cabinet for support, watching him trace endless circles in the brown liquid with the spoon.

"Sergeant Kearns says they'll have almost the whole force out there tomorrow," he said.

"Today," she whispered.

Her father looked at the clock and then turned his head.

"When's your mother coming back in here?" he asked, finally picking up the cup and drinking the coffee.

"Tommy's just off to sleep," she answered. "I guess she'll be in here when he's asleep for good."

She looked out the window of the back door at the row of tall hedges that had separated their neighborhood from the white people for as long as she remembered. While she stood there she heard her mother walk into the room. To her ears the steps seemed much slower than usual. She heard her mother stop in front of her father's chair.

"Jim," she said, sounding very timid, "what we going to do?" Yet as Ellie turned toward her she noticed her mother's face was strangely calm as she looked down on her husband.

Ellie continued standing by the door listening to them talk. Nobody asked the question to which they all wanted an answer.

"I keep thinking," her father said finally, "that the policemen will be with him all day. They couldn't hurt him inside the school building without getting some of their own kind."

"But he'll be in there all by himself," her mother said softly. "A hundred policemen can't be a little boy's only friends."

She watched her father wrap his calloused hands, still splotched with machine oil, around the salt shaker on the table.

"I keep trying," he said to her, "to tell myself that somebody's got to be the first one and then I just think how quiet he's been all week."

Ellie listened to the quiet voices that seemed to be a room apart from her. In the back of her mind she could hear phrases of a hymn her grandmother used to sing, something about trouble, her being born for trouble.

"Jim, I cannot let my baby go." Her mother's words, although quiet, were carefully pronounced.

"Maybe," her father answered, "it's not in our hands. Reverend Davis and I were talking day before yesterday how God tested the Israelites, maybe he's just trying us."

"God expects you to take care of your own," his wife interrupted. Ellie sensed a trace of bitterness in her mother's voice.

"Tommy's not going to understand why he can't go to school," her father replied. "He's going to wonder why, and how we are going to tell him we're afraid of them?" Her father's hand clutched the coffee cup. "He's going to be fighting them the rest of his life. He's got to start sometime."

"But he's not on their level. Tommy's too little to go around hating people. One of the others, they're bigger, they understand about things."

Ellie, still leaning against the door, saw that the sun covered part of the sky behind the hedges and the light slipping through the kitchen window seemed to reflect the shiny red of the tablecloth.

"He's our child," she heard her mother say. "Whatever we do, we're going to be the cause." Her father had pushed the cup away from him and sat with his hands covering part of his face. Outside Ellie could hear a horn blowing.

"God knows we tried but I guess there's just no use." Her father's voice forced her attention back to the two people sitting in front of her. "Maybe when things come back to normal, we'll try again."

He covered his wife's chunky fingers with the palm of his hand and her mother seemed to be enveloped in silence. The three of them remained quiet, each involved in his own thoughts, but related, Ellie knew, to the same thing. She was the first to break the silence.

"Mama," she called after a long pause, "do you want me to start setting the table for breakfast?"

Her mother nodded.

Ellie turned the clock so she could see it from the sink while she washed the dishes that had been scattered over the floor.

"You going to wake up Tommy or you want me to?"

"No," her mother said, still holding her father's hand, "let him sleep. When you wash your face, you go up the street and call Hezekiah. Tell him to keep up with the children after school, I want to do something to this house before they come home."

She stopped talking and looked around the kitchen, finally turning to her husband. "He's probably kicked the spread off by now," she said. Ellie watched her father, who without saying anything walked toward the bedroom.

She watched her mother lift herself from the chair and automatically push in the stuffing underneath the cracked plastic cover. Her face looked set, as it always did when she was trying hard to keep her composure.

"He'll need something hot when he wakes up. Hand me the oatmeal," she commanded, reaching on top of the icebox for matches to light the kitchen stove.

25

THE CLOSET ON THE TOP FLOOR

They were all wearing white raincoats, but hers was a kind of pale blue, making her stand out from the rest. At the time she was too busy to worry about raincoats, trying to move her luggage from the car to the seventh floor of Wingate Hall. And she was becoming frightened too, looking at all those white faces pressed against the windowpanes.

"Don't worry about it, Chicken . . ." Her father reached over and patted her on the arm. "We wouldn't be sending you here if we didn't think you could keep the pace. Just think . . ." He smiled at her. "You'll be the first one to graduate from Green Hill. Is everything out of the trunk now?"

She looked at her father and wished he would stop calling her Chicken. He loved her, she knew that, but she was tired of being the Experiment. She tried to remember how it had been—before. And she wondered how it would be, when it was over: how she would feel, seeing nothing but dark faces day after day. She had lasted through four years of high school and in four more years she would be through. She could come or go, taking or leaving them as she pleased.

Her father had worked hard, petitioning the trustees and threatening a court suit to get her in this college, and she had felt ashamed for not wanting to go. The school had a good reputation of course, but who in her right mind would want to go to a Southern girls' college? At least Green Hill was a private school and there would be no photographers hounding her. Her father said most people didn't even know she was coming. Lord knows he would change that. Suddenly she felt herself tightening up and she tried to remember the breathing exercises the doctor had prescribed for her.

"Thanks, Daddy," she said. "I think they'll have someone to carry up the foot locker." She leaned over and kissed him.

"Now Winifred, you be careful." A woman's face appeared at the window. "If you need anything, call home. For heaven's sake, don't wait like you did last time. We can afford the telephone bill." Her mother was quiet for a moment. "I'd love to see your room, dear, but climbing those steps wouldn't be good for my headache." Then, as slowly as it had risen, the head sank down on the foam rubber pillow and pastel yellow sheet spread on the back seat of the car.

Watching the head rise and fall, Winifred felt nausea well up, then down, in her throat. Her mother was allergic to dust and traveling made her uncomfortable. Still, she followed her husband on civil rights jaunts across the Southeast. She didn't mind sacrificing her health for the cause.

"Well, that's it, Chicken." Her father slipped a check into her hand and adjusted the rearview mirror. "Don't forget to write Aunt Millicent—she worries about you."

Good Lord, she thought, first Chicken, now Aunt Millicent. She suddenly wished the car would go home. "Okay Daddy, I won't forget."

He turned the key and the motor sputtered. "You get out of this rain—don't want you catching cold." Her father put the car in gear and turned into the street, but not before a chubby hand rose from the back seat.

Winifred watched the car turn the corner, picked up her portable hair dryer, and walked toward the dormitory steps. She listened to the raindrops falling on her coat as she walked hunched over, shielding the animal in her arms. He was a pink dog with orange eyes and she was afraid he would get soaking wet because the plastic bag didn't cover his fur completely.

Winifred registered for classes the day after she arrived. As her father had warned her, everyone pretended she wasn't there. Her roommate's name was Norma Parker. She had had the room all to herself until Winifred and the pink dog arrived for the second quarter. Winifred would have preferred a single room, but her father insisted that she be treated as any other student. So she had to take her chances with roommates. Norma was tall and slender with curly blonde hair, and her best friends didn't look like Winifred either. Ellen and Bonnie lived down the hall from her and they had been friends since high school. All three were chemistry majors and Winifred didn't see much of them since all of her classes were in the liberal arts building.

To decorate her room, Winifred had moved in with a whole zoo. Aside from the dog, there was a small tiger with leopard spots guarding the dresses, a yellow bunny three feet high named Mandy, a green duck, and a fuzzy lamb. The animals were the first things she looked for when she woke up in the morning. As she crawled out of bed she always had a vague notion that something was wrong. When she was unable to remember anything that bothered her, she would check the calendar on her desk to make sure of the date. With the date pressed into her mind, Winifred would carefully button her robe, make up the bed, and begin the seven a.m. procedure.

First she would open the top dresser drawer, find her underwear, and arrange the pieces on the bed. This morning she tiptoed to her closet—Norma never got up before nine—and brought back a green pleated skirt, green blouse, and green sweater. She put these clothes on top of the underwear, but not before she carried the bar pin from her jewelry box and pinned the clasp on the blouse collar. Quietly she picked up the soap and towel, opened the bedroom door with just two squeaks, and walked down the hall.

At that hour of the morning the dormitory lights had not yet been turned on, and the porcelain on the water fountain almost glowed as the light from the end hall window shone across the surface. She walked to the middle shower before anyone else was up. The first week of school she had tried all three showers and the one nearest the door had a broken soap holder. The soap slipped through, fell on the tile, and melted under the force of the water. The shower on the other end sprayed too fine and she disliked the peppery streams of water shooting into her ears. So she had decided always to be the first one in the middle shower every morning. And she had been too, she thought happily, removing a shower shoe from her beach bag. Only once had Edie Roddey gotten up early to study for a biology exam and beat her to it. Thinking of Edie Roddey upset her, and Winifred stayed in the shower longer than she meant to. She had to rush back to the room and comb her hair to get to breakfast by 7:40. By the time Norma awoke, Winifred was sitting in the basement of the library between the bound copies of *American Girl* and the *American Journal of Sociology* studying history.

Everybody was in a sorority but Winifred. She didn't mind. Somehow she had become used to not being invited and when she received an invitation to a sorority tea—by mistake, of course—she very casually threw the envelope into the wastepaper basket.

She had a difficult time trying to think of something in which to major. Her mother had suggested drama but Winifred didn't see how she could play the maid's part for four years. She was fairly adept in biology, but the department scheduled field trips throughout the year. And even if the motels were supposedly integrated, she hated to be involved in testing them. So she had to major in something that didn't involve people or embarrassing scenes. Finally, in the blank to fill in a major, she wrote "History." There was nothing embarrassing about doing library research—she had nothing whatsoever to worry about, studying medieval Europe.

Winter came and on the campus the number of camel-colored boy-coats with raccoon collars increased by one. Regardless of the season, Winifred dreaded Sundays. Every other day of the week she had no trouble deciding which hat to wear with the boy-coat; no one on the campus wore hats. In cold weather, or when the wind was blowing, everybody wore a triangle scarf and Winifred had a scarf to match each of her winter skirts. But on Sunday mornings she had to wear a hat and if she wore the same one two Sundays in a row, she shuddered to imagine what people would think. She couldn't possibly hide—everybody saw her when she walked into the chapel.

Her pink plaid hat box overflowed with hats so that choosing one for church was a terrible decision. She was standing on a chair in the closet, staring into her hat box, when Ellen and Norma came into the room. They obviously had been discussing something for a long time and they didn't see her or the chair missing from the desk. "It's not that she doesn't look nice in brown," Ellen said. "Heavens, anybody can wear camel, or beige, or whatever you call it. But with that raccoon collar and her short neck, nobody can tell where the collar stops and her hair begins."

"Well, the hair is hopeless. There's not a thing you can do about that, but she could at least take off the collar. You look at her and all you see is a brown blimp."

"Don't talk so loud—she'll be here in a minute."

Winifred, leaning on the top shelf, almost squeezed the color from the gray felt hat she had decided to wear. They were talking about her. Why hadn't they told her? Noiselessly she pushed the felt hat back into shape and clutched it in her hands until Ellen and Norma left to find Bonnie for a three-girl game of bridge. When she was sure they were gone, she gave the half-shut closet door a sharp push with the chair, being careful not to drag her coat on the floor. With the scissors from the right side of her desk drawer she began clipping stitches. In fifteen minutes there were the same number of boy-coats on the campus, but one less raccoon collar.

The boy-coat disappeared in the spring and was replaced by a gleaming white, double-breasted English raincoat which Winifred's parents had sent out from the store. Nobody ever mentioned her parents. The hostess would call her name over the intercom every other weekend and she would disappear into the beige car. If she didn't go home, they usually took her out to dinner and bought her a cake, or some cookies, or some other sweet to take back to the room. But she always came back looking unhappy.

"Gee," Norma said to her one evening, "you must really miss your folks." Winifred thought that she looked impressed.

She went home sometimes for a weekend. On Friday afternoon, by the time Norma returned from assisting in the chemistry lab, all of Winifred's bags would be packed except the largest suitcase. She preferred to carry home the two weekenders and the pink plaid hat box. On her bed in a neat bundle, ready to be carted downstairs, were her radio and steam iron. Winifred just looked at her when Norma asked why the iron, the radio, and the dictionary had to follow her home.

"Yes, of course we have an iron," Winifred told her, "*and* a radio *and* a clock. I just like to use my own." She didn't pay Norma any attention when she overheard her telling Ellen about the portable dictionary.

One night when Winifred was out with her parents, Norma decided to stay in the room and study. When Winifred came in, she saw her lying on the bed, reading her chemistry book. "Do you smell something chocolate?" Norma asked, breathing deeply. Winifred didn't bother to answer but shook her head "no," swallowed an aspirin, and began undressing for bed. Then, feeling around in the

33

bottom dresser drawer, she took out a suitcase key on a long black ribbon, and picked up a square white box that had been hidden under a blue sweater on the bed. Softly she tiptoed to the closet, pushing the desk chair in front, avoiding the eyes of her roommate, who was still reading her chemistry manual.

In the closet Winifred turned a key in a lock and a suitcase snapped open. In about five minutes, smiling strangely, she came out of the closet and began brushing her teeth, according to a prescribed pattern. The toothbrush swung ten swishes to the right, then ten to the left, and the bottom row all over again. She gargled deeply in her throat for exactly fifteen seconds and then she was ready for bed.

Norma closed her book. "I'm going to the basement for a Coke," she said. "I'll probably watch television with the people down there."

By the time she had located a dime, Winifred was turning back the sheet and fondly patting the two blankets. She placed the pillow at the foot of her bed for her feet, and another pillow at the head. That done, she pulled the bed from the wall and tucked the cover on each side securely under the mattress and away from the floor. "Bugs come off the walls," she explained, "and the floor gets awfully dirty with you walking all over it."

"Do you mean 'you' collectively speaking or just me?" Norma asked.

Winifred didn't answer. She had overheard Norma telling Ellen about the ceremony she performed to the God of the two white pillows who protected the bed from bugs.

And for some reason that Winifred couldn't understand, it upset Norma greatly to see the pink dog with orange eyes covered up for the night in a plastic dry-cleaner's bag.

Although the late show was over when Ellen and Norma returned from watching television, Winifred had not fallen asleep. The room was dark except for the light from the streetlamp slipping through the venetian blinds. She heard Norma open the door but because the cover was wrapped around her head she didn't see her walk inside.

"Come in and look at Winifred," Norma whispered. "Would you believe it's eighty-six degrees outside?"

Ellen crept over to the blanketed hunk in the bed, swelling strangely at both ends. "Golly, do you think it would pop if I touched it?"

"Sh-h-h," Norma cautioned her. "She could be awake under all that cover staring up at us right now."

With that thought they were overtaken by a fit of giggling. Winifred's eyes didn't move, but the body in the bed went up and down with the regularity of a breathing exercise.

"Guess what," Norma said between giggles. "She's got some kind of key she hides in that bottom drawer and I could have sworn she locked up a package tonight."

"Well, let's find out what she hid." Ellen already was walking toward the dresser.

"We shouldn't bother her things."

"Oh, don't be silly."

Winifred could hear them rambling through her drawer looking for the key. Then she heard a chair being carried to the closet, and in her mind she saw them trying to fit the key into each lock. She lay under the covers waiting for one of them to speak. She knew they would find the lock the key would fit, although she had hidden the pullman on the very bottom of the shelf.

Norma spoke first. "Hurry up before I drop this luggage."

Then there was silence. There was no use pretending; even under her blanket Winifred could remember every object they would see. In the first white cardboard box, probably with dabs of frosting stuck to the carton, was a fudge cake. In the next box were a dozen chocolate chip cookies, and then a whole mincemeat pie. They would open her other boxes, too, and they would find the food she had saved all year.

Winifred listened to them whisper inside the closet. Ellen had the nerve to wonder how Winifred could ever be hungry, and they actually expected her to offer them something to eat. They could never understand that eating everything spoiled the whole plan. She had eaten a chocolate chip cookie just once, to count the chocolate chips inside. Then, multiplying by eleven, she had tallied the approximate number of chips in the package of cookies. Now they were disturbing everything.

"Norma?" Ellen asked, her voice sounded puzzled. "Do you think all of them are like this, or just her?"

"I don't know," Norma answered. "Our maid takes food, but she never really tries to hide anything."

Finally Winifred heard Ellen say good night, but she didn't even listen as Norma replaced the key in the pocket of the lavender pajamas and crept to bed.

Winifred packed her radio, her steam iron, her clock, and the dictionary every two weeks all year, and she began wearing the suitcase key around her neck. Once when she came back with a sweet potato pie and climbed up to store the dessert in the suitcase she could have sworn that someone again had tampered with the cookies. Norma never said anything about the cakes and cookies, so Winifred never asked her about that night.

Still, she worried all day thinking that someone else had discovered the suitcase, and to make sure that nobody else bothered her collection, she started staying in the room all day—between classes and meals. At night she would crawl between the covers and lie awake, waiting to hear footsteps. She had made up her mind that if they bothered her suitcase again, she would say something.

In the middle of the third quarter, Norma moved two doors down, with Ellen and Bonnie. Three-girl rooms were illegal, so of course she had to sleep in her own bed in 708 with Winifred, but she moved all of her books and some of her clothes into 712. Winifred never seemed to mind; she even held open the door every time Norma left with another bundle. Besides, she worried because Norma was concerned about her. She happened to be standing outside the door one day when Norma was whispering to Ellen.

"But suppose something is wrong with her," Norma said. "I mean seriously."

"Look, she wouldn't be here if she was completely out of it."

"I don't know. Maybe her folks don't know she has these queer ideas."

"They see more of her than you do," Ellen answered. "Besides, who would you tell? Suppose you turned her over to Student Health and they found out she was all right? Boy, would she be mad at you. You know colored people aren't like us."

"Well, if her parents are happy, I guess I should be."

And then Winifred had swung open the door.

"Hi!" they said in unison. She grunted and walked straight to her desk.

Now, most of the time, Winifred lived in the room alone. She arranged the furniture the way she wanted to arrange the furniture. She pulled her bed away from the wall— permanently. At any hour of the day, the cover was tucked under the mattress, army style. Since most of Norma's clothes were no longer on the rack, Winifred began studying in the closet. Reading in the closet really made a lot of sense, because there were no windows inside and she didn't have to worry about catching cold. She thought about moving in the bed, too, but the bed and the desk would not both fit, and she didn't want to close the door completely.

Everybody supposed Winifred was getting along all right. They never really saw her anymore, because after a while Norma persuaded Ellen and Bonnie to put their beds together and she slept in 712. Then the weekend rolled around and, as usual, the hostess called her name over the intercom. But Winifred didn't come down. There was no way she could have known she had company. Nobody can hear the intercom in the closet. When Winifred didn't answer an all-call, the hostess sent somebody upstairs to try and find her. It was a short search; she was always in the closet.

A few days after the all-call, the housemother paid a visit to 708. When Winifred didn't answer her on the intercom, she rode to the seventh floor, walked right into the room, and knocked on the closet door. She stood in the doorway, letting in air, talking and talking, but Winifred ignored her. In fact, the only thing she remembered about the conversation was that the stupid woman imagined she was straining her eyes reading in the bad closet light.

She accompanied Winifred to the infirmary, and after the nurse assigned a room, sat in the visitor's chair while Winifred unpacked. "Are you sure you don't want an aspirin?" she asked.

Winifred saw no need to answer.

"If you like, we can call Norma to come down and visit tomorrow afternoon."

Winifred checked the corners of her bed to be sure they were tucked under, hospital style, and pulled the cover halfway down. Then she began putting her cosmetics in the cabinet above the sink. Unfortunately the house-mother's chair was beside the sink so she was forced to stand beside her and listen to her chatter. Before she was halfway unpacked, a nurse walked her to a lounge for some silly picture tests, the Name-the-Story kind everybody gets sooner or later in the infirmary.

This one doctor kept coming in and asking her whether she minded being the only Negro in the college and whether Norma was her friend, and why she hadn't been to class in such a long time. Stupid questions, really, but she decided that the best way to get around the doctor was to ignore him completely and pretend she was in her closet—alone.

39

So whenever he started infringing on her thoughts, she pretended she was cutting the closet light on again, then off, then on—which made his interviews pass very quickly. She finally discovered that if she would make up stories for their pictures, they would stop bothering her. So she did.

Winifred was sent to the infirmary on Thursday. The following Saturday she was ready to go home. Hardly anyone on her floor was awake when she started bringing her things down from the seventh floor. Moving took a long time because she herself insisted on carrying the big suitcase. All of her father's hints that she was too weak to carry heavy objects and calling her Chicken wouldn't change her mind one bit.

Winifred walked down the stairs carrying the largest piece of luggage and the dog. Of course, riding the elevator would have taken less time, but she almost hated to leave her closet behind. She didn't have a chance to say goodbye to Norma and Ellen. By ten-thirty they had not come by her room; she didn't bother to walk down three doors to 712. Besides, the stairs were at the other end of the hall.

After twenty minutes, the luggage was in the car. "Well, Chicken, this is it," her father said, slamming the trunk top. "I told those people you only needed a rest. They acted like you weren't good enough for their school. Don't worry—we'll get you back."

She looked at him and tucked the pink dog under her arm. Her father held open the car door, she crawled into the front seat, and he locked her in. Then, as the beige car turned into the street, the orange eyes of the pink dog sitting on her lap looked up at Winifred.

BEFORE TWILIGHT

The car turned down the dark road, plowing between rows of ripening cotton, stopping in a small cleared-off place and scattering ashes between the cotton bolls. The motor sputtered and the ashes settled, covering the green Chevrolet with hazy gray particles that almost were invisible in the night air.

"We'll see you tomorrow, Jenny," Hank said, turning to the girl sitting in the corner of the back seat. He waited until the tall thin girl slammed shut the car door and was climbing the porch steps to the unpainted frame house. Then the car started off, lighting a path in the middle of the dirt road.

Jenny opened the screen and was knocking at the door before she remembered. "Hank," she hollered, running to the edge of the porch. "Hey Hank!" But the car continued chugging along the road. From the porch she could see the taillights flickering in the darkness. As she stood near the porch beam, the light escaping from the living room window shone on two paperback pamphlets. Jenny held them so the glow outlined the words on the cover—*Freedom Now, Americans All*. Suddenly she turned the titles of the two books inside, facing each other. Feeling around in her dress pocket for the door key, she looked for a safe place to deposit the pamphlets.

Not that Mama would care, she reasoned, but still there was no sense in taking chances. Mama's brother Harold had gone around telling everybody that membership in CORE was dangerous in this part of the country. He almost threw a fit when she even mentioned the word.

She was about to turn the key in the lock when she heard footsteps approaching the front door. She started to tuck the papers in the crevice behind the geraniums, but before she could move the window box, the door opened.

"What kept you so long, honey?" The tightly curled hair of the woman speaking glistened under the living room light.

"Nothing Mama, I went over to Willie Mae's house," Jenny said, shutting the door behind her.

"All the way back from Willie's at this time of night? Jenny, when you going to learn not to be walking by yourself after dark?" As her mother frowned, she watched the wrinkles deepen into dark brown folds.

"Hank had the car and he brought me home." She tried to edge her way toward the curtained entrance that led to her room.

"He give you those books?" her mother asked. Impulsively she reached for the top pamphlet in her daughter's hand. Before Jenny could stop her, she was turning the pages of the first book.

"Oh," the woman said. "Oh." Jenny noticed that her face looked almost chubby in the living room light. She watched the shadow from her fingers as they slid across the printed letters on the jacket front. Her lips moved but no words came out. Congress of Racial Equality—she whispered the words again and looked up at Jenny.

42

"We're not trying to start up a chapter," Jenny said. Her words barely were audible. But before she could finish, her mother interrupted.

"Your uncle told you better," she said, sitting down on a folding chair. The bulk of her body seemed to overshadow the bent sofa and other chair in the room. Jenny looked down at her mother's hands, seeing the knuckles swollen in the middle of each finger. She knew what she was thinking about. The father of one of her friends had found the charred body last spring. Since then she guessed everybody had just stopped talking about voting.

"When I heard you talking about that group I figured you'd show at least a little sense, but you're not going to be hurting yourself because of them. Especially on account of that Hank. Seems like he'd know better by now."

Jenny looked past her mother, who had stood up again, at the place on the wall where the flowered wallpaper was peeling. "But Mama," she whispered, "nobody said anything about starting trouble."

"Jenny, honey," her mother's voice was sad, "this is Spring Gap. Remember? Alabama is paying for your tuition and without that scholarship you couldn't put one foot in a college nowhere."

"But Mama, if I lose the scholarship I could work some to make up." She looked at her mother waiting.

"No, there's no sense in going out your way to tempt trouble." Her voice became harsh. "You'll start working in somebody's kitchen and want to get married, and then the babies'll start coming. You'll be just sitting here like me." For a moment her mother stopped talking, as if she were engulfed by the shadows that fell on the unfinished floor. Then suddenly she was looking at her daughter again. "No, Jenny, as long as you're living here, you'll listen to me."

The two women stood under the lightbulb facing each other. Jenny knew her mother was frightened because in her world of pots and pans and narrow back doors nobody but a crazy person went around even talking about CORE. Finally the woman turned away from her daughter and walked into the kitchen. Jenny stood motionless, watching the shadow disappear behind the kitchen door. Then she dropped the two pamphlets on the sofa and quietly opened the screen door.

She wished she had thought to get a sweater, the air felt unusually cool for August. But almost all of her clothes were washed and ironed and ready to be packed for school. Mama probably would have a fit if she wore one of those washed and ironed sweaters before September tenth. She stepped around the pile where the ashes were dumped from the kitchen stove, thinking of poor Hank, who always managed to drive right into the dust pile. Funny, she thought, how things never seemed to come out right. She had enough scholarship money to cover a whole year at State, and she even had a watch, but here she was into something again.

Jenny folded her arms and hugged her shoulders to get warm. The school told her she was deficient in algebra, but Willie Mae said that if she got arrested she could study math in jail. In spite of herself she smiled. She and her friends had thought about sitting-in for two weeks now, ever since Hank came back from Birmingham talking about the CORE meeting he went to.

She began walking toward Bubbles's sandbox. In the dark, the sand seemed almost luminous, like the pamphlets under the light. She always had the whitest sandpile in the neighborhood because her father used to bring home the fine-grained sand from the construction company where he worked. She stood over the rectangular box, looking at the toys Bubbles had left in the sand. Here and there along the edges of the box were wobbly letters, mostly "B's." Bubbles was learning to write her name, but she didn't have very much time to help the little girl.

Just standing there looking at the sandpile she realized how much she still missed her father. He used to help her make the hard letters, like the "S's." Seemed like he'd been dead much longer than six years. Now she and Bubbles played the same game with the alphabet letters. Sometimes when she was thinking by herself, she wondered how her mother could forgive them for not sending the ambulance right away and then carrying him right past the big hospital to reach the one that would take him.

With her right foot, she moved Bubbles's rubber spade around in the sand. She wondered if he would understand how she felt now. Hank said they couldn't depend on anybody else to do things for them. She knew he was right, but being right didn't take away the fear inside her. Her father used to tell her that someday she would be proud to have been raised in Alabama. Already she knew better. Jenny sat down on the edge of the sandbox, running the dry sand through her fingers.

She couldn't blame her mother. Having to take care of Baxter, Bubbles, and herself was kind of hard on her. But since Baxter had gone to the army, she hadn't even had time to miss him. Today she hadn't even been home long enough to see if there was a letter from him.

She stood up and began walking toward the front door at a slower pace than usual. She wished her mother liked Hank better, but she thought anybody who got expelled from school was terrible. She tried explaining that the fight wasn't his fault. Everybody knew he couldn't just stand there while that boy from Linwood called his sister a tramp. Well, she guessed she should be glad her mother liked Bobbie, although she wasn't about to tell her who punched a hole in Mr. Wright's tire last Easter. Poor Mr. Wright still talked about how parking an empty car wasn't safe on her side of town.

Jenny realized that she was tired of standing up. After working all summer, she decided that cleaning for Mrs. Wright was an all-day job. By the time she'd caught a ride home and cooked supper for herself and Bubbles, she usually just climbed into bed. She wished now she had stayed home tonight. She could have spent a peaceful evening reading the new book Mrs. Wright lent her.

Sitting down on the bottom porch step she thought about Hank trying to talk them into sitting-in. Everybody started kidding him asking if he was Martin Luther King or something, but he kept insisting he was violent. Which was funny then, but sometimes when she was thinking, she wondered whether he was serious. Hank always could take kidding, but none of his friends, not even her, would tease him too long.

Still, there weren't too many kids her age left in Spring Gap. Almost as many kids as nails in the step she was sitting on right now. Some of their friends had gone up north to work, but most of her girlfriends were married and the ones she played with in elementary school had babies now. She ran her fingers over the five nailheads in the step. Out of the seven kids left, four were going downtown tomorrow to try to get served at the Rose Crest Tea Room.

She'd often heard Mrs. Wright say that the Rose Crest Tea Room was the only place in town where she didn't mind eating out. She and Mr. Wright left the kids with Jenny and had dinner there all the time. All at once she chuckled aloud. Hah! She could see Mrs. Wright's face if she plopped down beside her in the great Rose Crest Tea Room.

"Pardon me," she would say, haughtily taking a seat, "but would you pass the menu." Mrs. Wright's eyes probably would bug out completely when she ordered chicken à la king. Why, the poor lady more than likely would turn redder than she already was.

Suddenly she realized her finger hurt from rubbing the wooden steps. She had never been arrested before. Once her civics class paid a visit to the county courthouse, but that was in the ninth grade. The jail looked so shabby that she was afraid to walk down the rickety steps to the cells in the basement. Jenny was thinking about the roaches people said were in the jail when her shoulders straightened up. Somebody was calling her. She ran to the porch and quietly locked the front door behind her.

By the time she reached her room, she heard an angry voice talking in the kitchen. "Bubbles, have you washed up yet?" She knew then that Mama wasn't calling her. "But Mama," a small voice answered, "I don't got no more soap."

Bubbles and Mama were fighting the soapsuds. Honestly, she'd never seen a child that hated to wash so much. She remembered the time when Bubbles had liked to wash her own self. While Mama was out of the kitchen the little girl dumped a half a box of Rinso Blue into the tub of water and dived in. Poor Bubbles peeled for weeks.

Following the sound of voices, Jenny heard herself agreeing to put Bubbles to bed, and in twenty minutes the house was quiet. She wandered from room to room, just thinking. Finally she picked up a *Time* from last December, turned a few pages, and decided to undress for bed, taking the magazine with her to read herself to sleep.

As the bright sunlight shone in her face, Jenny decided that morning came too early. While Bubbles slept contentedly on the other half of the bed, she squirmed beneath the sheet. She turned over toward the door and heard her mother piddling around the kitchen. She heard her starched housecoat swish to the door.

"Want your breakfast now?" To her ears the voice sounded tired.

"Uh-uh, not now Mama," she yawned, "I don't have to be at work until ten today. I'll eat later."

Jenny felt vaguely uneasy. She was glad Mama couldn't see her face because she could always tell when one of them was lying. She turned over and buried her head under the pillow until she was certain her mama had gone to work.

She got up then, scorched the bacon, and fried Bubbles an egg. While she was cooking she tried to decide what to wear downtown. She remembered that Mrs. Wright always wore a hat when she went out for lunch, but her

Sunday hat was packed already and she couldn't risk getting the straw dirty. Jenny unwrapped her black leather pumps from the brown wrapping paper and slipped them on. She hoped nobody would notice she was barelegged. Finally, she decided to wear one of Bubbles's ribbons, then she wouldn't need a hat.

At ten-thirty she combed Bubbles's hair and put lots of peach jam on the bread so she wouldn't get too hungry before Mama came home. She knew Mrs. Johnson would give Bubbles something to eat if she stayed next door all day. She gave the child a peach to carry in her hand, patted her on the bottom, and shooed her next door.

The walk down the cotton road to the main highway took exactly three hundred and eighty-two steps. She timed herself once when she had nothing more important to think about. Today her feet kept dragging as if they were stuck to the red dirt. She stopped to examine a cotton plant, pulling gently at the white stuffing between the brown dry leaves. This was the funniest kind of weather they were having, still cool enough for a sweater. She walked to the end of the field and waited for Hank and the car.

Willie Mae and Bobbie were already in the back seat when Hank drove up. He decided that parking on the colored side of town would be better than parking on the main street, in case anything happened. Then nobody would bother his father's car. So they parked by the Baptist church and walked in pairs the half mile to town. Jenny wondered if the others were as nervous as she. Hank and Bobbie were walking in front; she and Willie Mae followed a few paces behind, sort of like an army formation.

She was looking around at the fields she'd seen a hundred times before when she happened to notice that Bobbie's hip pocket was bulging very oddly. She watched intently as he unwrapped a caramel, popped the candy into his mouth, and dropped the wrapper on the ground. As they walked, he continued unpeeling caramels, making her almost laugh aloud. Bobbie, whose mother had seen to it that he grew up on manners, didn't even realize he hadn't offered anyone any candy. Jenny felt much better.

As they walked across the countryside, Jenny remembered that she loved this time of year. The cotton was spilling out of the bolls and some people had started storing in their hay for feed. They waved to Mrs. Nelson, who tried to find out where they were going as she cooled tomato-filled mason jars on her porch railing. Jenny looked again at the mound on Bobbie's pocket, which had become flatter and flatter. Suddenly she was tempted to say something, he had just reached back and no candy was left. She held in her laughter but in a few minutes the chuckles had turned into a strange fizz that invaded her body.

They were nearing the downtown section. Hank and Bobbie turned down Lee Street, past the Methodist church and the mudhole where she had dropped her library books in the sixth grade. The book she hadn't found probably was still down there. They came to the fire hydrant with the peeling paint and all of their initials carved on the surface. After seeing this same street for seventeen years she imagined she could walk the route with her eyes closed. Like they used to do when she was small and she and Willie Mae took turns leading each other down the road. But this time as they walked, she tried to see everything so she always could remember the street, just in case.

The group was downtown now and her heart quickened at the possibility of just stopping at the street marker and turning around. But she kept walking mechanically, up the hill, past their town park with the graceful weeping willows, until they arrived at the rock monument honoring the confederate dead.

"All right everybody." Hank was talking. "We're almost here now. You girls powder up and we'll be ready." Jenny looked down and discovered she was wearing only one glove. Quickly she put on the other one. Then she pulled out a handkerchief and wiped the dust from her shoes. Willie Mae fluffed out her hair and they were ready to leave.

Salems were on special at Knox Drug Store. The girls stretched out on the long green grass made her aware of how hot she was inside. They passed the drug store and stopped at the "Don't Walk" sign. Nobody paid them any attention. For some reason she was glad of that. They passed window after window of bright smiling girls standing up to their ears in raccoon and boy-coats. She thought of something to tell Bubbles—the mannequins looked just like the mouse people in her storybook.

Seven more steps and they were directly in front of Seller's Department Store. The boys held open the door and on their right were the stairs. As they climbed to the first landing, the red carpeted steps became a blur of faded color. She heard Hank say something to Bobbie and his voice sounded too loud. She wondered if her nose was shiny, pushed a strand of hair out of her face, and stumbled on the last step. They were on the third floor. There right in front of her eyes was the tea room. The music coming from the hi-fi speakers near the door was just as soft and tinkly as she had remembered.

Hank looked for a side table, and they followed him in the dining room. Some of the people stopped eating, looked hard, and quickly left. Most of the other diners who had not yet looked up went right on with their meals. Hank pulled out her chair, Bobbie helped Willie Mae, and they all sat down.

A waitress swinging a handful of menus came halfway up to their table, stared at them, and almost ran through the kitchen door. She reached up to hasten the closing of the swinging door, but not before Jenny saw a tall hefty man follow the waitress, who stood at the crack between the door and the wall pointing in their direction. The man nodded and walked to their table.

Hank spoke first and very quickly. "We'd like four Shopper's Specials," he said.

"You must be mistaken," the man interrupted, "your snack bar is downstairs. Now if you will kindly leave . . ."

"We would like the Shopper's Specials," Hank insisted.

"I'm sorry but we have no facilities for your people up here." The man smiled. "Now if you will please leave, someone will escort you downstairs. We will be glad to serve you in the basement."

No one moved. The man disappeared through the same swinging door. Jenny sat across from Hank running her fingers through the pink squares on the checked tablecloth. While the man was gone, Jenny looked around. The tea room was nice, she decided. All of the lights were soft pink and cast a hazy glow on the tablecloth. She thought even brussels sprouts would taste good in a place like this. She turned to look at the people in front of her, patting their faces with the pale pink napkins and leaving their plates half-finished. They watched the people leave the dining room, in little groups, sometimes alone. Once a woman brushed against their table, and Jenny was sure she bumped them purposely. In a matter of minutes the Rose Crest Tea Room was empty of white customers. The rosy light continued to glow but there were nothing but quiet tables and vacant chairs to bask in the warmth.

While they sat there Hank tried to say something funny. "Maybe we should have brought our own lunch," he said seriously. They all laughed nervously. The Shopper's Special never came; still they sat in the tea room, the fourth table from the rear.

Two policemen entered the room. Jenny could see them without turning around, standing by the door. One was tall and fat and the other man looked like an ordinary white man, kind of colorless leaning against the pink wall. In her mind she immediately named him Rose Petal. She watched the fat policeman bend down and whisper to Petal, who snapped to attention beside the door. Then the other man walked over to their table.

"Which one of y'all is in charge here?" Jenny noticed that his badge needed polishing.

"No one is in charge, officer," Hank said. "We came to eat lunch."

"Well, get your gang together, boy, and let's go down to the office."

They were no trouble—he asked them to leave so the girls stood up and Hank and Bobbie slipped all four chairs in place.

The policemen escorted them from the dining room to the stairs. No one was left in the tea room to watch the procession. But with the appearance of the policemen, a small crowd had formed on the third floor near the banister. Jenny turned around and faced the stairs; she hoped nobody she knew saw her. Not that she was ashamed, but she wanted to tell her mother herself. Her hearing all of a sudden from one of the neighbors would be horrible.

Jenny barely could hear the whispers in the crowd. Once she heard somebody yell something about a "coon." From the corner of her eye she could see a teenage boy who was about her own age. As they walked down the steps something hard, probably a spitball, hit her on the back. She heard "nigger" and the word did not disturb her, but when she looked down at her fingers she had bitten the top off her thumbnail.

When they reached the ground floor, the officer marched them down the main aisle, past the perfume counter where Bubbles liked to be taken every Saturday morning just to smell. As the officer led them past the department store she almost stopped from habit to drop a penny in Blind Markie's tambourine, but she was pushed past the jewelry store, then Sears. The blades of the electric fan outside Meyer's Hardware Store looked like spun silver and tracing the arc made her head ache. They stopped walking and a few feet ahead was the county courthouse.

This time of day the afternoon sun shone directly over the courthouse, increasing the glare on the asphalt shingled roof.

She wondered for a minute if the tar on the roof was as sticky as the tar on the main downtown street. Jenny glanced down at her brightly polished shoes, she was glad they didn't have to cross the street. She had heard the colorless policeman call the other one Johnson. And Johnson was the one who opened the side door to the police office and shoved them inside.

The room was neat and to her practiced eye clean. Even the sand in the metal ashtrays was a dull grayish brown. She looked at the blue wall, watching the sunlight filter through the venetian blinds, making deep shadowy slats on the gray linoleum floor. She saw only one policeman on duty, who barely looked up as the four of them walked in.

"Afternoon Captain Waymer," Johnson said. Waymer put down the *Sports Illustrated* and swiveled his chair to the front of the desk. "What you got here," he said, looking at them with the same sullen expression Jenny had seen on the boy's face at the store. The policeman sat them down on the row of folding chairs near the window. There was one chair left over and she placed her handbag there.

Before the officer in charge could ask any questions the telephone rang. Jenny guessed it was the Seller's manager because the captain said he would call back if a signature was needed. The four of them took turns answering questions, but with each answer they gave, one of the three policemen managed to twist their words. After an hour Jenny just stopped talking and then they started yelling at her. When Bobbie tried to explain that she was tired they started hollering at him too.

Then the pale policeman started calling them names, each one, especially Willie Mae, who he said was a turnip

55

nose. Jenny tried to blot out the sound of his voice and began concentrating on the tile covering the floor, but the flecks and the lines seemed to merge and she had to grasp the bottom of the chair to keep from toppling over.

Jenny watched Hank reach into his pocket, from habit she guessed, and pull out a cigarette. He had just lit the match when Johnson reached over and pulled it from his mouth. Without saying a word he took Hank's hand with the lighted cigarette and slowly ground his fingers into the ashtray. No one dared give Hank a tissue and he refused to wipe his hands on his good suit.

Then Waymer started back again: "Who put you kids up to this?"

"Nobody," Hank answered, pausing to make noticeable his omission of "sir."

"Well, let's go somewhere where you can decide." As he spoke he reached into a desk drawer, pulled out handcuffs, and snapped them on, one by one. Another officer grabbed Hank and Bobbie by the shoulders. Jenny and Willie Mae were just pushed in line behind them, down a flight of stairs into dark musty air. She thought of that story her English teacher read once, all about the underworld and the goddess who changed the seasons. Her legs felt not exactly trembly, but the way she used to feel when she was little and had done something wrong she would be spanked for. She breathed deeply and made up her mind to turn around and see everything at once. In the darkness, Jenny saw that only a part of the basement had been turned into cells, but there were enough cubicles for each one of them to be alone.

She was the last one to be guided to her cell, which was farthest away from the single half window. Although her eyes had grown accustomed to the dark light, her ears still could not pick out any noises in the cell. She stood by the bars waiting for the officer's footsteps to disappear up the steps to the main floor, above her head. For an instant she tried to imagine the policemen trying to balance themselves on top of her head. Then she began counting silently to herself, trying to let ten minutes pass before she spoke.

When she was certain the policeman was gone she called softly to Hank. Even then Jenny didn't know why she called except that she wanted to hear Hank's voice. But before she could ask him anything the footsteps returned. "Cut out the noise," the voice said. He came closer and she could make out his hand on his hip. Jenny realized he had been standing at the top of the steps waiting for one of them to speak.

The officer turned to leave again, but since she could not be sure he was gone, she said nothing. The stillness in the jail was beginning to bother her. She waited to hear some kind of outside noise, music, the paperboy, or even just the sound of people walking uptown. She wished she could think of something to keep her mind busy, to keep herself from wondering what the Seller's man was going to do.

Once when she was younger and had gotten angry at the neighbor girl across the road, her father had tried to get her back in good spirits by playing the wish game, which he said was much better than starting up a fuss. "When I grow up," she'd said, "I'm going to be an axe and cut off all of

Maggie's hair." Her father had laughed and said good little girls didn't grow up to be axes. She wondered if he would think good little girls went to jail.

Jenny was thinking of other games she used to play when she became aware of footsteps. She saw Johnson standing in the door. "Captain says he wants to talk to you boys alone." His words came out slowly, as if he was grinning between each syllable. Swinging the keys, he opened Hank and Bobbie's cells and led them up the steps. Jenny's knees seemed to sink beneath her and she slipped to the edge of the cot. In a few minutes she could hear footsteps shuffling back and forth. Then there was a terrible scraping sound as if something was being dragged over the floor. She knew the walls were too thin.

Jenny heard the dragging sound for what seemed like hours. She kept wondering what time it was and wished her mother had let her wear her graduation watch before she went off to school. She sat farther back on the cot until she remembered about the bedbugs. Gingerly she stood and began examining her skirt, but the handcuffs kept getting in the way and she wanted to sit down.

She must have sat in the cell for hours wondering what Willie Mae was thinking about. Her fingers made a rhythmical tapping sound to the tune echoing in her head. The kids at the meeting Hank told about sang freedom songs, but she didn't know the words to any of the new songs except the major one. "We shall overcome, we shall overcome," the words followed the thud her fingers made on the mattress. She used to hum the song sometimes while she worked. And Mrs. Wright asked her if all Negroes sang under their breath. Only the word hadn't come out Negro, she imagined it was closer to nigger.

Jenny thought about college and wondered if any of the other freshmen would have jail records. Nobody in her family had ever been arrested before. Except that cousin on Mama's side and he didn't count because he was really a stepcousin. The picture of the new dormitory in the college bulletin flashed into her mind. And then she wondered if she would be there to enroll.

She held her breath and listened closely. In the darkly lighted basement, she could hear distinctly the sound of breathing in the cell at the other end of the room. She hoped Willie Mae's head didn't ache like hers. The dull throbbing pain became intense and she realized her head wasn't the only part of her that ached. She wanted to go to sleep, but her body felt brittle, like she would break into a hundred pieces if touched. Jenny didn't know how long they sat in the hot dusty basement, but when she heard steps coming down the stairs, the sky had darkened and the hotness had settled into an uncomfortable warmth.

Taking his time, Johnson unlocked Willie Mae's cell and then hers. He herded them together, up the steps toward the main room. Immediately she saw Hank; his eye was puffy and there were bruises on his cheek. Bobbie was sitting beside him, his head slightly bent so she could see the cut above his eyebrow. She traced with her eyes the imaginary line where blood had dripped from his forehead, down onto his torn shirt. She felt sick all over again, even when Hank reached over and touched her arm. He started to whisper something to her, then both of them saw the little black man who had just walked into the office, standing by the door.

"Good evening, children," he said. "The officer tells me you children are a little confused. I told him you all weren't doing nothing but playing games."

Jenny didn't move at all. They had agreed not to tell anybody their plans. She couldn't imagine what Reverend Honeycutt was doing there, he was the last person in whom they would have confided.

"How come you children not working your jobs?" he asked. "You know you colored children need to work to keep out of mischief. Ain't that right, now?"

She watched the preacher smile up at them as if he was sharing a big joke. Reverend Honeycutt was what her mama would call a bad taste in the mouth. Jenny was determined not to listen. Preacher or no preacher she knew God would forgive her this time.

They sat in the office for fifteen minutes watching the minister. He had conferred with the Seller's man and the policemen, he said. And they all agreed that to press charges would start up publicity, which neither they nor you children wanted. Reverend Honeycutt did not look at any of them as he spoke, his eyes were straight ahead on the blank wall.

As the preacher paused for breath, Captain Waymer began talking. Jenny watched the red veins in his neck ripple in and out of his shirt. Ashamed—ashamed—his words came out in puffs—they should be ashamed of trying to start up trouble. Jenny focused on a crack in the ceiling, she did not look down until the captain stopped talking. Then he glanced at the clock on his desk, took off the handcuffs, and pointed to the door. "Next time," he said, not having to finish his sentence.

Reverend Honeycutt softly closed the door behind him and they were out in the twilight. Nobody said anything to him but he tried to speak. "Children," he kept mumbling, "children, I know what you're thinking . . ." but Hank and Bobbie pulled Jenny and Willie Mae away and they left the old man standing in front of the newsstand next to the courthouse.

They went the back way, across some cotton fields, to the place where Hank had parked the car. The walk did not seem nearly as long as before. While they walked between the cotton plants, Jenny felt the wind rustling on her back, but none of the plants around her moved. Then she looked down at the chill bumps on her arm. By that time they were in front of the car. Willie Mae lived closest to town, then Hank dropped Bobbie at his house, and she was alone with him.

"They say the first time's always the hardest," he said, looking straight ahead. She nodded her head, which could mean yes or no, and looked out of the window. Last night this same road had looked so different to her eyes. In the twilight she saw that there was no place for anyone to hide. As they rode, she sat in the front seat thinking about the funny way the dark covered everything when suddenly she almost cried out—the next time, oh God, the next time. Suddenly all the feeling she had held in during the afternoon spilled out. Jenny tried to stop the first tears but in seconds she was crying and her whole body was caught up in the sobs.

"Hey, do you feel all right? They didn't bother you and Willie Mae, did they?" Hank slowed the car and pulled over to the side of the road. At first he fumbled in his pocket for a clean handkerchief but then he turned toward the window until she was ready to drive again. In a few minutes she opened her handbag and pulled out a soft tissue.

"I'm okay," she whispered, "I was just thinking."

When he gave the signal to turn down her road she reached over and pulled on the steering wheel. "That's all right, I can walk up to the house." As if he understood, Hank stopped the car.

"Want me to wait until you get to the porch?" he asked.

"No," she tried to smile, "thanks anyway."

She stood by the last cotton row waiting until Hank's car blended into the dust, way up the highway. Her mama, she knew, probably would not be coming home until later, on Thursday she always had to stay because of the bridge club meeting. Even this far from the house she could see Bubbles sitting on the front porch steps.

Jenny looked at the open country around her. The air was dry and as she lifted her head, she seemed to be overshadowed by the sky. She was outdoors at one of her favorite times of the day, after the sun had set, but still not late enough for the darkness to invade all of the daylight. She looked around her at the cotton plants, which were heavier and more listless than they had seemed this morning. She stooped and touched the dry red soil that had been plowed and weeded so carefully. She imagined they would have rain soon, September always came with rain.

Jenny tossed the clump of dirt she had picked up back into the field and started down the road. She saw Bubbles jump from the porch to the ground, and then the little girl was running to meet her.

"Jenny," she yelled, running at full speed, "how come you just now getting home?" She stopped running long enough to make a jump for Jenny's knees.

"Stop Silly Billy Bubbles, you'll get my dress dirty!" They were both laughing as Jenny tried to salvage a white glove that had slipped to the ground.

"Silly yourself," the little girl said, still giggling. "I didn't like Aunt Johnson's dinner so I come home. Know something?" she said, turning her eyes upward. "I bet I been waiting for you a billion hours."

"A billion hours I bet," Jenny said, echoing her words. Pushing Bubbles in front of her, she walked around the ash pile and toward the front door, thinking of what to fix for supper and how to explain to Mama.

HEALTH SERVICE

"Mama," George Frederick whispered, "when we gonna stop and rest?" Sweat was running in little rivulets between patches of hair down to his brow and she noticed he needed a haircut.

"Where's your hat, George Frederick?"

"I don't know," he shrugged his shoulders, "I couldn't find it when we were leaving."

Libby frowned at him and swung the baby onto her shoulder, carefully pulling the ragged flowered bonnet over his face to keep out the sun. If he had a hat at least nobody could tell he needed a haircut. She looked down at the children who clustered around her, wishing she could hurry up and see the white, peeling sign that said "Health Clinic." All she saw over the tops of the children's heads was the flat dusty road and the grayish red dirt that settled between the toes of her sneakers and made her children's canvas sneakers stiff with grime.

"Mama, I'm getting tired." Wicker caught hold of her hand and tried to slow her down.

"We're almost there now," she said. "When we get up to the filling station, we'll rest. And don't any of you start begging me for a Coke either, we can't afford none."

The small group of children looked at her sadly. "Can't we even split one?" Wicker asked.

65

His mother patted the baby on the back and ignored him. The little group walked along much slower than before and a few yards ahead Libby could see the curb of the service station and the row of chinaberry trees that lined the turnoff.

Stopping at the Esso station always made her feel a little uneasy. Back when she was first married and Hal was still going to school some, he used to work there after classes. Still, the station was a good halfway place to stop on the way to town and the kids liked to see the cars go up and down on the elevator.

She walked slowly, changing the baby from arm to arm, but before she could settle him comfortably on her shoulder they were at the station. The children ran immediately to the trees and played under the dark green leaves that made a pleasant canopy of shade. She sat on the curb, far away from the main working area, rocking the baby, who had started to fret.

The baby was a solid lump in her lap and she was too hot even to care. Libby watched her children, who, now that they could rest, were chasing each other around the chinaberry trees. She was just sitting still, staring down at the curb, when she saw Matt's grinning face and waving hand pointing toward her.

In school Matt and Hal had been best friends. When Matt graduated from high school the white man, Mr. Sommers, had kept him on at the station. He had a good job and she used to go with him in elementary school. Last summer Matt sent them an invitation to his wedding when he married that girl from Chesterfield County, but she couldn't go because they didn't have any extra money to buy presents.

She watched Matt look around to see if any customers were coming and then he bypassed the gas pumps to the curb where she was sitting. He stooped and peeped at the baby.

"Sure nice he takes after you." As if he had spoken a magic word Calvin smiled and his dark eyes followed the oily finger that Matt swung over his head.

"That boy of yours come back?" he asked, suddenly becoming serious.

She shook her head no.

"You know where he is?"

Again she shook her head.

"That damn son . . ." But before he could finish Libby pulled his arm and pointed to the children, who had stopped playing to watch their mother.

"I don't want them hearing none of that." The children stood waiting until their mother shooed them away.

"Hasn't sent you any money either, I bet." Matt squatted on the curb beside her. "If you need anything right now, you let me know, and if you don't hear anything from Hal soon, you see those county people."

"We don't need to be on no welfare," she interrupted.

"Hell, anybody can be in trouble for a while, beside you got to feed those kids."

"I got me a job working in town." She tried to keep her voice from breaking.

"Your mama's not going to keep that baby forever, she's getting too old to be picking up after little children."

"That's not your business," Libby answered quickly. "Nobody told you to get mixed up in my business."

67

"All right, all right." Matt stood and in the sunlight he appeared as a black shadow hovering over her and the baby. "But if you need anything, promise me you'll let me know."

Libby sat on the curb not looking at him, trying to keep her tears from falling on the baby. She'd promised herself she wouldn't be bothered thinking about Hal and here she was crying like a fool baby. While she sat still letting the heat dry her tears, Matt treated all four children to soft drinks. He made Meetrie bring one to her and then they were ready to start walking again.

The county clinic was on the second floor of the courthouse building. As the children climbed the steps she tried to freshen them up, sticking in Wicker's shirttail and trying to keep Hamlet still enough to brush the Coca-Cola from his pants. Not until she passed a clear glass pane on an office door did she see her own reflection. The shoulder of her cotton dress was wet where the baby had burped. She herded the children together and let Meetrie lead them up the stairs past the main waiting room into the cubbyhole that served colored.

Nine other people were in the waiting room ahead of her, and there were only two seats left. She took one chair, and Meetrie and Wicker squeezed into the other seat. Libby reached over Wicker, who was leaning on the chair's arm, and picked up a copy of the *Post*. The magazine was the same one she had read when Wicker had hay fever. Maggie Haliday, one of the maids in this building, told her once that the magazines were only put in here when the white people were finished. She saw a *Life* on the other side of the room, but didn't feel like walking to get it or starting up one of the children, all of whom had chosen this moment to be quiet.

She looked around at the other people waiting to see the doctor, trying to decide if she knew any of them. One of the women, the one with the hair in little sausage curls, reminded her of Hal's aunt. But, of course, she wasn't; Hal's aunt lived in Bethel. The woman looked up at her and smiled. Libby smiled back.

"All these children yours?" the woman asked.

"Yes." Libby turned Calvin around in her lap. "This one," she said, pointing to Meetrie, "will be ready for school next year."

"One more off your hands," the lady began, chuckling, "but I guess you'll have enough on you anyhow."

The woman had a thyroid condition, she said, and whatever the doctor gave her didn't do any good. Last night, she'd had one of those attacks, and the first thing this morning she'd come to this place. And look at her, she'd been here since eight-thirty, and already it was eleven minutes to ten.

While she talked, a nurse came in and asked who was next. A pregnant woman stood and shuffled toward the gate that separated the waiting room from one of the inside offices. When the woman was safely inside the office, the nurse turned and pointed a finger toward Libby.

"You," she said in an expressionless voice, "keep that child out of the ashtray."

Libby turned in time to see George Frederick digging in the sand of a tall cement ashtray. She was too embarrassed to do anything but grab him and sit him down beside her. The other children were becoming restless now, and she knew that if the doctor didn't see them soon, they would be a problem in such a cooped-up space.

"All your children sick?" the woman asked her.

Libby sensed that she just wanted someone to talk with.

"No, they're pretty healthy," she said. "Mr. Johnson said positively Meetrie couldn't go to camp unless she had some kind of shot. He said, with the others running around outdoors all day, they should get shots too. I guess the nurse will know what to give them."

"She doesn't look old enough to be off from home by herself." In response to the woman's thoughtful stare, Meetrie began wiggling in her chair.

"Oh, she's not going away from home, she's just going to day camp. Mr. Johnson, he works with the Community Fund, got her a scholarship," she said proudly.

"White folks are always packing off people's children to camp. Seems like they could think of something better to do with their money."

Libby nodded, and both women were silent.

"Your husband work around here?"

"No, he's working upstate."

"How come he left you by yourself?"

Suddenly Libby was tired of listening to the woman. She certainly wasn't going to get a complete stranger mixed up in her life.

"Calvin here was too little to travel, so I stayed with the children." Her words were curt but the woman paid the tone no attention.

"Guess you miss him, but with all those children it's a good thing he's up north working. I bet he sends you more money than he brought home when he was working here."

Libby did not say anything, but shifted Calvin to her other shoulder and picked up the old copy of the *Post*. From her usual way of feeling time pass, she guessed they had been sitting in the waiting room for over an hour. A man with a swollen foot began smoking and, since there was no ventilation unless the door stayed open, cigarette smoke hung heavily in the air.

She wanted to ask the man to stop smoking because the baby was coughing, but he was so much older than she that finally Libby decided to walk up and down the hall to get some air. She ordered George Frederick and Meetrie to watch out for the younger children and walked out the door.

She had just started down the hall a second time when the same somber-faced nurse stuck her head out the door. Immediately, Libby was conscious of someone sniffling.

"Your kid's in here raising sand," the nurse said. "We ask you people not to deposit your children in the waiting room. When only one's sick, why don't you leave the rest at home?"

"Meetrie started it," she heard Wicker say.

Just as the nurse shut the door, she saw Meetrie lean over and kick George Frederick. Then Meetrie fell on top of the boy and began pounding him with her skinny fists.

"Meetrie," Libby screamed, "get off that floor!"

She looked for someplace to put Calvin, afraid to put him on the chair because he might roll off. George Frederick was still on the floor and she hated him for pretending to be hurt. Quickly she bent down to pull up both children and almost dropped Calvin.

George Frederick's yellow pants had splotches of dirt from where he had rolled on the floor. She pushed the children together and made them sit in the chair. The funny thing was that they hadn't disturbed anyone in the waiting room; everybody sat quietly, hoping to be called in to see the doctor.

Libby felt the minutes ticking away, wishing that some of the people in the crowded waiting room would leave and come back tomorrow. If the nurse didn't call for them soon, she knew they'd have to go home. She hadn't thought to bring anything for a lunch and they couldn't afford to buy anything out of the cracker machine.

Libby could hear feet moving around in the next room, and each time the footsteps approached the waiting room she felt her muscles becoming tense. The children were getting edgy and George Frederick had started sucking his thumb, the same hand that had scooted in and out of the sand. She started to reach out and remove his thumb, but decided that at least this way he was quiet.

She raised forward on the edge of her chair to relieve the strain on her back, feeling the cloth of her dress stick to the plastic back of the chair. Calvin had fallen asleep but he seemed to be heavier when still. Libby knew he would be hungry when he awakened, but there was nothing to feed him that she could afford. She found herself offering a prayer to be next, feeling that right now she would promise God anything if she could hurry up and leave this clinic.

It occurred to Libby that thinking and dreading today so much probably made her nervous. Her mother was bound to ask if Hal had sent her an anniversary card, and all this week she'd expected to hear something from him. Then this morning came and she stood ten minutes on the front porch waiting for the mailman, who rode by without even leaving one of those advertising circulars. She felt her stomach grumble and swallowed hard to stop the noise. If she was hungry, she knew the children soon would be begging for something to eat.

As a last resort she decided to think only of happy things, but that too was impossible. Everything she thought about seemed to have happened after she was married and not before. She looked down at the baby, remembering when she had sat in this room pregnant with Meetrie. It was in the hospital that her mother, seeing Meetrie for the first time, had slipped her own bent wedding ring onto Libby's finger because Hal had not yet bought her one. She looked down at her finger, seeing the narrow gold band, dull after six years. Sometimes she felt that she had a wedding ring and that was all.

In the middle of her thoughts she was aware of someone pulling on her sleeve.

"Mama," Wicker whispered, "I gotta go to the bathroom."

"Get Meetrie to go with you and unbutton your pants."

Meetrie looked up at her mother. "I don't want to go in there all by myself."

Libby didn't much blame her. The lightbulb usually was out in the toilet and, regardless of the disinfectant, the room smelled awful.

"Mama, I gotta go bad." Wicker was standing on one foot and then the other.

Libby stood and grabbed him by the hand. She couldn't take all the children with her or she would lose her place in line. Yet, if she left them alone they were bound to start up something. The toilet for Negroes was all the way down in the basement, and if she didn't get Wicker there soon, he was likely to wet right in the middle of the floor.

Suddenly the woman she had talked with earlier was at her side.

"You take him on downstairs," she said, picking up Calvin, "and I'll watch them up here and save your place."

Libby smiled her thanks and hurried Wicker from the room. Knowing that George Frederick would have to go by the time she returned, she pulled him along.

Coming back upstairs Libby walked so fast her legs ached when she reached the second floor. She couldn't risk having the little boys see all those candy and snack machines. Maybe if they didn't see food they wouldn't be hungry. The big clock over the main door read twelve-forty-five—they already had been waiting over three hours.

After the lady had been so nice to take Calvin, Libby felt she ought to introduce herself.

"I'm Alma Courts," the woman answered, "and he was a real sweetheart." She settled in her chair, expecting Libby to continue their conversation.

Although talking to Mrs. Courts helped time pass, Libby didn't want to be questioned too closely. She found her place in the old magazine and began reading.

She had not finished the first column when the nurse popped her head inside the door. "You people go on home and come back Monday," she said.

"Huh?" a man said, and a few people raised out of their seats. "I can't come back on Monday." His voice was joined by a chorus of "me neithers."

Libby stared at the nurse as if the woman were crazy, and

she wanted to knock that silly starched cap from her head. She couldn't come back on Monday and bring all of them. There was no telling when she'd have another Saturday off; the Nelsons hardly ever went away for the weekend.

"The doctors are leaving early," the nurse continued, as if no one had interrupted her speech. "You come back on Monday and they'll try to see you." Then she closed the swinging door and the people in the waiting room heard a key turn in the lock.

"Well, ain't nothing we can do," the man with the swollen ankle said, "'cept come back. I already lost three days off the job, don't guess one more day will make no difference." He stood and grimaced in pain, shifting his weight to the foot that was not hurt.

Libby stood, and immediately the baby began hollering. She felt the rubber pants and saw that they were heavy. There was nothing to do but change him in the waiting room. Mrs. Courts looked at her sympathetically and wiped Calvin's slobbering mouth with a slightly soiled Kleenex. "Sometimes I wonder why more of us ain't dead. I could of had an appendix going loose inside me and it wouldn't made no difference to them."

"You know anybody going to Fir Town?" Libby spoke loudly enough for everyone in the room to hear.

"No," Mrs. Courts said, "don't know nobody with a car going that way." Since no one else seemed to be paying her any attention, she stationed herself by the door. Nobody was going even part of the way in her direction.

Libby prodded George Frederick forward and handed Meetrie the diaper bag to carry down the steps. The clock on the first floor said two-thirty, the wrong time of day for her to try and catch a ride. Nobody she knew who worked in town got off from work before four on Saturdays.

She hustled the children out the door and headed toward the corner. While they were walking, Meetrie pulled away from her side and started to run across the street. Libby gave the child a jerk that almost made her lose her balance.

Meetrie stood still, rubbing her arm and looking as if she might burst out crying. Libby knew that when one child started up, the others also found something for which to yell. She bent down and touched Meetrie's head, waiting anxiously to see if Meetrie would stop sniffling.

For an instant, Libby thought about keeping straight up the main street and walking around the shopping center. She hadn't been window shopping in ages, but seeing new clothes wasn't worth the trouble of keeping up with her children. Besides, it was way past time for them to eat, and the sooner they passed somebody's peach tree the better. She shifted the baby to the other arm, caught hold of Wicker, who was walking slower than anyone else, and started home.

MINT JULEPS NOT SERVED HERE

The house, hidden in a grove of fir trees, was made of wood, wetly painted so that the boards almost glowed in the dark. Because wood is so plentiful, most of the people who lived in the community surrounding the Forest Preserve preferred brick houses. Only people living within the forest had wooden homes, and they were few in number. If the census takers knew of the family's existence, Mr. Mack, the head, would have been classified as a dragger. Since chopping down trees was illegal in the Forest Preserve, he had to wait for a natural calamity, such as a thunderstorm, to uproot trees and shrubbery. Then he dragged the dead trunk, or as much of the wood as he could chop and carry, to his backyard. Once a year, usually in the spring before the beginning of the tourist season, Mr. Mack took the animals and dolls he had carved from his dragging to the main craft shop in town.

The women who owned the shop were always pleased to see him. His squirrels and pigs were very popular with people shopping for souvenirs, driving through to the western states. He never said anything other than to discuss prices and ask about the advance on his commission. He never tipped his hat or said thank you or even called the women by their names. But of course one could not expect too much from his kind, no matter how respectable he looked—the ladies knew that. And when the customers asked about the artist, the sisters were quick to point out that he was the town's talented Negro citizen.

"We get along with him awfully well," the fatter of the women would say.

"Yes," the other sister usually completed the dialogue, "we can count on seeing him once a year, like clockwork. I don't understand places like the South. We never have racial trouble here."

Mrs. Mack never came into town. Her last trip down the path occurred several springs ago. Mr. Mack brought the bicycle from under the lean-to to drive to the hospital for the birth of their son Alvin. Alvin, one of two living beings they brought from Mississippi, died three days after birth. Her doctor could not understand what extinguished the baby's thin cries. When she had seen the stiff little body for the last time, Mrs. Mack heard the physicians talking in the corridor of the shining hospital.

"It's almost as if the little fellow was afraid to breathe," one doctor said.

Mrs. Mack shut her ears, knowing that the doctor spoke the truth. She could do nothing but be grateful that her infant son would be buried in this quiet land. Their other son, called Rabbit, grew into a healthy child with long limbs like the trees he climbed. Now that he did not require careful attention, her days were spent in cooking, and in cleaning the house—a house that belonged to her.

She seldom thought of her white family in Mississippi. The baby boys whose diapers she changed between cleaning and cooking were no longer a part of her mind. Ever since she and Mr. Mack shut the cabin door for the last time she had succeeded in putting the town out of her thoughts. The town with all of the pale faces that ruined her baby frightened and angered her. But she and Mr. Mack knew better than to become angry in their town.

At first they decided to stay, hoping that holding him and cuddling him would make their son forget the circle of bright faces in the Mississippi field. He had come home from playing, shirt torn, pants caked with red dirt where the boys from town had sat him down and pinched his nose, threatening to stop his breathing. They had thrown him one from the other, sometimes dropping him the way a child bounces a rubber ball. By some miracle he had limped home, letting the boys take with them his power to speak.

They could take no chances with other children. A voiceless child is after all powerless. So, during county fair week when she was pregnant again and the whole town was beset with confusion, they put on their best clothes, left the furniture and starched uniforms in the cabin, and walked into town. At the bus station they purchased tickets to Jackson. A usual event—all of their friends had relatives to visit there. At the Jackson bus terminal they walked straight to the map on the terminal wall. Mrs. Mack closed her eyes and pointed to the state where they would live. When the bus arrived at the town, they walked out of it, feeling their way toward the Forest Preserve.

During the summer the weather was warm in the day. Life in the forest was like being at home, except for sleeping on the leaves. By the time fall came, Mr. Mack had begun building the house, adding to the two rooms year by year.

A sturdy house he built, he himself hauling the logs and painting them white. Somehow he had managed, Mrs. Mack never understood these things, to tap a power line so that they had electricity for the small stove. Mrs. Mack did not mind the limitations; candlelight was a small fee for her own life.

And hers was a good life. She was comforted with the thought that Alvin was at peace in his new world, and Rabbit seemed to find some quiet in the woods, away from the pale faces in his head. If she had her way he would never meet any people of the other kind—at least not until he was old enough to understand that some colors were naturally evil.

She could hear Rabbit now in his own room, banging the two tin cups. The cups had been her measuring utensils until one day she dropped them and their clatter on the smooth floor entranced her son. He refused to give up the cups, and when he saw others of varying sizes he insisted on holding them in his chubby hands, measuring the two people around him. The din from the next room, muffled by the wooden beams that separated the kitchen, was a constant reminder that he was at home, safe with her until he grew old enough to protect himself.

Rabbit sat on the floor, legs tucked underneath, straddling a sunbeam from the open window. His head faced the screen, the afternoon sun warming his wide nostrils, making his eyelids blink. It was time to feed the bear. Mixing the milk from the box with the same brisk motion he had observed in his mother, he poured the liquid air into the smallest cup. Bearlie would not open his mouth until he pushed a finger in the orange slit and forcibly brought the cup to the bear's face. He held the cup just so, until Bearlie had drunk. He turned the cup slowly in the sunlight, at once washing and rinsing, the silver color bouncing in his hand. He put the cup to his ear and listened to his mother's footsteps in the next room. She would soon be in to look at him, when the soft swish of her broom no longer scratched the floorboards. Her feet would thump toward him in the blue slippers. He could feel her shadow behind him.

"You're quiet today, Rabbit."

Her voice was puffs of soft breath tickling the hair on his neck.

"Do you want to see the picture book?"

No, he did not want to see the picture book but, because she would sit down beside him, he would turn the pages, his fingers walking slowly, stopping at pictures until she grew tired and returned the *Ebony* to the shelf.

"Come on in the kitchen with me."

She seemed to sing as she spoke, standing at the door waiting. He looked quickly at her, then at the window, comparing her to the sunlight beyond the sill. Then slowly he brought the chunky legs together and sprang up, bouncing Bearlie in his arms.

"Will you pass the milk, Mrs. Mack?"

Her husband softly touched his wife's hand. Before he spoke she already had begun sliding the pitcher. They did not need words between them. For Rabbit, who should grow up knowing his parents had Mister and Mistress attached to their names, they spoke. Rabbit was too busy shaking canned milk into his oatmeal, turning the paste into soup, to notice them. Mr. Mack had raised the spoon to his mouth when the strange noise made his hand tremble. He looked at his wife to see if she had heard and found her eyes paralyzed, his fear caught in her eyes. Surely no one had driven a car into their part of the Forest Preserve. While they sat, stiffened, waiting to see if the noise resumed, Rabbit did not seem to hear the sound. He continued stirring his cereal in wide swoops, pouring syrup into little wells of oatmeal. When he had finished his bowl, scraping the sides with two flat fingers, they had not heard the noise again. The family finished the meal in silence. Days and nights were not counted, each passing evening brought the darkness more quickly to their supper table.

The leaves were coming down, sometimes in great bunches, leaving the trees behind the grove, arms up in the air. His mother said the trees had to undress for the winter. After a while he had come to believe everything that she told him. Whatever she said was always so. Soon the trees would be covered with green, making the cool spots for him and Bearlie, away from the sun.

He was walking with Bearlie, stopping sometimes to wait for a quivering leaf. Then, just when the red wrinkle was coming toward him, the wind would blow away the leaf. He was at the top of the hill now, looking down at the path his father kept cleared of grass. He saw the woman walking and knew immediately she was part of the strange noise he had heard past the trees. He had listened to the crunch of leaves and twigs—someone walking who did not know his way around the woods.

She walked in sunlight, and the bits and pieces of fallen sun were woven in her hair, playing games there. At once he wanted to reach out and touch the curls, to see if the sun would rub off, but something about her made him hush. She was a strange kind of person, such a funny color. Perhaps he had seen someone like her, but his head would not bring the pictures from the whirring circles into focus. If he reached out perhaps she would remember, but she did not look up at his outstretched arm. She walked past his fingertips toward his house. Then suddenly he ran, determined to leave the stranger behind.

Mrs. Mack was measuring oatmeal for muffins when she saw him running, charging straight toward her. He was clutching the bear so tightly all of the stuffing in one arm had coagulated near the top, making a shoulder droop. He was trying to show her something, his eyes glancing at her, sweeping the Forest Preserve, and back at her. Something had frightened her baby. She reached down to comfort him and saw the woman walking up the path toward them.

She pulled Rabbit toward her and at the same instant used him to shield herself from the creature.

"Hush, Rabbit, it's all right."

See what you have done to my child. Her eyes carried even harsher words over Rabbit's head.

"What do you want?" Mrs. Mack spoke, surprised at the strength of her own voice.

"Good morning." The thin lips spotted with pink smiled. "I'm Rosemarie Langley from the County Service. We didn't know you people lived so deep in the forest. Goodness, you really have a long drive into town."

Mrs. Mack stood in her doorway. "We don't go."

"But your husband comes in to sell his exquisite carvings."

"He goes, but we stay here."

"We found out about you people through your husband. One of our caseworkers clerks part-time at Sears and saw your husband purchase a boy's snowsuit. Just by chance she mentioned the suit to me and I started wondering why a snowsuit that big wasn't in school, and here I am." She was suddenly breathless, but her teeth became bigger with each smile. "Oh, I'm not here officially. Today was such a nice day for a drive. I parked the car by the picnic grounds and decided to try and find you people."

"Our boy doesn't talk so there's no need to send him to school. Might as well not go if he never says nothing."

Miss Langley took a step nearer the door. "Have you had his hearing tested?" she asked. For a moment she looked as if she might peer inside Rabbit's head.

"He hears a lot of things we don't hear. He just don't say nothing about them and we like him the way he is." Mrs. Mack's voice was stubborn, and with each step the caseworker took, she retreated farther into the kitchen, dragging Rabbit on her apron.

"May I come in?" Miss Langley asked.

"Looks like you're here already." Mrs. Mack was surprised at herself a second time. At home she wouldn't dare talk like that to one of them, but the woman did not pay attention to her curtness.

"Now that I'm here, please may I sit down? What lovely wood. Did your husband do the carving on this chair?"

"He made all of the furniture."

"You're very fortunate to have such a talented husband. Is your son artistic too?"

"He likes to look at books and he likes to feed the squirrels. When he gets older I guess he'll learn to use a knife."

Rabbit still had not looked up, keeping very still while his mother smoothed his hair, stroking away his fear.

The woman's voice made a strange humming sound, reaching into every corner of the kitchen. "When he comes to school, of course he'll learn to read and write. Then we can give him tests to see if he has an artistic bent."

"He doesn't need to go to your school. When he decides he wants to read the picture book, one of us will teach him the words."

"Oh, you mean you're educated." Miss Langley colored, her cheeks matching the pink lips. "I mean, you and your husband went to school?"

"I can read a cookbook and he knows how to read a road map, but all that's behind us now. We don't have no use for your learning. Those we know who had it never had much use for us." She smoothed her son from her apron. "You're sitting on his chair. He don't like the others, please move."

"Oh, I'm terribly sorry." She stood and fluffed the cushion she had crushed.

Mrs. Mack picked up the shivering Rabbit and sat him down. Perhaps warm cocoa would soothe him, cocoa with a pink marshmallow floating on top. She dragged his chair to the stove while she mixed cocoa. Together they watched the caseworker.

"Such a cozy little place, do you mind if I look around?" Miss Langley pulled away from the table and Rabbit immediately clutched his mother's skirts. She pushed back the curtain. "Only one bedroom? Thank heavens you have two beds," she said, shaking her head. "But do you really think that's wise? Having him sleep in the same room with you?"

Mrs. Mack felt herself blush. Shame on her for making such talk, even if she didn't come right out and say her thoughts in front of Rabbit.

"It's not good to have a child exposed to too much," Miss Langley called from the bedroom. "Why, half the juveniles we have in court are there because they grew up too fast."

Mrs. Mack continued stirring the cocoa. The woman couldn't possibly think she preached something new. The thing to do was not let them grow up at all, keep them away from people who came prying, looking into affairs not concerning them.

"I'm fixing my baby some cocoa, would you like some?" When the woman nodded she brought the cups from their hook and reached for the marshmallows.

"My, what handsome mugs. I bet your husband carved those too."

"The cocoa will take a while," Mrs. Mack answered, rejecting the compliment. She pulled a chair beside Rabbit and again both of them stared at the intruder.

She had such pretty hair, not knobby and crinkly like his mother's. She wasn't even sitting near the door and it shone like his book when light fell on the pages. His mother didn't like her either and she really had done nothing but walk into his room. And other times she smiled at him, the teeth locked together as if they guarded a big hole. He dug his fingers into the arm of the chair, wondering how Bearlie would look covered with some of her hair. He would like to take a single strand to cover Bearlie's gray fur. Then, when night came, the brightness of Bearlie's new coat could light the darkness around his bed. He could smell the cocoa, feel the bubbles bursting in the pan as if the cocoa had hiccoughs. Then his mother poured three cups and allowed him to reach first. With the cup in his hands, his tongue darted out to catch a precious drop oozing down the side into his palm.

"Thank you, Mrs. Mack. It really smells delicious."

There was silence. Mrs. Mack watched the pale fingers pick up the cup and hoped she would burn her tongue. Why couldn't those people leave her family alone. Why did they always have to come inside when they were not wanted, looking with icy eyes, freezing everything, trying to make everybody in the world like them. Every last one of them made her ill.

"How old is your son?"

"Nine going on ten."

"Why, Mrs. Mack, do you realize that other children his age are halfway through the fourth grade?"

"There's nothing you can teach him that will help preserve him."

"Why, Mrs. Mack, we try to turn our children into useful citizens. Surely his heritage is worth preserving."

Rabbit looked from one to the other, two bright shining eyes peering over the cup attached to his nose.

"We have such a good group of parents who come to our family meetings. Perhaps you and Mr. Mack might come. We have an Indian couple who go quite regularly. I'm sure the others wouldn't mind you two at all." She smiled at Rabbit, and Mrs. Mack's swallow of cocoa suddenly turned cold in her mouth.

Mrs. Mack said nothing; she wished the woman would leave. Truthfully, she dared not wish her away. She would not only return with more of her own kind, bringing the sheets of paper and asking questions while one of them marked Mrs. Mack's answers in little boxes. Out of her head came memories of the surveys—women from town walking through her door after barely knocking, holding their noses, and brushing the chairs before they sat down. She would not live through that time again. She would not let them force Rabbit to talk in their words with their reason. Her son was much healthier chasing pictures inside his own head. He did not need this pale woman.

"Would you like some more cocoa?"

"Goodness no, this cup is still so hot, I can hardly drink." She smiled again.

Mrs. Mack looked over at Rabbit sitting drowsily in his chair. The cocoa had made him relax, his fat palms drooping over the arms of the chair.

"It's past his naptime," she said, shaking Rabbit gently on the shoulder. "Come on now, let's go to bed."

"May I help you tuck him in?" Miss Langley stood and waited to follow the boy and his mother. She watched Mrs. Mack turn down the sheet and slide Rabbit between the covers. "My, what an exquisitely carved headboard," she said. "Don't tell me. More of your husband's handiwork."

Rabbit had fallen asleep, his face on the pillow as static as the ducks and squirrels on his headboard. Mrs.

Mack walked from the room; the social worker tippy-toed behind her.

"Good," Miss Langley whispered when they had returned to the kitchen. "Now we can talk. You never can tell what little children might overhear." She smiled with half her teeth hidden. "I would suggest that you bring your son down to the county clinic early next week. We can run some tests and, if necessary, enroll him in a special school. Why, if the county has to send a social worker after you, there could be all kinds of trouble."

Mrs. Mack nodded, watching her husband walk up the path, straight to the back of Miss Langley's chair. He walked silently, accustomed to hunting small game. Now she watched him stop and sniff the air. He could always tell when one of them was in the vicinity. "They're not like us," he always said, "they even smell different." She watched him creep to the lean-to on the side of the house where he stored the carving tools. Satisfied that she need not explain to him, she turned her eyes toward Miss Langley.

"My husband should be returning soon, maybe you ought to talk to him."

At that moment Mr. Mack walked through the door. He put the bag of hazelnuts on the floor. The wooden mallet he used as a nutcracker was anchored on top.

"I'm glad to see you," Mrs. Mack said. "This is Miss Langley. She wants to bring Rabbit down to the clinic, and she wants us to go to some meetings."

Miss Langley turned her smile to face him. She saw the heavy mallet coming down, but even then her eyes did not believe. He hit her four times, because she was, after all, the fourth visitor.

"I didn't think you were ever coming," his wife said, putting brown paper bags under the body's head to catch the blood. She began scrubbing the floor with soda before the stain set in the wood.

"Too bad Robert had to see her," he answered, picking up Miss Langley. "I'm really sorry. If I'd known she was here pestering you, I'd have come straight home." He opened the screen door. "Will you please bring the shovel? It's on the side of the house."

She finished scrubbing and carried the bucket to the porch, tossing the pail so that pink sudsy water melted into the ground. They walked past the fir trees, deeper into the Forest Preserve.

"Here?" he asked, depositing the body on the ground.

She nodded and handed him the shovel. "At least this one is full grown," she said, remembering last winter when the boy with spotted glasses was lost from his hiking group. He came to their door for something hot to drink, cold to his toes, he had said. He was surprised to see people living in the middle of the woods, and then Mr. Mack knocked him unconscious, dragging his body to the front yard. The Forest Preserve was so large, he knew the search party would not reach their part of the woods until morning. By then he had carried the stiff body to a spot close to town. The newspaper account that Mr. Mack read said the boy apparently fell, struck his head on a rock, and wandered dazedly before collapsing. He froze to death overnight. The other two did not matter, they were old ladies hunting mushrooms and herbs, so they said.

Mrs. Mack watched her husband uncover the hole then drop the shovelfuls of dirt over the slender body, completely covering the golden hair. She wished he would hurry up—darkness would soon catch them. She had to get home and sweep the air out of the house. Anything, she thought, to remove that terrible odor before bedtime.

KEY TO THE CITY

"Nora, want to eat your breakfast with me?" Her mother's starched uniform swished as she walked to the door.

"All right, Mama, I'm getting up now." She watched her mother push aside the curtain that separated her bedroom from the hallway. Then she swung both feet to the edge of the bed and stood up. The little girl who slept beside her did not stir as Nora pulled on her blue jeans and tiptoed from the room.

In the kitchen her mother already sat at the table. "Babycake still asleep?" she asked. "That child ought to be completely worn out getting ready for this trip. You'd think we'd been to Chicago and back."

Nora slipped her egg from the skillet to the plate. "At least Mattie isn't so much trouble," she said, "but the two of them sure don't help my packing."

"I wish I could help, but Mrs. Anderson is not going to let me off early."

"She still mad about you leaving?"

Her mother nodded and Nora watched the wrinkles around her mouth deepen into soft brown folds. "Time for me to be leaving." She looked at the battered alarm clock on the center of the table. "Listen, honey, be sure and get the eggs before the girls get up. The chickens deserve a little bit of peace." She picked up her handbag from the kitchen chair and walked out the door.

Nora rinsed her plate in the kitchen sink, and taking the wicker basket from on top of the icebox, opened the screen door. Immediately the hens scurried around her, giggling with cackles as they flapped across the front yard. She looked down at the basket in her hand. Here she was gathering eggs like she did every day of her life and tomorrow the family was leaving for Chicago.

Her daddy had a good part-time job, he said, but he'd gotten so busy he no longer had time to write, not even to send a card for her graduation. She felt strange knowing she would see him in a few hours. Tomorrow morning she and Mattie and Mama and Babycake planned to ride all the way from Still Creek to Chicago without ever leaving the bus except when they all had to go to the bathroom.

Mama probably would have a time with Babycake. Her little sister got sick whenever she rode for a long time, and they couldn't wash her very well in those bus station bathrooms. She knew her daddy would meet them at the downtown Chicago bus station; he would be awfully glad to see them. A lot of people around Still Creek said he'd left them and wasn't going to send for them or even see them again. She had known better. If he said he would send for his family, he would. Besides, when he first married her mama, he promised they'd get away to Chicago. Which was really why Mama took on another job instead of staying home with the kids. With both of them working full-time, she figured she could save some money.

At their graduation exercises, the principal had announced the two members of the class who would go on to college. Nora's going to college was the reason they were moving. Her parents said she could go to a branch of the city college practically free and finish up her education. They had planned to move "one of these days" for as long as she could remember.

Nora could repeat their special family formula backwards, frontwards, and even sideways. They had talked about it ever since she was a little girl. Mama and Daddy would get jobs up north, and with the money she herself could earn, she would eventually get through college. Then she would put Mattie through, and Mattie would see that Babycake graduated. And of course if any other sisters or brothers came along, they would do the same thing for them.

She waved to Mrs. McAuley, who was hanging out clothes next door. Her wash, like their family's, was conspicuous with the absence of a man's blue work shirts. Nora wondered if Mr. McAuley would ever come home, but the neighborhood's early morning sounds blotted out the memory of him. Behind the chicken coop she could hear the grinding noise of Mr. Johnson's tractor. How funny to think that in a few hours she would no longer hear that familiar sound. Leaving was just a day away and even thinking about it made her throat feel a little funny.

By the time the eggs were gathered and set up high on top of the icebox, Mama had long since been off to work. Nora made Mattie and Babycake mayonnaise and egg sandwiches for breakfast. After they were through eating, she tried to persuade the two little girls to play house outside. But in an hour they were tired and wanted to help her.

"Go on, Mattie, go back outdoors and play." She tried to keep her impatience from showing.

"But we don't got nothing to play with," Mattie said, determined not to leave. "Margie and Tanker-Belle are all packed up and you said we won't see them again until we get there."

Mattie's brown eyes began watering as if she were going to cry. Margie and Tanker-Belle were the two dolls of the family. Tanker-Belle had been one of those fancy toaster cover dolls that some well-meaning aunt on Mama's side had sent as a Christmas gift. Which would have been nice, but they didn't have a toaster.

Mattie had practically confiscated the doll and for reasons known only to Mattie had named her Tanker-Belle. She had spent most of her time since Christmas in the Pretend House back of the pecan tree. Tanker-Belle was rather frayed now, after having spent several nights in the rain.

Now Nora explained to the little girls that at last the doll was going to have a nice long rest. She had packed Tanker-Belle immediately after breakfast while Mattie was busy with something else. She was now inside the big roasting pan with the dictionary and the kitchen forks. But Mattie insisted that she knew Tanker-Belle was lonesome inside the turkey pan.

"I'll tell you what, Mattie," Nora said as she tried to comfort the sobbing child. "Look on my dresser and get a nickel out of the blue bag. You go find Babycake and you all walk up to Mr. James's store for a double orange popsicle. Then go play in the Pretend House until lunchtime."

96

"Can I, Nora! Oh, can I?" Mattie's smile stopped the tears running down her cheeks. She raced out of the little hallway jumping over boxes and through the bedroom door for a nickel. In a second she was calling Babycake and the two little girls started up the road.

Five dollars and ninety-five cents worth of graduation money was left. Nora kept a mental record of her savings since June. Her habit of saving was a reaction, she guessed. Her father had all the good intentions in the world but whenever they needed money he never had enough. That was one reason why her mother had taken the responsibility of moving the family.

She stooped down and began cramming some books in another cardboard box, in a hurry to move on to something else. By the time the little girls were finished with the popsicle, it would be time for their naps. Nora tied a string around the box and made a double knot. If she could have just an hour by herself, she could finish the packing.

She had begun scrubbing the kitchen floor when suddenly a noise that sounded like a rock hitting the wire of the chicken coop made her drop the rag and run to the back door.

"Babycake, you and Mattie stop bothering the chickens. We won't get any eggs if you keep on; what's wrong with you all anyway?"

"Babycake wants all the popsicle, Nora. And you gave it to me, didn't you, Nora?"

By the time Mattie explained about the popsicle and how Babycake had gotten angry and thrown a rock at the chickens, Babycake was crying. Mattie, upon seeing

Babycake's tears, had begun crying herself and Nora stood there, outdone. Here she was faced with two squealing little girls and her with all that work to do.

"I can tell," she said firmly, "that it's time for two naps. Give me the popsicle and you can eat it after you've had a nap." She marched her sisters through the back door, stopped to deposit the ice cream on the kitchen table, and continued toward the bedroom. While she undressed her sisters, the popsicle lay forgotten.

In a quarter of an hour Babycake was asleep. Mattie, who was ready to get up again, decided she was not sleepy and began singing to herself. Nora had to stop packing again and tell her to be quiet. She didn't notice the popsicle until she saw the sticky orange drops on her clean kitchen floor. She wiped off the table and floor and swallowed what was left of the dripping orange popsicle. There was no getting around it, she'd have to spend another nickel for some more ice cream.

Nora worked all evening, sorting clothes, folding linen, and packing kitchen utensils. Finally, the boxes were ready to go.

In the morning the smell of freshly fried chicken lingered throughout the house. The two fryers Mama had killed last night plus the one Mrs. McAuley brought over would last them the time the trip would take. In the bottom of the lunch basket were three sweet potato pies and a brown bag full of the Georgia peaches that grew wild in their backyard.

According to the schedule propped on an empty milk bottle on the kitchen table, in a half hour everybody would be ready to pile in the Edwardses' car for the bus station. The Edwardses were going to keep all the house furnishings in their barn until Mama sent for the furniture.

The two big beds already had been dismantled and Mattie's roll-away cot was folded up near the front door. Nora walked from the hall into the living room. The whole house looked so empty, even her father's postcards were missing from the mantel over the fireplace. Suddenly she smiled. All of the furniture was covered with old newspapers their neighbors had saved, and four layers of the *Still Creek Bugle* couldn't possibly revive the sagging sofa cushions.

By seven-thirty Babycake had been freshly washed and ironed for the trip. She was commanded to sit still on the front stoop and announce the Edwardses' arrival. Mattie, who had been dared to get dirty, kept her company. The two little girls sat on the first step, facing the swing tied to the pine tree. Their sliding feet had trampled the bits of grass growing beneath the rope, and scattered in the yard were a few green weeds the chickens had not pecked away.

Babycake reached over and gave the potted Christmas cactus a goodbye pat. The leaves were shiny because she had poured water over them this morning—Mama insisted the plant be clean when Mrs. Edwards carried the pot home.

All at once there was a honk from the horn and a long lanky boy, the oldest of the Edwards boys, was running up the steps.

"Pop says are y'all ready yet?" Without giving them a chance to answer he started piling boxes in the trunk of the car. Babycake and Mattie were so scared they would get dirty and get left they did everything Nora told them to do.

"Mattie, pick up the little shoe box . . . Babycake, make sure we got the lunch. No, I'll take care of the lunch, you pick up the hat box over there." Their little house had never been so cluttered and then so empty. Come to think of it, their neighborhood seldom had seen such excitement.

Everybody in Still Creek was at the bus station to see the Murrays off. There was no need to ask how they'd gotten there. Those few people who had cars drove down and piled in as many neighbors as they could. Uncle Ben, Aunt Mabel's husband, was one of those who had walked the three quarters of a mile to the bus station. Mabel had caught a ride. Anyway, they were all there, a mass of black humanity overflowing the little waiting room marked "Colored."

In one corner of one half of Still Creek Bus Terminal, Mattie sat on an upright box as Aunt Mabel gave her pig-tails a quick brushing. When she had tied each end with a bright yellow ribbon, Mabel thumped Mattie on the neck and pushed her off the box toward her Mama's voice that attempted to round up the family.

Nora saw Aunt Mabel trying to catch Uncle Ben's eye. Mabel began to speak above the noise in the room.

"Haven't been this many people here since they brought that Jackson boy's body home," she said, "the one who was killed overseas three years ago."

While Uncle Ben and Aunt Mabel discussed the com-munity gatherings at the station during the last five years, Mama was getting ready to buy their tickets. Somebody got up so she could sit down and count out the money for four one-way tickets to Chicago.

Mattie was hanging over her shoulders, wide-eyed. "Mama," she breathed, "are we rich?"

"Hush, child, I'm trying to count." When she had counted out the correct amount of money four times, she tied what was left into a handkerchief and put it in the blue denim purse, which in turn went into her genuine imitation leather cowhide bag. Still counting silently, she made her way to the ticket window. When the man had given her the tickets and counted out the change, Nora felt like giving a glorious hallelujah of relief. At times like this she always felt something wrong was going to happen. She could imagine the fare going up and them without enough money, having to go back home.

With Mama talking to Aunt Mabel, Nora slipped out of the side door for a final look at her hometown. The Georgia landscape was shallow and dull and, to her eyes that had seen no other part of the country, beautiful. Even this early in the morning a thickness had settled over the countryside, covering everything with a film of fine red dust. She fingered the purse inside her pocket. Six dollars she had now—Mrs. Edwards had given her a dime to buy some candy in case she got hungry on the way.

The sound of voices inside the waiting room reached her ears. She could hear Aunt Mabel crying, louder and louder. The voices seemed to reach out and carry her with them. The bus—the bus must have come. Quickly she shut her purse and ran back toward the waiting room.

Sure enough there was her mother frantically hugging and kissing everybody and thanking them for all the good things they had done for the Murrays. Mattie was pulling Mama's hand and begging her to hurry up before they got left. Seeing Nora, her mother beckoned her to come and get Mattie and Babycake for a final trip to the bathroom.

By the time everybody had been pushed out of the waiting room, the men had most of the luggage stored underneath the bus. Then began the last-minute hugging and kissing and gift giving all over again. Nora felt a dollar bill pressed into her hand. She couldn't help the tears; Uncle Ben really didn't have any money to spare. She bent over and kissed the old man on his cheek.

The bus driver checked his watch and in a dry, matter-of-fact voice announced that anybody who was leaving with him had better hurry and get on because he was driving in exactly two shakes. Finally the steel door closed. In the rear of the bus, their noses pressed against the windowpanes, the four Murrays waved goodbye to friends and neighbors and to Still Creek, Georgia, "the original home of fine Georgia peaches."

After hours of riding, Nora lost track of the towns they passed. Still Creek seemed so far away and the slight jogging of the bus no longer made her head ache. The whole trip had become a kaleidoscope of sounds and colors. The small towns surrounded with ranch-style houses and green lawns were loose fragments she counted, like turning storybook pages in her mind.

At the next rest stop, Nora decided to stretch her legs in the bus aisle. Mama herself took the little girls inside for a glass of milk and a trip to the bathroom. When the bus started again, she began telling a fairytale to Mattie and then suddenly the accident occurred. Little Babycake had stuffed herself with too much sweet potato custard and she lost all her dinner on the back seat of the bus. They tried to clean up the seat with some old waxed paper, but they couldn't clean and pay attention to Babycake too.

Babycake started crying. Her stomach hurt and she wanted to go home. Mama tried to hush her, but the more she patted, the more Babycake cried. By the time the sourness had spread throughout the bus, Mama sent Nora up to the bus driver to ask him if he would stop and let Babycake get her stomach settled.

Nora stood up and held on to the seats, cautiously walking up the aisle, toward the back of the bus driver's gray-blue suit. After hours of riding, the jacket still looked freshly pressed, and he didn't even glance up in the mirror as she approached the driver's seat.

"My little sister's sick," she explained. "If she could get some air, my mother said she might feel better." She held on to the pole near the front steps, facing the back of the driver's gray head.

Muttering something unintelligible, he said no. He had lost enough time and would be stopping soon anyway. They would just have to wait like everybody else.

While she was standing in the aisle, the bus picked up speed and turned a sharp curve. Nora felt herself fall against two elderly women and although the bus was air-conditioned, one was struggling trying to raise the window.

"Niggers," she whispered, her voice grating, colliding with the growl of the motor.

Nora was not certain she had heard the woman speak, but even thinking of the word hurt her ears. Nobody'd ever called her a nigger to her face before. At least never with such anger. She looked into the woman's eyes, seeing the fierce look her father often described as belonging to white people. Fierceness that was hatred. She was conscious of the bus moving, jerking to a stop and then moving again but she heard nothing except the woman's words. It was as if the words formed an invisible cloak and only by pushing it away with her thoughts did she keep from being smothered.

She wanted to see her father now—have him take his wife and children from this horrible bus and put them down where they did not have to move ever again. What if . . . No, he would not do that, not after he talked so badly about Mr. McAuley deserting his family six months after they met him in Chicago. The McAuleys stayed in the city not even a year; in December they had come home. Even with the extra money allotted them because of Mr. McAuley's disappearance they did not have enough money to eat. She dared not even think.

Nora never knew how many rest stops the bus made. Once as she turned toward the window she realized the daylight had changed into darkness. She even forgot to watch for the sign telling them they had crossed the Illinois state line. Mattie wanted to play Cookie Jar, but she could not concentrate on the hand-clapping for trying not to remember those words. Nora was almost asleep when the bus turned into an entrance, pulled up to the curb, and stopped.

Because there were so many bundles to carry out, they were the last people getting off the bus. Babycake was the first one to see him. She caught hold of Mama's hand, yelling "Here we are, here we are," and started to run across the terminal to the man in the black trench coat. Nora had to hold her back. The man Babycake saw was not their father.

He was a little too tall, and when he passed the family, he just looked at them strangely.

They stood outside the big glass door with the little packages, waiting and looking through each crowd of people, but no one came.

"You people need help or something?" a woman asked. She walked as if she knew every inch of the ground surrounding the terminal. "If you need a taxi, I'll show you where to stand."

Nora shook her head. "No thank you, we're waiting for someone." Her eyes dropped to the pavement and for a while she was conscious only of shoes, so many different colors, passing, all walking by them. After fifteen minutes and two "May I help you's" Mama guided them through the revolving door and to a bench in the middle of the station.

"That way he can see us when he comes," she said, sitting down on the bench. Nora again braided Mattie and Babycake's hair and then there was nothing to do but wait.

Oh, why hadn't he come. He was supposed to be here, they had sent the letter last Friday. She had told him the exact time of their arrival. Twice she'd written it out.

Now Babycake was getting sleepy again. "Where's Daddy?" she asked. "Aren't we there now?"

"Hush up." Her mother motioned for Nora to unlace Babycake's shoes. "Maybe he can't find us," she whispered above the little girls' heads.

An hour passed. Nora stood. "Where you going?" Mattie asked. "Don't you get lost from us too."

"To check the luggage, it won't take long." Nora began

walking down the side of the terminal, near the shiny cigarette machine and past the magazine rack. Everything glittered with a metallic glow but the fluorescent lighting only emphasized the emptiness within her. She looked up and saw an overhead panel advertising a course in short-hand—gt-gd-jb . . . Then she met Elizabeth Taylor's gaze beneath the sign pointing to the telephone booth.

At once she was aware of what had happened. He was working overtime, and had overslept. She had the apartment building's telephone number from one of his first letters. She would call and whoever answered would tell her where to reach him and then he would come get them. With sticky fingers she loosened a dime from her money collection and lifted the receiver. The phone rang once, and a voice answered:

"McConnell's Drug Store—Hello? This is McConnell's Drug Store."

"Please," Nora whispered, "could I speak with Mr. Joseph Murray."

"Sorry miss, but no Joe Murray works here."

"Are you sure, don't you know him?"

"No, lady, but if you want to wait I'll check the list of people working in the building."

Then he was back too soon, and he was sorry, no Murray was even listed there.

Nora emerged from the booth and stood at the lockers, wondering if she should look outside, when she felt someone bump into her. She turned quickly, into a woman tugging on a small boy. "Excuse me," the woman murmured, pushing the boy ahead of her.

Abruptly pulling away, Nora ran toward the doors out to the sidewalk into the darkness. She tried to brush the air from her face but the fingers slightly touching her eyelashes came away damp. She stood outside, her eyes tightly closed, trying not to see them, all three of them huddled on that bench. Then her cheeks were dry.

Nora went back to the station bench and whispered to her mother, who was sitting quietly, Babycake's head nestled in her lap.

"Mama? Oh, Mama, did you know all the time?"

Her mother shook her head and reached for her daughter's hand.

"I couldn't know for sure," she said. "We had to work toward something. Don't you see? We wouldn't have ever gotten out if we didn't work toward something." Her voice was sad and quiet, as if she might slowly start humming Babycake to sleep.

"What are we going to do, Mama? They're bound to make us move out of here sometime."

"We'll just stay right in this spot," she said, covering Babycake with a coat, "just in case." She turned her face toward the suitcases and Nora, seeing that her mother might cry, was sorry she had asked.

"Tomorrow we can call the welfare people. Somebody there can help us find a place to go." Her mother spoke with her eyes fixed on the travel posters on the far side of the room.

That they never before had had to ask for help made no difference to Nora. She felt that they were pieces in a giant jigsaw puzzle, oddly shaped blobs that would never be put together. Here was her mother sitting so quietly, not letting anything upset her. But then that was not so difficult to do, she herself was not conscious of feeling anything. He loved them, he had to. After all, they were his, but sometimes loving became a burden. And if he had met them at the bus station, perhaps they would have become that to him. But they were supposed to be a family, weren't they? She was no longer certain.

Stepping over the suitcases piled near the bench holding Babycake, Nora began sorting bundles. She looked at the clock on the terminal wall, the silvery hands seemed fixed. Strange that it was morning already, outside the sky was still dark.

She'd probably have to babysit for a while, until Mama found a job and a place to leave the little girls during the day. She began fingering the string around the boxes. Today was Saturday and Mattie and Babycake's Sunday dresses would need ironing, but she'd worry about that later. Their hair ribbons did not have to be pressed, if she could ever remember where they were.

Slowly Nora put down the box. Her shoulders slid down the back of the bench. She couldn't press anything, she couldn't even remember where they had packed the iron.

THE VISITOR

The next train schedule written on Alice's blackboard would mark a departure. Why Katie would choose to ride the train was beyond her, but she would not complain. Jack did not have to spend plane fare for his daughter. Now there would be no reason for Alice not to accompany him to the national medical convention.

They were driving her car to the station. In his car with the top down the wind would muss her hair and she refused to meet his child looking like a freak. Her baby, Jack Junior, was still in school. His father wanted him to be excused but she saw no reason to upset his normal schedule. This child was only his half sister. Jack was already in the car when she came outside, the afternoon sun catching the shine of her hose through the mesh shoes. He was waiting, impatiently fiddling with the radio dial.

"Well, you certainly took your time."

They were not going to start this ordeal by arguing. She leaned over and kissed him on the neck and without thinking he reached up and brushed the spot.

"Sorry honey, but getting dressed takes a girl time."

"Does it, Alice?" His eyes were like Little Jack's and the picture of Katie too, the same intense brown. "Does it take all day to get dressed when you've done nothing?"

He was going to be nasty again. He had been the one who insisted she not return to work until Jackie was large enough to take care of himself. And they didn't need the money. He was the only Negro general practitioner allowed on the white hospital staff so he had no choice but to make money. How could she stand sitting around the house, he wanted to know, doing nothing but nibbling all day and becoming fatter and fatter. Even with a girdle, her most comfortable suit was a sixteen and a half.

She had tried becoming active in community work, but the neighborhood meetings always seemed to conflict with her pinochle games. Jackie was too young to be much help with the housework. True, she'd had her series of maids, but they just were not reliable. Madge quit two months ago to have her third illegitimate child. When Alice thought of giving her some old pillowcases, she opened the linen closet and discovered Madge had already helped herself to most of the new pastel sheets. All these months the woman had been slowly pilfering, quietly restocking her house with Alice's possessions. Since then she had decided to do the housework without a maid.

The station was only twenty minutes away and finding a parking place was no problem. If necessary Jack could do as she did since she attached one of his "Doctor on Call" signs on her car. Good Lord, it had been so long since she'd ridden a train she'd forgotten how dirty the station looked. She caught hold of her husband's arm and as they walked along she realized that he no longer guided her in public. Instead he seemed to pull her along, tugging at her elbow. That settled it, she'd have to go on a diet, but she thought *diet* repeatedly every day and the picture of a slender Alice was not convincing, even to herself.

Katie's train was late. By now her group was halfway through Linda Knight's pinochle luncheon, but just as well she missed that meeting. Linda was known for serving uninteresting snacks. They could go inside to sit down, Jack said, but the seats looked grimy and she certainly didn't want to get the new suit dirty. Alice considered asking him to get Cokes from the machine when a baggage cart drove past her and abruptly stopped.

"How you Mrs. Wilson? Come to pick up the Doctor's little girl?"

She thought the boy had left Columbia years ago, but she was looking into Monroe Jefferson Turner's sweaty face.

"Why, Monroe, you just crossed my mind today. Have you been working here very long?"

"Yes ma'am, since last September."

If he knew about Katie then news of her arrival must have spread all over town. The old rumors would be starting again. She looked at Monroe's coarse black hair; he had changed little since third grade. She had heard the talk when she moved to Columbia, teaching in the elementary school near the Negro hospital. Jack, everybody said, had married Sondra uncertain that the baby was his, but unwilling to let the child begin life fatherless. At the time she was not concerned, spending most of her time in the third-grade classroom, the windows overlooking an itching slum. The children that year were all dark, with big eyes that seemed expressionless until she learned their names and was forced to read their records for her reports.

Then one day in the spring Monroe Jefferson Turner was hit in the mouth with a baseball bat. Without thinking she grabbed him, half running, half dragging him to the emergency ward of the hospital, all the time thinking that the child didn't have anything else, please let him keep his teeth. Monroe Jefferson's front teeth were cracked right down the middle and he was snaggletoothed until high school, when he finally managed to buy a bridge. She first saw Jack in the emergency ward. She hadn't known his name then, but made finding out her business.

Getting the older teachers to introduce them at holiday dances was no problem. Then any man would have been proud to be seen with her. And after all these years her complexion was still the same—not light enough to look white, but a comfortable light brown color. She was small in those days. Hah! Anyone who thought she would be squeezing into a size sixteen with her best girdle would have been joking. But Jackie was almost ten now, and they had waited three years before having children.

She had insisted. It seemed such a shame to have to bear all of that weight when for the first time she had money to buy really good clothes. She still derived pleasure from walking into a store and having those snippety salesgirls speak of her as Dr. Wilson's wife.

She had only the best of maternity clothes, Jack saw to that. Suddenly she was conscious of staring at Monroe. Dear Lord, everything seemed so far away.

"Yes," she said, "we're here to get Dr. Wilson's daughter." Alice smiled, hoping he would tell all of his buddies that he'd seen his third-grade teacher and she was as pretty as ever. All size sixteen of her. As she waved Monroe on to the baggage room, she reached out to grab Jack's arm and immediately felt lonely when she clutched air. Trying to hang on to him so tightly was perfectly silly. Besides, she saw him now, leaning over the magazine counter, his coat wrinkled. He was talking very quietly to the man who sold magazines.

Until now hers had been a good life, considering the kind she had been brought up to expect. She had spent the first years of their marriage slipping into the doctor's-wife mold created by Jack's first wife. Through the years she settled into the pattern—joining the wives' auxiliary, even church organizations. Finally this spring she felt that she had completely erased Sondra's memory. She had been elected president of her sorority chapter and the news received national coverage in the *Afro*. Then the letter had arrived. Thank God Katie was to stay just for spring vacation. Alice knew she would be unable to take a stranger's visit any longer.

"If she's like her mother," she told Trude Williams on the telephone, "she has the makings of a real bitch. I imagine she thinks like Sondra, and you know what they say about trouble coming in small packages."

Then Jack appeared at the doorway, his face serious, as if he had heard. She had to laugh aloud, feeling the air push up from her throat making a hollow sound to let him know she was joking, of course. But it was the truth—Sondra was a bitch, even Jack's sister Joan did not like her. And didn't it stand to reason that this child, this Katie who had grown up with Sondra, would be just like her.

Oh, not that they looked very much alike, but you couldn't tell everything looking at pictures. Photographs, carefully posed, came every year. They were usually serious brown eyes, half-hidden under a mop of dark hair—the child had absolutely no style. But in her school uniform with the date stamped across the bottom, what could anyone expect? These pictures, which Jack kept in his wallet, one on top of the other, reminded Alice of the "Wanted" posters in the post office.

This year when the time came to see how much the child had grown, there had been no picture. Snatches of Sondra's letter still ran through her mind, phrases popping up when she needed all of her wits for pinochle. "Five years is a long time, she should see the city in which she was born." And how did she end it, as if Alice could forget? "I want her to be friendly with her brother." The child could never become close to Little Jack, and what her visit might do to him frightened his mother. He knew that Katie existed, but for him she was among the paraphernalia in his father's wallet, certainly not as attractive as the baseball cards in his own pocket.

For her Alice had cleaned the guest room, put dust covers over the velvet chairs, and undergone no special preparations. Very few people had stayed in her guest room. Jack's friends who came visiting in Columbia usually brought their children, and knowing of her aversion to noise and pets, stayed at the local hotel. Unfortunately Jack's daughter would have a birthday while she was here, so there was no way to keep quiet those two weeks.

Already she had engaged Larson's band for a birthday party at the Adelphi. Her nieces Carol and Cicely had promised to invite some of their friends, some of those nice-looking children that were always around her sister-in-law's house. Not that she was conscious of color, but light-skinned children looked brighter at spring parties. And this party had to turn out exactly right.

The station was filthy, gray soot seemed to cling to the windows and dull the tracks in the midafternoon sun. Perhaps Katie would not come. Sondra was just spiteful enough to have them make room, squeezing another person into the house, and then decide that Katie was too young to make the trip alone. The child should look presentable enough for travel; God knows Jack sent enough money to keep her fed and clothed.

She turned to watch her husband leave the magazine rack and stop at the ticket window. He raised his hand in thanks and made his way toward her.

"The train from Memphis will be here any minute. Don't look so sad, Katie's a big girl now. She won't be any trouble."

Exactly the problem—she was a girl big enough to observe and send home a complete report to Sondra. She could tell her mother about Jack's fat wife, not at all like the pictures they used to see on the Wilsons' Christmas cards. She could write about the custom-mixed make-up that caked between his wife's wrinkles. And she could tell her how Mrs. Wilson had to stay in air-conditioned rooms because sometimes, even in her own mind, she felt as if she were burning up.

"Of course, she won't be any trouble. I just hope she and Jackie get along. He's too sensitive for other children to pick on him."

"If you'd let him play with the neighborhood children he wouldn't be so sensitive about what you insist is baby fat."

No, they had come this far in the day. They were not going to argue here. She would not let him become angry with her until this child had returned home. Before Alice could answer they saw the train pulling into the station.

Her high heels clicked beside Jack, past the baggage cars and the few people waiting for disembarking passengers, until they reached the platform. Katie was the last person the conductor helped step down. Naturally, with her growing up in Memphis, Sondra would see that the child had no initiative. She probably had been standing at the window afraid to get off, not moving until the conductor helped her step down.

Katie was not a bad-looking child, a little too thin to be almost sixteen, and she was not well filled out. But some children were slow in developing, and she did have one saving grace, nice hair—a bit too long to be stylish, even for a teenager, but hair could be helped. At once Jack grabbed her by the arm, dragging her to meet his daughter.

"Baby, I'm so glad you came. Was the train ride comfortable?"

She pulled away from her father, not forcibly, but almost as if she were accustomed to slithering out of arms.

"Fine thank you."

So she was not going to call Jack "Daddy." She probably would spend the entire two weeks sitting wherever he sat, standing wherever he stood so that she would never have to call him by name from a distance.

"Look baby, you've never met Alice."

The cool brown eyes focused on her now, surveying, eager to write the report to Mother.

"Hello Katie, we're glad you decided to come." Should she hug her? Katie extended her hand and Alice was saved from doing anything but squeezing it, a little too warmly maybe. She could feel the child withdrawing, but Jack need not know.

She was alone with Katie while Jack waited for the baggage.

"Goodness, you must be tired, that's an awfully long trip for someone who's just finished midterms."

"How did you know about my exams? Do you read the letters I write to my father?"

Those eyes staring at her made Alice uncomfortable. "Of course not, but my husband tells me what you're doing as a matter of course. I feel rather awkward about this Katie, but Jack thought you might wonder what to call me. Most of my girlfriends call me Kitten, why don't you use my nickname?" She smiled at Katie, who seemed to be looking past Alice's shoulder.

"I'd rather call you Mrs. Wilson if you don't mind. I've always thought of you by that name."

So this was her impression. The second Mrs. Wilson as in the radio program, brought to her by a short, skinny girl, cemented with the enemy in Memphis, and whose father probably would side with her against her stepmother.

"Let's go have a Coke while your father puts the luggage in the car." Neither one of them would have to talk while they drank, and those eyes could stare at their reflection in the mirror opposite the soda fountain.

"I hope you like lemonade," Alice said. "Little Jack is allergic to soft drinks, so we drink lots of fruit juice."

Katie took a big swallow of her drink. "Is he allergic to many things?" Alice thought she detected a slight smirk on her face. The child was unnerving, she reminded her of a wizened old lady in a child's body. She was just about to list Jackie's allergies when Jack returned.

"Let's go," he commanded, slipping his arm through each of their elbows. Katie crawled into the back seat and was silent during the drive, except to utter a polite "uh-huh" each time Jack pointed out a local landmark. In another twenty minutes they were home, waiting for Jackie to come from school and meet his sister.

Katie did not seem to be impressed by the guest room. She hung up her clothes and sat quietly in the den, not touching the scrapbooks Alice brought her, containing Jackie's baby pictures.

But for Alice, Katie's birthday would have been another ordinary day. She opened her presents immediately after breakfast, said thank you, and put them away. Alice hoped she would perk up during the birthday party.

"Heh Katie, Mama says do you want to go downtown with us? Aw, come on and go. She says we can have lunch at Honey's and if you don't come I have to stay home with you."

As she scraped leftover omelet into the garbage can, Alice listened to her son. Without moving she could see the top of his head, bobbing outside Katie's door. Such a contrast there was between the children, even if they did resemble each other. Jackie seemed to be more alive. Oh, there was life in Katie, but life incapable of surfacing, breaking through her distrust of other people.

When Alice asked about the class ring she wore around her neck, she shrugged and said, "Just a good friend." The child did not take easily to teasing but that came, Alice knew, from not having many friends. She seemed to like both Carol and Cicely, spending most of her afternoons at their house, but she preferred to spend her evenings sitting on the covered chair reading a book. Even the thought of tonight's birthday party did not engender any enthusiasm within her.

Alice tried to help her look decent so she'd fit in with the neighborhood children, but her efforts were thoroughly frustrated. Incidents like yesterday morning seemed to occur and reoccur.

"Katie," Alice said yesterday, "I have to go to the hairdresser this morning. They have some awfully cute hairstyles for girls your age, how would you like to have your hair cut? Irene's an excellent stylist."

She should have known the suggestion was useless as she watched the brown eyes freeze.

"I'd rather not cut my hair, at least not until I ask Mother if it's all right."

"We could call her tonight if you want to."

"Oh, but that would be too expensive. Anyway I think I like my hair better when it's long."

"Katie, you can at least come and get it set." Alice was quickly losing her temper. "Surely that wouldn't hurt you, to be away from your book for just an hour. You've got such nice hair and it's time you were concentrating on an image."

Later, rethinking the scene, she could have kicked herself. Katie very casually put down the book.

"If you don't mind," she said, looking very bored, "I think I'll stay home. I have some letters to write."

And that was the end of the hairstyling. If Jack didn't mind presenting her to his friends as she was, there was no reason for his wife to be upset. After all, she was not the girl's mother.

Now as she washed the breakfast dishes, she thought of Katie's birthday party. The party would be well put together even if Katie were not. All they needed to do now was pray that the weather stay beautiful. The thought of God being on her side made Alice smile. Heaven knows He was probably the only one.

"Jackie," she called from the kitchen, "don't you bother your sister. Let the birthday girl do whatever she wants to do."

Pink and green lights blinking and fusing made the room a kaleidoscope of color. Streams of light settled on Alice standing at the door of the Adelphi's main lounge. The party would not begin for half an hour yet, but unaccustomed to letting other people polish last-minute details—a leftover she had inherited from her one-parent childhood—she had come to make certain everything was in order. The party had to be a success. She was, as everyone said, a perfectionist.

Joan's oldest daughter, Carol, promised to come exactly on time and make sure Katie met the people she and Cicely had invited. Katie could not be persuaded to come early. There was nothing for her to do, she said, and besides, Alice wanted her hair in a French twist, didn't she? Don't worry, she'd get there, her father would bring her shortly before nine-thirty. Carol offered to help with her make-up, but

Katie had never worn any and saw no reason to start now. Just thinking about the child exhausted Alice. Really, she had never seen any one person so ungrateful.

After dinner this evening she tried to make Jack see his daughter's lack of social grace, but making apparent the obvious facts had been a mistake.

"I spent all morning downtown with your daughter. All morning, I tell you we looked for a party dress, and she didn't see one, not one that she wanted. It wasn't a matter of money, I told her the dress was a birthday present from us."

Just then Katie wandered into the room and picked up a letter box from the sofa. Twice during the day she had sneaked up on Alice telling first Trude, then Joan over the telephone how flat-chested Katie was, and that she refused to let Alice buy her a padded bra. Ignoring them, Katie left the room.

Jack did not put down the evening newspaper. "Why didn't you let her decide what she wants for a present?" he said. "Maybe she isn't interested in new clothes."

"Be serious, Jack. A new dress with price tag, no question? Why, when I was that age I was never so lucky. Every extra cent my mother made went to send me to college. Even when I didn't want to go to school, she wouldn't let me spend that money."

"She's obviously not like you."

Just the way he said it made her ache. Biting her lips to keep from saying anything, she had taken the salad bowls into the kitchen and begun cleaning the refrigerator until he left to check on a patient at the hospital. He hadn't even thought to order flowers for the party. So, at the last minute she called the shop and ordered an orchid for herself and a corsage of rosebuds for Katie. If she wore the flowers, attention would be directed to the top half of her dress and hopefully no one would notice that the dress was inches too long.

Alice straightened the tablecloth and wiped her hands on the panels of her dress. Now the problem was out of her hands. She walked around the room waiting for the band members to slip into place. She had heard them practicing downstairs when she arrived.

"Hi Aunt Alice, I got her here on time and in one piece." Carol swept into the room, dragging Katie behind her. "What shall I do with the guest of honor, put her on the stage?" Surprisingly, Katie giggled.

"You look lovely, Katie," Alice said. She did not, of course, but Carol's eyeshadow was a definite improvement.

"Mom and Dad are coming later, Aunt Alice. They're waiting for Cicely's date to come for her. Heh, here comes somebody now."

Katie stood at the door between the two of them until the last guest arrived and the pink lights were hazed with a film of smoke. When every name had been checked on the party list, Alice stood at the door alone, surveying the crowd.

Cicely had pulled her dress above her knees, and tomorrow when she mentioned the unladylike behavior her niece would declare she could not dance in such a straight skirt. She saw Jackie at the punch bowl again, but maybe he was getting a cup for someone else. Satisfied with the panorama, she decided to go sit with Joan and her husband, who had come, as Pete said, to observe the orgy.

"Hello, hello, glad you made it out tonight. How does it feel to be the aging mother of two beautiful daughters?"

"Girl, I don't even want to talk about them. They're Pete's children. I'm too young to be their mother. I'll own up only to Pattie. She wanted to come tonight and felt very hurt that she was not invited."

"Be sure and take her some birthday cake, she probably likes frosting better than she likes parties." Alice pulled up a chair and sat down. From this table, near the center of the party, she felt as if she were the reigning queen.

"Where's Jack?" Pete leaned over his wife, his elbow trailing dangerously above the chip dip.

"At the hospital, where else? You'd think he would be here for his daughter's coming-out party, but some baby decided to come into the world."

"Too bad," Joan said, "he does have a bad habit of leaving before a party ever begins." She began chuckling, a deep spontaneous laugh that Alice always envied. "Watch it, sweetie, you're making the dip unfit for human consumption." Joan very carefully moved the bowl to the center of the table.

If any person could dethrone Alice, Joan would be the one. Sometimes her sister-in-law actually unnerved her. She never seemed to be upset about anything and Alice wondered how she could put up such a good front. She and Pete both were just schoolteachers and the two oldest children, with a year's difference in age, would be in college together. She always thought they often borrowed money from Jack but she was afraid to ask, being almost certain he discussed her with his sister.

"I saw Katie through the crowd and she really looked adorable. Did she seem excited about the party, Alice? I couldn't help feeling she would have enjoyed a smaller collection of people."

Joan always was so practical. Too practical. She certainly didn't have the vision necessary to plan a party like this one. "Every girl ought to have one big party," Alice answered. "I always regretted that nobody could afford to give me one."

Joan's eyes followed Pete's carrot stick into the dip. "Where is she now? We'd like to wish her a happy birthday."

"She's around in this crowd and I'm counting on your girls to make sure she has a good time."

"I don't think they'll be still long enough to even miss Katie, if she were missing. Cicely came over to point out some boy in her history class and I could swear he's not the one who brought her tonight. We haven't seen Carol since she left home." Joan laughed again.

Sometimes Alice wished she could be as unconcerned about things as Joan. Her house always was in a state of confusion and the disorder only attracted people.

The band broke into a rock-and-roll piece that sounded vaguely familiar. She watched the guests bounce, all they seemed to do was bounce and shake on the dance floor. One of her nieces had started some kind of step, her arms waving, and everybody began following her. She saw Carol and the Williamses' son. Now there was a nice boy, but of course Katie didn't particularly like him. Where was she anyway? She could at least dance and pretend to have a good time. Alice stood and tried to see through the knot of people on the floor. Katie was not in the group.

She really did not blame Jack's daughter. She too would have been nervous among so many well-dressed children. When she herself was being initiated into Columbia society, she always had been afraid that she would say something out of place or really act like she was from Ebston, Georgia. Now, she knew how to fit in with anybody of importance.

"Heh Mama." Jackie was tugging at her elbow, and unthinking, she pushed him away.

"Mama." His voice was insistent.

"Yes, Jackie, what is it?" Her voice was curt and in case anyone heard she reached down and smoothed the top of his head. She watched him frown and wipe his hair with a fat palm.

"Good night Mama. All I wanted to tell you was that some lady wants to meet Katie and I couldn't find her anywhere. She sent me over to ask you."

"I thought she was sitting at one of the side tables. Haven't you seen her at all tonight?"

Jackie shook his head. "Mama, when can I go home?"

"Aren't you having a good time?" She watched his eyes above his pudgy cheeks. "Max will be serving very soon and then you can eat and then we'll see about going home. Now go talk to those people, I'm going to check the ladies' lounge for Katie."

"Lovely party, Alice."

She waved to Winston and Trude Williams, and to some people she bypassed going through the door. So far she was pleased with her party. Occasions like tonight made her despise the *Clarion* for not covering colored social events. A reporter for their community paper had taken a picture of Katie and herself greeting the guests. She herself had written the caption. "Alice Wilson, charming wife of Dr. Jack Wilson, is shown with her lovely . . ." She pushed open the door to the women's lounge.

Katie was sitting on the sofa, her legs crossed beneath the full cotton skirt. Alice picked up the long white gloves that had slipped to the floor.

"Are you all right? If you felt ill why didn't you tell me?"

Katie did not look up. "I'm all right," she said. "Those people are enough to make anybody sick."

The sensible thing would be to ignore the child. Alice certainly could not force her downstairs, but if she left her here, the first person out of the ladies' room would spread knowledge of Katie's discontent throughout the whole party. It was a wonder she hadn't already been discovered. Perhaps she could shame the child into returning downstairs.

"Don't you think you should go back down and meet the guests who came late? They came to talk with you."

Katie shook her head. "No." The freshly curled hair dipped again over the book.

"The civil thing to do is to look at adults when you speak to them." Alice grimaced. That sentence hadn't come out exactly right—she sounded like an old maid schoolteacher.

"Oh?" Katie closed the book over her index finger and looked straight at Alice. The eyes were smiling, the only sign of life in the carved face.

"Can't you say anything? Here Jack's spent all of this money so you can meet some decent people and you decide to read a book. Now you get up from there and come down and act like you're enjoying your own party."

"I think I'll go home." Katie stood and waited as if she expected Alice to unblock the entrance.

"If you go anywhere you're going downstairs to talk to those people." This child with her skinny body actually had the nerve to be stubborn.

"I don't feel like being sociable. I would like to go home."

"Now listen, Katie, be reasonable. At least stay long enough to blow out the candles and cut your birthday cake."

"Let those people eat as much of my cake as they want. Jackie can blow out the candles and choke on the frosting for all I care. I'm ready to go home."

"Oh no you're not, you're going downstairs." Alice reached out to change the child's mind.

Katie jerked away. "Let go of my arm. You're hurting my arm."

Then she opened her mouth and Alice was certain the scream could be heard downstairs, above the band, which thank God was playing another noisy piece. In the moment that Katie screamed, Alice had loosened her hold. Now she stood mutely as Katie brushed past her and ran through the door. Surely the child would tell Jack, and she did not want to think of his reaction. Alice sat on the red leather sofa, waiting to compose herself. Only when she heard voices coming toward her from the stairs did she stand.

"There's our hostess." Trude Williams and Ingrid Hamer were coming through the door.

"Jack's downstairs," Trude said. "He has a baby due and just popped in to see how things were holding up."

Alice edged toward the hall. "I should go see that my handsome husband gets a glass of punch. If he's on hospital duty, he'll need nourishment."

"I sympathize." Trude nodded her head wisely. "Where's Katie? We didn't see her downstairs." She looked straight into her compact and Alice wondered if she had heard the scream.

"Katie didn't feel well and wanted to leave early."

"What a shame that she's missing her own party."

Now she could only hope that Jack never discovered Katie walked all those blocks by herself. For one thing she was thankful—they apparently had not heard the girl cry out. Perhaps the noise did not travel down the stairs. Strange that outside the women's lounge the air seemed heavier, the weight of the party creeping up the stairs, invading the second floor. Jack was talking to his sister when she arrived, his suit coat rumpled, his hair mashed down by the golf hat.

He turned as she approached. "Spare me from such affairs," he said, and as usual she could not tell whether he was serious. A different sense of humor was one of the problems involved in marrying an older man. She decided to play safe and smile.

"Katie wanted to go home."

"Home? In the middle of her party?"

"She didn't feel well, Jack, and one of the boys offered to walk her home. Nothing serious, I think the air will help her headache."

Alice looked at her sister-in-law and her husband, but they did not look as if anything out of the ordinary had happened.

"I think I'll call," Jack said. "Are you sure she has a key?" He reached for another sandwich from his sister's plate and strode toward the back room.

"Too much excitement," Joan murmured. "Poor thing, she's probably not used to such late hours."

For the next two hours Alice wandered from table to table explaining that Katie did not feel well. She had been almost asleep when Jack called to see if she felt better. Please try to stop by during the week. No, Katie was not staying long enough because her school begins in a few days.

Lies, lies, they were the center of her life. One of these days she would stop playing games, but when the games ended she too would be finished. Only that knowledge kept her running in these ridiculous circles.

At midnight the yellow dresses and the blue dresses, all of them, began filtering out of the room, stopping to thank the hostess for the party, hoping Katie would soon recuperate. Alice felt as if she would scream. Jack long since had returned to the hospital, leaving a message at the back desk not to wait up for him. Little Jack was still awake, filling a paper cup with the fresh fruit decorating the punch bowl. She had one of the waiters get their coats from the checkroom.

"Come on baby, take the cup with you and let's go home. I'm ready for bed, you should be too."

Sunlight sifted through the venetian blinds, horizontal stripes slashing the organdie bedspread. Alice reached for the alarm clock on the nightstand. Had she slept that late? The second bed was untouched; Jack must have spent the night at the hospital again. She should call, but if he were hungry he could send out for something hot to eat.

"Mama?" Jackie stuck his head through the door, the sunlight reflecting on his glasses. "Mama, you'd better come see Katie. She says she's going home."

Alice put her hand to her face. She remembered now and knew why there was a dull sensation running through her body. The child probably would create a scene.

"Did she say why she was leaving?"

"Nope, just said she was going home."

"Run outside and play, Jackie, I'll see about Katie."

She was awake at once, her slippered feet padding down the hall toward the guest room. Both of Katie's suitcases were spread open on the floor and the girl stood at the dresser, carefully sorting her possessions. In one pile were the clothes she had brought with her, ready to be lifted into her luggage.

"Good morning, Katie. What on earth are you doing packing so early? Next Tuesday is a long way off."

"I'm not staying until Tuesday. I'm leaving this evening."

"But why?" Alice felt weary having to go through this routine. She had been so careful not to make her unpleasantness concrete. And except for last night she had succeeded. Perhaps she could convince Jack that the child had hallucinations. She herself had told him she did not feel well.

"You know your father will be very disappointed if you don't spend the entire two weeks with us. He was so happy when you decided to come. Since you haven't talked to him yet, why don't you stay?"

Katie looked up for an instant, as if consciously deciding whether to ignore her question. "When he comes home for dinner, I'll talk to him. The train doesn't leave until seven."

"Katie, you can't leave without any money, how are you paying for your ticket?"

"My ticket is round trip and when I called, the agent said a reservation was not necessary."

So she really was being defiant, thank God for that stubbornness. Alice would play the role, step by step, until the end.

"All right Katie, you're old enough to know what you want to do. I'll call your father."

The receiver was almost weightless in her hand, and she dialed the number without thinking.

"Hello June, this is Mrs. Wilson, let me speak with the doctor."

Then there was the familiar click when June switched lines, followed by a brisk "hello."

"Katie's leaving, Jack. She wants to go home today. Yes, she feels fine, but I think she's really homesick. Honey, you can't expect her to adjust so readily to our life." Alice was not conscious of what she said; the voice speaking was detached from her body.

"Two weeks away from home, for the first time in her life—that's a long time. I don't see how she could help but have a good time. It's not every week that a sixteen-year-old has a huge party given especially for her. She wants to go home, it's only normal."

When he hung up, she stood perfectly still, patting the receiver with her other hand.

The guest room was almost spotless when Alice returned. On Katie's bed, beside the girl and the book she was reading, was a pile of clothing, every item Alice had bought for her.

"Aren't you taking your new things?" she asked.

"I've packed my clothes."

"If you don't have room we can put the new clothes in a dress box."

Katie ignored her suggestion.

"Your father will be home at three, he'd like to come earlier but he has an office full of patients. You know how busy he is during the week." Alice was silent for a moment. "Is there anything I can get for you?" The child could not be persuaded to talk.

"We'd better call your mother and tell her you're coming home."

"I've already called her." Katie looked up. "Don't worry, I reversed the charges."

There was another uncomfortable silence before Katie spoke again.

"If you don't mind I'd like to finish this book, especially since I have to write a report for school."

Alice stood at the foot of the bed. Katie did not move, not even to turn a page. Finally Alice left the room, closing the door softly behind her, standing in front of the barrier with her hand on the brass knob. She could not will her feet to move, and when she heard the quieted sobs only a few feet away she felt guilty, yet horribly pleased. Her hand started to turn the doorknob and stopped. There was nothing she could do; Jack's daughter was his problem.

Alice cooked dinner, an especially nice one she thought, to celebrate Katie's going away. Katie stayed in the guest room until she was called to eat. In spite of the pineapple-decorated ham, dinner was a quiet meal. Alice tried to add some life to the table but Katie sat quietly at her place, toying with her food, and speaking only when someone spoke directly to her.

"Baby, are you sure you won't stay for just a few more days? You don't have to stay until Tuesday. Aunt Ethel and Uncle Roger haven't seen you since you were a baby. They'll be awfully disappointed at missing you." Jack had pushed his plate to the side and leaned over the table. "Alice, Jackie, and I really looked forward to having you come. Won't you please think about staying?"

"I've already told Mother I'm coming home." Katie was folding and unfolding her napkin.

"We can call again."

"No, I should go home."

"All right, Katie." Jack seemed resigned and the meal was completed in silence. Only Alice and Jackie ate the strawberry shortcake, helping themselves to the bowl of pink whipped cream. Jack suggested that Alice tell Katie goodbye at home and let him take her to the station.

"I haven't had too much time to spend with her," he said. "I counted on these two weeks."

"It's time for you two to be leaving if you're going to make the train." Alice began carrying the dinner dishes to the kitchen sink. "Jackie, you help Katie and your daddy get her things into the car."

Alice watched Katie disappear into the guest room. The child probably would be too timid to eat in the dining car, even if it were integrated. And since she had such a long ride ahead, Alice had packed sandwiches, fruit, and leftover birthday cake in an old Eastern Airlines flight bag. Hopefully the container did not give the appearance of a lunch.

She gave the flight bag to the girl as they stood on the front porch.

"Come back real soon, honey." Alice bent to kiss the smooth cheek, instead her lips rested on the head of thick hair.

While Jack stowed the luggage in the trunk and opened the car door for Katie, his wife and son watched from the front porch. Alice stood with her arm around Jackie's waist, touching the roll of fat over the belt encircling his pants. There was no need for silence, yet the air around her was dry.

The house, safe and silent, stood behind her. Conscious of the image they formed in Katie's departing eyes, Alice sucked in her stomach and purposely stood tall. She watched Jack back out of the driveway, the lines of his face set—a look she had seen when he was determined to accept an unpleasant situation. Watching him made her feel curiously relieved and for the first time during their married life she was certain he would never destroy anything that she valued. Perhaps Katie's return was a good omen. He already had lost one child; he would not risk losing someone else who was a part of him.

Her fingers reached up and nudged Little Jack's chin. "Wave goodbye," she whispered, "wave goodbye to Katie."

BANAGO KALT

Riding on the train from Basel to Zurich, Millie scarcely had taken time to sit down. She stood at the window now, her nose pressed against the window glass, staring down at the lakes that were scattered across the countryside. Through the polished window she gazed at the picture-postcard valleys, each surrounded by gray-green mountains and dotted with flowers.

Now that she was in Switzerland she no longer had any doubts as to whether she should have come. Usually in the summer she was up to her neck in freedom work but this year she suddenly had an overwhelming desire to leave everything. She was sick and tired of sitting-in, and standing-in, and after that minister's dog bit her, even kneeling-in. Sometimes she just felt so boxed in living in the South. At this moment all she had to do was look through the glass at the green country on the other side to feel free from herself.

Earlier this afternoon her group of American college kids had arrived by jet in Basel. Millie loved Switzerland at once. She could have stayed all day at the open-air cafe where the group drank coffee before splitting up to meet the families with whom they would live. So many things were different from home, even little things like the giant-sized advertisements that covered American billboards.

All over the Basel train station and on sidewalk posters, side by side in groups of three was the same picture of a little boy drinking Banago Kalt. One of the kids who spoke fluent German discovered from a waiter that Banago Kalt was something like Kool-Aid, only made with milk. She knew immediately she would feel at home in Switzerland from seeing those darling old ladies with the long aproned skirts drinking big glasses of chocolaty Banago Kalt.

Millie looked over her shoulder at the two American girls who were no longer looking at the countryside. They didn't seem at all excited. She smiled, thinking of the way her next-door neighbor would have described Karen and Rita: being white, they were just without soul. At first she was worried about Rita, who was from a small Texas town, but immediately all three of them were good friends. They really were nice girls and she was glad they fit together so well.

She, Karen, and Rita were going to live with a Swiss family through the Family Friends Experiment. Supposedly the Experiment was a highly selective program, and the other girls were amazed that she had been accepted after applying in May. Millie didn't expect to have any difficulty with her application. At the small Virginia college she attended, every now and then somebody wanted "one" to represent the school in the public eye. She figured the Experiment would be no different from a newly integrated college.

In fact, when the director wrote her acceptance letter he kept stressing how delighted they were to have a bona fide civil rights worker in the group. She, he said, could give Europeans a true picture of American life. The funny thing was she didn't give a damn about the Experiment's goal of understanding new peoples. Her parents just weren't the type to give her money to bop through Europe on her own; she, in turn, was not one to knock herself out babysitting and save all of her coins for travel. The Experiment was a happy compromise.

Their Swiss family, the Borbachs, was at the train to meet them, standing in front of three Banago Kalt signs. Mr. Borbach was of average height with a kind of roly-poly cheerfulness; his wife was half a head shorter than he. They had no trouble finding each other—the girls' eyes were drawn to the couple by the wild yellow and brown sunburst stripes in Mrs. Borbach's linen dress. Mr. and Mrs. Borbach greeted the girls with fluent English, in direct contrast to their nonexistent German. Heinz and Ursi, the children of the family, smiled at them but would not let go of their father's hand. Since they did not look surprised to see her, Millie assumed the family had been forewarned by the American office.

The girls shared a large room on the second floor of the Borbach house. From the front window Millie could see a blaze of red geraniums that seemed to sprout from every neighbor's window box. The children, who had lined the driveway when they arrived, were still playing in front of the house. They certainly did stare at her, but then they could have been looking at Rita. She still wore her hair teased in the high bouffant style and she wore mascara to bed rather than go to the trouble of making up her eyes in the morning. Karen was rather plain and looked like she drank a lot of milk. Millie didn't know what they thought of her, but she imagined she fit somewhat in the middle of the group.

Mrs. Borbach had placed a big bowl of zinnias on the dresser, and even the flowers made her feel this would be a great summer. It was going to be such a relief to talk to people without trying to figure out if they were for or against the cause. For once in her life she might not have to whip out the twenty-five-words-or-less speech of Negro life in Cadbury, Virginia.

"Come on kids," she turned to Karen and Rita who were lying on their beds, "let's finish unpacking so we can help Mrs. Borbach with dinner." As members of the family they were expected to help out with all household tasks. The girls were washing the supper dishes when Mrs. Borbach told them in her halting English that there was a surprise for the evening.

"You go sit on the balcony steps," she said, shooing them out of the kitchen.

The girls had not been sitting still for a minute when a jangly, discordant sound filled the air. Suddenly they saw a band marching down the street preceded by a group of boys rolling a flower-decorated beer barrel toward the Borbachs' garage. The band was followed by a stream of people coming from all over the neighborhood, and everybody crowded into the Borbachs' front yard for a summer concert. Millie could hardly contain herself. The scene was just like a travel folder, a real European street festival in her own yard.

The concert started with a rousing march. She was standing by the hedge with Karen and Rita, tapping her feet to the Swiss music, when suddenly a strange man came up, grabbed her by the arm, and pushed her past the band to a spot under the front porch light.

The next thing she knew he was comparing the color of his arm to hers and motioning to the crowd to notice the similarity in browns. He seemed to be thoroughly delighted that he was almost as dark as she. Millie saw no reason for anyone to be so pleased with his suntan. She considered escaping into the house via the front door but by this time they had attracted the whole audience's attention. When the band burst into a polka, he swept her into a wild dance in the middle of the street. Which would have been fine, except that they were the only people dancing.

At the end of the band's number he refused to let go of her and carried her back to the yard. She immediately yelled for Mrs. Borbach, who assumed Millie wanted a translation of the man's conversation. The Swiss woman listened and explained that Millie was the first dark girl he had ever seen in Switzerland. He considered it quite an honor to dance with her. Mrs. Borbach suggested that he was "How do you say it? Intoxicated?" But that was no excuse. The man kept smiling and pointing to her all night.

Karen thought he looked like he might have been Portuguese or something, and Millie wished he would return to his homeland full of dark girls and leave her alone. She spent the rest of the evening standing by the beer barrel with Rita and Karen, waiting for the neighbors to end the party and go home.

After the street party she and the other two girls spent most of their time following Mrs. Borbach around Herrliberg. Although most of the younger people commuted to Zurich offices in the morning, there were many older people who seemed genuinely pleased when the girls took their pictures. Aside from "please," "thank you," and "hello," the only German phrase they had mastered was "May I take your photograph please?" If these phrases were not appropriate, they soon learned that a series of wild hand gestures would get across the idea.

Millie did not like to wander around the town by herself. People kept staring at her and when the three of them walked down the street somebody was bound to come along and point at the "Americanos." When they came to her though, the word changed to "Indiano." The other day when they were buying meat at the butcher shop Mrs. Borbach told her that the butcher wanted to know if she lived on a reservation in the United States. And then at the bakery the clerk asked in French if in August she were returning to Africa or the United States. Although both she and Rita were Southern brunettes no one ever confused their names. It was poor Karen with long blonde hair who repeatedly was called "Rita." At any rate, everybody in Herrliberg seemed to know that the two Americanos and their Africano-Indiano friend were visiting the Borbachs.

Every morning Mr. Borbach announced the next day's plans to his captive audience at the breakfast table.

"Tomorrow afternoon we are going to climb the mountain," he said one morning with an air of finality.

Millie, buttering her fourth slice of brown bread, scuffed the floor with her new hiking boots. The girls had bought the boots two days before and were wearing them around the house to soften the stiff suede.

"How high?" Rita asked, leaning across the jam pot and focusing intently on Mr. Borbach. Early in the morning she never had in her contact lenses and the Borbach children did not understand why she recognized them in the evening and not in the morning.

"Not too high for American girls." Mr. Borbach looked at his wife and smiled.

Millie and Karen avoided looking at each other. They had discussed the possibility of becoming ill. Their idea had been squelched by Rita, who wanted to climb just one mountain so she could write home what Karen termed the Great Adventure. She and Millie went to bed Thursday night praying for rain.

As the newspaper had predicted, Friday morning was bright and clear. If they were lucky, according to Mr. Borbach, on Saturday morning they should be able to see three mountains from the top of the one they would climb. They would like the Drusberg, he said. In the winter men from the Swiss army used the paths for ski runs. Tonight he had arranged for them to sleep in the hayloft of a ski house near the foot of the mountain, and Saturday before dawn they would begin climbing.

Herrliberg was two hours behind them and the sun was sinking when Mr. Borbach stopped the car on a narrow gravel road. Millie looked through the brush surrounding the road, but she didn't see a ski house anywhere in sight. Mr. Borbach handed out their knapsacks and pointed to a small hut halfway up a mountain.

"All the way up there?" Rita squealed. "We have to walk?"

"Only a forty-five-minute walk," Mr. Borbach commanded.

He and his wife began walking and the three girls started to follow them. After the first fifteen minutes Millie's feet felt as if they were stuck to the ground. Rather than walking straight up to the hut they seemed to weave up the mountain-side. She wondered what in God's name was in her knapsack. Because of the weight on her back she could no longer walk straight, her stomach leaned toward the ground.

She looked up to see Mr. and Mrs. Borbach several hundred yards ahead, waiting for them. Karen was just a few feet behind her, but Rita, who at the last minute had stuck into the knapsack her curlers, giant economy-size hair spray, and movie camera, was barely moving. Almost as if there had been a signal, she and Karen stopped. "To wait on Rita," Millie panted, hoping the Borbachs understood.

"Come," Mr. Borbach called after ten minutes. "We are almost there."

By the time the girls reached the ski house ten minutes after the Borbachs, no one was speaking. They were too busy gulping air and trying to steady their shaking legs. Rita lay prostrate on a wooden bench. Karen and Millie, too tired to look down at the view, sat leaning against the railing, facing the front door. They evidently were the only persons staying at this place and from the porch she could hear Mrs. Borbach discussing the price of supper. Millie didn't ever want to move again. Only fools climb mountains.

They were sitting quietly when suddenly a short stocky man with a mass of long black hair appeared at the door.

"How do you do," he said in careful English. He stopped in front of Millie and smiled: "If you speak slowly I can understand you."

She was too tired to do anything but return his smile. Then he paused and, pointing to Millie, said to Karen: "Tell her that I speak a little Arabic but I do not know the language of the South."

Millie looked at him wondering where in the hell he thought she came from. Then he bowed to both of them and left the room. "May I present your royal-blooded Arabian highness." Karen bowed and crossed herself. For no reason except that they were exhausted, the whole scene became funny. When Rita woke up to ask what was happening they were too tickled to explain.

Supper was ready in twenty minutes and since she had not carried her knapsack from the yard to the porch Millie was the last person to come inside. She was dragging her pack across the porch when the same man crept up behind her.

"When the others go you must stay," he said, touching her shoulder as if to ingrain his command.

She looked around for Karen or Rita but they already were inside the house.

"There is a man on that hill who wants a black girl." He pointed to what looked like another mountain peak. "I will call him," he said, nodding his head vigorously. She watched fascinated as he took down a strange animal horn and stepped to the side of the porch.

The incident diminished her appetite considerably. Even Mr. Borbach asked if she were feeling ill. In spite of herself she kept glancing at the door, waiting to see if the man fond of black girls would appear. She had just managed to whisper part of the story to Karen when the ski house owner towed into the room the most bedraggled creature Millie had ever seen. He was barely more than five feet high and he wore the cotton shirt and grubby trousers real mountain people often wear. His bare feet were dirty and almost the color of the black beard that fell to his waist, in a strange contrast to his bald head.

The ski house man brought him over to the table. Millie, uncertain as to what she was supposed to do, immediately spilled her soup in her lap. Karen was busy stuffing her mouth with bread to keep from laughing aloud. Millie listened to the Borbachs talking with the men, trying to understand the rough-sounding words. Mrs. Borbach was always saying these mountain people were strange. That man might actually expect her to go off with him.

Then Mrs. Borbach translated. The man had come over to meet Millie and he was so kind as to bring his accordion to play for the American visitors. Millie, sandwiched between Karen and Rita, spent the next two hours listening to Swiss mountain songs. All during the concert Karen punched her in the ribs and each time that man was staring straight at her.

She sat as close to the door as possible and when the time came to say good night she conveyed her thanks for the entertainment from across the room. In certain instances Millie did not believe in taking chances. The thought of being spirited away to spend the rest of her life on the next hill was not a matter to take lightly.

The next day was fresh and bright and excellent climbing weather according to Mr. Borbach. Long before the sun had appeared they were ready to begin walking. The cows evidently awakened with them and for a long time after they had passed the grazing herds they could hear the tinkling of cowbells in the distance. With Mr. Borbach leading and Mrs. Borbach closing the gap at the end of the line, they finally reached a place where even the cows did not graze.

Millie sat on a small clearing drinking wine tea. This high everything seemed to be smothered by the blue sky, and the three other peaks looked as if she could jump across to touch the snow that covered them. They were down the mountain in time for lunch after only one delay. Rita left her camera on the mountaintop and they had to wait half an hour while Mr. Borbach returned to retrieve it.

Wherever they went in Herrliberg people stared at the three girls, and usually the lens of Rita's movie camera was staring right back at them. Sometimes Mrs. Borbach asked them to walk across town to the new supermarket to buy small items not on her weekly grocery list. Armed with German-English dictionaries, and Mrs. Borbach's carefully written, divided-into-pronounceable-syllables shopping lists, they invaded the store.

The clerks always were helpful and extremely interested in Millie. The last time they went shopping Karen was putting the groceries into the shopping bag when the clerk stopped them. He gestured toward Millie's arm, smiled at her, and slipped a huge chocolate bar into their basket. "Two chocolates," he said.

"I guess they're kind of surprised to see us all together," Rita said when they were walking home. "Millie, you ought to start a race riot."

She thought about Rita's suggestion because she wrote home describing the problem that kept occurring. Although she meant to amuse her parents there was something vaguely disturbing about having people take so seriously what she said. Quite often when they were visiting with the Borbachs' friends, one of the Swiss would want to know about her life in the United States. Was she in any danger of being lynched, they wanted to know. She felt so responsible trying to answer them because they respected her word as law. Millie could not bring herself to play up the violence that headlined the Zurich newspaper. She certainly was as surprised as they when she found herself telling a group of high school boys there were several Southern white people she would regard as close friends.

Each morning the girls awakened to eat breakfast before Mr. Borbach left for work, but this morning the continuous slamming of a car door woke Millie instead of Ursi's timid knock. She crawled out of her bed to trace the origin of the sound and from her window saw a boy about their age throwing bags out of a car. The Mossimans' oldest son, the one Mrs. Borbach was eager for them to meet, must have come back from Germany.

The Borbachs and the American girls were invited over to the Mossimans' for supper to celebrate Jurg's return. Although he didn't speak English he seemed to be a really nice guy. Still, Millie was surprised when Mrs. Borbach told her Jurg would like to take her out to dinner. Would she like to go, Mrs. Borbach asked. "He says since he does not speak English so well he will have to use his hands." Millie swallowed her smile and said of course she would date Jurg.

She, Rita, and Karen debated whether she should carry along her pocket dictionary. A dictionary was not the most romantic thing to carry in her handbag but it was practical. "Use your hands," Rita said, giggling. When Jurg came over to get her, Millie could have sworn she heard Rita's movie camera grinding away through the living room window.

Jurg was fond of horses, at least she understood that much in the strange mixture of English, French, and Swiss German that they spoke. They had dinner at a riding club and Millie had become so accustomed to being stared at she made her entrance with more than usual grace.

The restaurant owner, a personal friend of Jurg's, was a chubby man, the kind people usually tend to associate with food. Jurg introduced her and he promptly decided to sit at their table. Mr. Gachnang also did not speak English, but every now and then he would address a question to her in French. The rest of the time he sat across the table beside Jurg, gazing intently at her.

Suddenly he leaned across the table and made a face at her. After a few seconds' hesitation she realized he was asking her to open her mouth.

"She has good teeth," he said in French to Jurg. Then he smiled again and jumped up. When he returned to their table the voice of Louis Armstrong had invaded the room.

Millie would have tried to start a conversation but without her dictionary she was lost. Mr. Gachnang continued talking to Jurg and every once in a while she would hear the word "Americano."

"You are mélangée?" he asked, turning toward her.

For a minute her mind went blank. She couldn't remember what "mélangée" meant. Then it dawned on her. No, for heaven's sake, she was not a mixture.

He pointed to her hair and gestured wildly. "It does not stick out like Africano. Indiano?" he asked hopefully.

"No, American Negro."

He shook his head in an effort to tell her she did not understand.

"North America," he said, "you understand?"

She nodded yes.

"Denmark?"

Again she nodded her head. They went through a list of five countries before he came to Switzerland and pointed to himself.

Yes, she agreed, she knew the country.

"India," he yelled triumphantly, "you, you." In his excitement he was leaning over the table almost in her dinner plate.

Again she shook her head. "Americano Negro." She made the words very distinct. The little man was becoming annoying and she wished he would just let her be what she was.

Millie looked at Jurg through the myriad of bottles resting on their table. He did not drink much because it was not good while he was driving. Still, Mr. Gachnang brought out bottles to sample in honor of her. Swiss girls didn't drink except at home, and she and Karen had figured out that most people were so surprised they drank in public that they were offered wine from shock. Mr. Gachnang was still smiling at her as if to say he knew all about her hidden relatives. With an effort to be social she returned his smile. That must have been the magic action because he immediately jumped up and disappeared into the back room. She hoped he was not returning to the jukebox. Already she had listened to Louis Armstrong's only record five consecutive times.

"He is hah-hah," Jurg said confidentially.

She nodded in agreement. "Hah-hah" certainly was the exact word to describe Mr. Gachnang. Suddenly she was aware of someone standing behind her.

"A present for special girl." Mr. Gachnang stood with his hands behind his back. She didn't have the heart to wonder about his surprise. People were always giving her things and Rita threatened to complain of discrimination.

When Mr. Gachnang placed his gift beside her plate she began to shake with unsounded laughter. She now owned a box of cigars, Swiss made.

Evidently Mrs. Borbach had told Jurg she had to be in early for the morning trip to the Zurich museum. Immediately after they listened to Louis Armstrong one more time he took her home.

"How'd it go?" Karen asked as Millie crawled over her feet to get into her own bed.

"Have a cigar," she whispered and collapsed in laughter at the foot of Karen's bed.

As the time to leave became closer Mr. and Mrs. Borbach's friends invited them to several parties in their honor. Talking with the people, even those that didn't speak English, was fun and they didn't mind answering the sometimes ridiculous questions. All of the Swiss girls, even little Ursi, were fascinated by their clothes. Did all of their blouses have those funny collars, they would ask, reaching out to touch the drip-dry oxford cloth. Sometimes they had trouble keeping the conversation on a noncontroversial subject. Mr. Borbach's brother Rato had very definite opinions concerning modern American classical music, and unless they avoided becoming entangled they usually ended up in an argument.

When they were undressing for bed after a sausage roast at Rato's house Rita turned unexpectedly quiet. "You know when I get so involved in those silly arguments I see how much of a tourist I really am. I just like American things best because they're ours. I mean I love the Borbachs but sometimes . . ." And suddenly, becoming embarrassed, she stopped talking.

Millie looked up, surprised. Rita very seldom said anything that caused a person to think and when she did it was somewhat of a shock.

"Yes," Karen said, walking across the room to flip the light switch. "It's like drinking Hershey's cocoa instead of that Banago stuff."

In the darkness Millie did not speak. She lay awake long after she heard the quiet breathing on either side of her. Before sleeping she waited for the bells to ring from the tower of the Catholic church. At home there were no church bells and she felt how easily "home" slipped into her thoughts. At home there were things she often did not want to think about but were so much a part of her she knew she never could ignore them. She thought of one of her friends, half-joking, half-serious, asking what she would do when picket signs were no longer in style.

Millie slipped from the bed and tiptoed to the window facing the lake. The lights on the opposite shore slid into the water, casting an air of serenity about the town. These two months had passed so quickly. She knew the street signs on each corner and she could call by name the women who sold flowers by the railroad station. Yet she was not a part of this town, and she did not regret being an outsider. She only had to remember the lights from the lake shining through this window to know someday she would return to Switzerland, but here she was not at home.

WHEN THE APPLES ARE RIPE

Mrs. Gilley lived in the second gray house from the corner. When Jonnie Anderson was playing in his backyard, he could see the house, stuck between piles of red dirt left by the construction crew enlarging the road. Sometimes old Mrs. Gilley would come out on the porch, inspect her three gardenia bushes, and go back in again. Jonnie saw the top of Mrs. Gilley's house more often than he saw Mrs. Gilley. He couldn't go on Saturday mornings when Doug went up to cut Mrs. Gilley's grass and sometimes drive her to the doctor's office. He didn't even have a real watch so he could tell when Doug was coming home. Mrs. Gilley was sick a lot and his mother didn't want him bothering her. And he was forbidden to play in Mrs. Gilley's yard unless she asked him. So, Jonnie would climb into the swing and sometimes Doug would push him from behind until he was almost as high as the green hedge separating the Andersons' yard from the Stewarts'.

When Jonnie-Boy was swinging as high as the swing would go, he could see Mrs. Gilley's yard with the apples from the big apple tree rotting all over the ground. If the wind was right, the pungent apple smell carried over into their backyard. Sometimes the two brown dogs would be on the porch. Doug said that they caught rabbits for her to eat and she herself caught the mice that replaced the chicken in mice and rice soup. From up high, the dogs looked like a part of the window shades that were always pulled down.

Lots of times when Jonnie didn't eat dessert because his mother hadn't baked anything, he would be given a nickel and sent to the neighborhood store. Now, with his parents always talking about Doug, his mother seldom baked. They gave him nickels, it seemed, just to get him out of the house.

Almost every trip he would meet Mrs. Gilley with a brown paper bag in one hand and some meat scraps wrapped in newspaper in the other. He knew that the bags held bones because once Mr. Potter, who kept the small neighborhood store, told Mother he saved the bones and scraps for Mrs. Gilley's dogs. She carried home the bones every evening that she came to the store for her medicine. Since they lived so far out from the drug store, Mr. Potter had Mrs. Gilley's prescriptions filled.

Jonnie was always very polite to Mrs. Gilley. If he saw her coming and couldn't duck, he would walk up quickly, speak, and hurry past her. He was not chicken as Doug insisted, but anybody speaking to Mrs. Gilley always had the feeling she was looking at something straight past him. Sometimes Jonnie-Boy wanted to turn around and look too.

She did not seem to belong on their street. The other old ladies he knew, even the ones with blue hair, did not look that old. Mrs. Gilley was partially bald. The few strands of hair still growing on her head were a reddish brown and mixed gray. When he was smaller, Jonnie always thought she'd been scalped.

"What happened to her head?" he asked his mother.

"Mrs. Gilley is old," she answered, "and sometimes old people lose their hair thinking about something new." But she did not seem to mean what she said, and asking him to bring the dustpan, she began sweeping the kitchen.

His mother felt sorry for Mrs. Gilley. Quite often he heard her telling his father that she'd like to do something for the woman.

"I'm afraid she's not going to last very long," his mother said, lifting the spoon from the mixing bowl and watching the liquid drops fall into the batter. "I suppose it's a good thing though. I don't think she would really like living in this day and age. Can you imagine what it must be like for her? Every time you pick up a paper or turn anywhere, they're talking about the Negroes."

She pointed to the other cabinet. "Jonnie, hand me that bowl. Gracious, I still remember my mother saying how Mrs. Gilley's mother kept their servants in line. And they loved her for it, every one of them."

His father grunted, and folded the paper. "I imagine it's very pleasant to sit on the porch and wave the world down the street, knowing your only son is safe in his grave."

"Jim!" His mother turned, quick tears specking her eyes. "Don't even play that."

"I'm sorry," he answered. "I wasn't thinking of Doug. God, Carolyn, don't you think I know he's my son too."

Then they were quiet looking at him.

Today his mother did not seem concerned with Mrs. Gilley and while he stood around the kitchen, she paid him no attention. Even Doug had gone out by himself on the bike. Since he usually did not come home until dinnertime, there was nothing for Jonnie to do but go outside and swing until someone called him for supper.

"Would you like to go get new library books tonight?" his father asked. Before Jonnie could answer, the front door slammed and Doug stuck his head in the door. "Be in as soon as I wash up."

His mother rose and brought another plate to the table. Reaching over to thump him on the head, Doug sat down across from Jonnie-Boy.

"It seems to me," his father said when Doug had taken his place, "that you could get to your meals on time. If you were doing something constructive, I could excuse your being late."

"I'm sorry," Doug answered, sliding the butter dish to his plate, "but the orientation program is important. We can't just go down there and not know anything about the area."

"Have you ever considered the idea that you don't have to go?"

Jonnie's father put down his fork and stared at his son.

"I suppose you know it's all over town."

"What's all over town?" Doug's words were slow and patient as if he were talking to a child.

"That my son is going down south to help a bunch of people that don't even have sense enough to help themselves. Now sooner or later they're going to integrate everything. I know that. But sensible people with a future don't get involved." Doug did not answer. "If you have to get involved in politics, why don't you stay in another part of the state? There must be something you can do in Maryland without getting your name spread all over the paper."

"Please," his mother interrupted. "Please let's not discuss anything now. Dinner is the only time we're together in the day. Can't we even eat in peace? As a family?"

They finished the meal in silence. Jonnie-Boy, carrying the dishes from the table to the sink, heard his father and brother talking in the den. Then the front door slammed and he knew Doug had gone again on the bike. Frowning still, his father came into the kitchen and watched his mother.

"What are you doing now?" he asked.

"Fixing a plate for Mrs. Gilley. Surely you can't object to that?"

"Good Lord, Carolyn, is it so strange that I want to keep my son in school and not see him hanging from a tree in Mississippi? Do you think Mrs. Gilley would want a dinner from you if she knew you were raising a rebel? A Gilley from Jackson County?" Immediately he began to laugh, a strange sound it seemed to Jonnie, not like laughter at all.

He waited for his mother to cover the plate with aluminum foil. Sometimes, like tonight when they had something especially good for dinner, or something easy to chew, Jonnie would carry over the supper, running because the vegetables might get cold. Looking at his mother's face he wondered if she was thinking of Mrs. Gilley or if talking to his father made her seem so solemn.

His father always said Mrs. Gilley had nothing but background. And these days family background wasn't worth a damn. He could sympathize with Mrs. Gilley he said, because she and the Andersons had one thing in common. No matter where they lived they were Southerners by temperament. Most of their relatives and all of Mrs. Gilley's still lived in Virginia.

Sometimes when he came to run an errand, if she felt like talking, Mrs. Gilley would set him down on the porch steps. Then she would give him a licorice cough drop from the box in her pocket and tell him about her family's house. Far too many rooms for an old lady like her, she said. She could remember when there were picaninnies running around wherever she turned, making all that noise while she tried to get her grandmother comfortable enough to sleep.

Then she would become quiet because they had sold the house. "Well, there was really nothing else to do," she said, "I certainly didn't need all that room." Somebody told her, or wrote her once, she no longer remembered, that the little colored children were going to the school that carried her grandfather's name. Jonnie-Boy had nothing to say. He would sit sucking on his cough drop, trying not to cut his tongue when the candy was thin, waiting to be dismissed.

The family ate dinner around six-thirty. So, in the fall, everything was almost dark before Jonnie could get up to Mrs. Gilley's with the plate. The streetlight glinting at the corner was not bright enough to light all of Mrs. Gilley's yard. He walked fast until he got to the front of her house, and then dodging the shadows from the trees, he ran until he found the walkway. The stones that used to be arranged neatly in a crisscross pattern had long since been rearranged by too many feet. Here and there a stone was missing or split into chunks with strands of grass growing between the pieces.

He walked on the grass, lifting the plate high in the air because there was no telling when one of those dogs would come out and start barking. Once the biggest dog whom Mrs. Gilley called General Lee snapped at him and made him drop the plate. Tonight the dogs were not even in sight. The General had been surprised when a car he was chasing rolled in reverse and hit him. It was a wonder he didn't get killed, but Mrs. Gilley bandaged him up and kept rubbing on ointment that Mr. Potter ordered from the drug store.

Sometimes Jonnie-Boy did not mind carrying Mrs. Gilley's dinner; but when the apples were ripe and scattered all over the ground, he hated to walk in the yard. Mrs. Gilley did not have a porch light and trying not to drop the plate he couldn't see his feet to avoid stepping on soft apples. The apple juice always spurted on his ankle, making him itch and he couldn't scratch and hold the dinner too. Tonight he walked slowly, feeling around for any stray apples with the toe of his tennis shoes. Stepping over the snail lying wetly on the board of the second step, he reached the porch and knocked on the door.

Mrs. Gilley, who was hard of hearing, always took a long time to answer. When she finally unlatched the screen door, she grabbed his head and pushed him toward the corner of the porch nearest the streetlight. Satisfied that he was not one of the boys who broke the stems of her sunflowers and threw the blossoms onto the street, she invited him in the house to exchange the new plate for last week's plate.

Mrs. Gilley's living room spilled out on the front porch. And if her lot hadn't been so small she probably could have decorated the front yard. The mahogany rocker and footstool near the porch banister matched the other dark furniture in the living room. Jonnie stood across from the faded sofa.

The tapestry cushions, propped against the window, blocked what little light came through the yellowing window shade.

"Have a seat young man," Mrs. Gilley whispered. Jonnie-Boy sat on a hassock near the fireplace and looked up at the pictures on top of the upright piano. He was about to trace the diamonds in the carpet when he saw something he had never seen in Mrs. Gilley's house. Cautiously he rose and looked at the neat stack of magazines on the floor. There were copies of that magazine Doug read, the one his father hated. He could not imagine why Mrs. Gilley would have Doug's magazines. He was just about to turn a page when Mrs. Gilley came from the other room and saw him gazing at the floor.

"See a mouse?" she asked, bringing the clean plate down to his level. "They come out sometimes when the room is quiet like this."

He held out his arms and she carefully placed the plate in his hands. "Tell your mother I thank her," she said and guided him out of the door. Mrs. Gilley stood behind the screen until he was past the apple tree and out in the street light, carrying the blue plate in front of him.

On Saturday morning after breakfast, his mother called him back to the kitchen.

"Hurry up," she said. "We're out of Spic 'n' Span and you have to go to the store."

Jonnie-Boy's mother made him pin the dollar bill inside his shirt pocket. "Spic 'n' Span comes in a can," he sang to no one in particular.

"Hold still," she said.

On the front porch steps he reached up to the mailbox and took his hat from the magazine holder. Jonnie-Boy put on the cap, bent down, and began thumping every other pink flower growing along the walkway. He was about to walk up the street when he suddenly remembered the watch. That was funny, he'd forgotten he ever had a watch. But it was buried somewhere around here, right under the orange marigold on the end.

Jonnie-Boy wriggled his fingers in the reddish-brown soil until he touched something hard. All last month he practiced extra hard learning to tell time. When he finally could tell the time and read the hand on the left side of the clock he'd asked his father for a watch. They had given him one all right—one Doug had outgrown. A stupid Mickey Mouse watch with a red strap.

He fished the watch out of the dirt and began brushing it on his pants legs. The red band had turned a funny color and poor Mickey's face was now a strange tan. Satisfied that the watch was almost beyond recognition, he reburied it in the same hole. He smoothed over the dirt, pulled some grass to stick on top, and ran down the driveway up the street to Mr. Potter's store.

He walked a block, stopped, and sniffed the air. He still could not smell the rain coming like Mrs. Gilley. He guessed his mother was right. "Rain," she said, "is in other people's bones." He was almost up to her yard now and not a thing was moving. He heard his father say that the niggers could march to Washington and back, past Mrs. Gilley's yard and she would never budge to find out who was singing "We Shall Overcome." One of the dogs was draped across the old rocking chair on the porch.

He was about to walk another few feet when he noticed a

clock standing on Mrs. Gilley's porch. The clock, the color of mashed peanuts, was mounted on a low table with four wheels like roller skates. Two little knobs looked like they were attached to a drawer and the long glass front sparkled, out of place on the front porch. Jonnie-Boy was not sure but he thought that was a dish towel dangling from the top. He went to the edge of the yard for a closer look, and then hurried up the street to the store. He had never seen such a big clock on anybody's front porch.

Ten minutes later he was on his way home, carrying two brown paper bags. Mr. Potter asked him to deliver yesterday's bones to Mrs. Gilley because she had not come after them herself. Now, over the top of the bags, Jonnie-Boy could see Mrs. Gilley, sitting on the side of the porch nearest the apple tree, reading one of those magazines. She did not seem to notice him until she heard his feet squashing apples near the porch.

He looked at Mrs. Gilley trying to think of something to say when she spoke.

"Good morning young man." Her voice was harsh like she had not yet gargled with her mouthwash.

"Morning Mrs. Gilley," Jonnie-Boy answered. "Mr. Potter sent you yesterday's bones for the General and that other dog. He said he hadn't been able to get away to the drug store."

"Thank you young man, put them on the banister."

He plopped the bones on the railing and stopped to look at the clock. The wood, smooth and freshly polished, was cut into swirls which rushed up and curved at the top like dragons' heads. It was such a big clock. He was about to reach out and touch the surface when Mrs. Gilley spoke.

She looked at him and at her magazine. "There comes a time," she said, "when one can no longer pretend situations do not exist. You might tell your brother that I thank him for the reading literature."

Jonnie-Boy nodded and turned to pick up the groceries.

"Wait one minute young man, and I'll send your mother some fresh fall leaves."

He started to say "no thank you." If there was anything his mother did not want it was a handful of leaves. But Mrs. Gilley bent over and began clipping leaves from the gardenia bushes. She had a hard time trying to find enough green leaves. Of the bunches of leaves some had begun to wither and turn brown.

Without turning to face him she began to speak. "I assume your brother is commuting this term. Is he still doing well at school?"

"He's not going to school now," Jonnie said. "He doesn't want to go back to college."

"Well, what does he want to do?"

Jonnie hesitated. "Go to Mississippi but nobody wants him to go. Daddy says he's silly to get mixed up with those people, but he still wants to go." He felt vaguely uneasy as if he had broken a family confidence.

"So, Douglas will be a fighter for freedom." Mrs. Gilley stopped clipping to look at him. "I think that is what such people are called in the magazines."

"Yes ma'am," and Jonnie was silent.

"When does your brother leave?"

"He's catching the bus Sunday morning." And even

saying the words he felt a strange loss. Before he had always known that Doug was coming home at Thanksgiving or Christmas. Now there seemed to be no more holidays left.

When Mrs. Gilley had a fistful, she reached back and wrapped the leaves in a dish towel hanging from the clock. So it was a dish towel. While Mrs. Gilley polished the leaves one by one, Jonnie-Boy stared at the clock, his eyes following the swinging pendulum.

"Do you like my clock?" she asked, fondly patting the wood. "It's my third clock you know. I have one in the bedroom, one on the back porch, and one in the kitchen. Two months before he died, when Mr. Gilley and I were married, my grandfather gave this one to me. This is the kitchen clock," she said, "I try to air it out once a year. Grandfather was fascinated by clocks."

Mrs. Gilley was looking over his shoulders at the vacant lot across the street. "I kept only one of his tin watches, the others are buried with him. When my father considered my brothers young men, each one received a watch. Why, my brothers would no more have thought of being careless with their watches than they would have courted a northern girl."

Jonnie watched Mrs. Gilley slowly pull the knobs of the clock drawer. "Of course until it was sold I kept the big gold watch in the safety deposit vault at the bank. But this one went all through the war with my grandfather. He never did believe in letting those foreigners get close enough to touch his watch."

The drawer glided all the way out and she pointed to a small grayish-white box. "Young man have you learned to read a watch?"

Jonnie-Boy nodded his head.

"My father used to say," Mrs. Gilley said, resting her hand on the porch banister, "every young man ought to have a confederate flag, a horse, and above all a watch." She motioned for him to lift the box. "I can still hear him lecturing my brothers, telling them that a man's honor is like his watch, on duty twenty-four hours of the day."

Jonnie-Boy's hands wiggled with excitement. He was almost afraid to touch the box, but suddenly the top was off and there was the watch. He couldn't help smiling, there was exactly the kind of watch he'd always wanted—the kind that was in those pioneer stories. The watch was round and shiny silver with a long silver chain. And there was a clasp to pin it inside his pocket. He wanted to run his fingers over the case and around the silver numbers but with Mrs. Gilley standing there he hesitated to pick up the watch.

"Don't you have a watch?" Mrs. Gilley asked, looking down at his wrist.

Again he shook his head.

"I thought all youngsters had watches these days." Then without warning she closed up the graying top and shut the clock drawer. "Thank you. Tell your mother I send my regards."

Jonnie-Boy picked up the bag of groceries and Mrs. Gilley stuck the leaf bouquet on top. Until he turned the corner, she stood alert on her porch, waiting to see if a leaf slipped to the ground. His mother wondered where he had been but she knew he was not far enough from home to get lost. She said how nice of Mrs. Gilley to send the leaves and promptly stuck them in an empty mayonnaise jar. After all of the change had been accounted for and some of the dirt brushed from his pants bottom, his mother fixed him a picnic lunch to eat out of doors and out of the way.

Everybody went to bed early that night and when Jonnie-Boy awoke he could smell cinnamon buns baking in the kitchen. His mother made a plain loaf for Mrs. Gilley, cut off the crust, and wrapped the soft bread in a clean dish towel. Jonnie-Boy would deliver the loaf after dinner.

The kitchen windows were wide open when the family sat down for breakfast. Pushing the curtains aside, Jonnie sniffed the air and didn't smell a single drop of rain. He was still somewhat sleepy from trying to stay up and listen to his parents last night. They spoke softly though, as if they did not want him to hear. He was sure he heard his mother crying, just before Doug came upstairs to dress for bed. And then he didn't remember anything else.

He slid into his place being careful not to upset anything. The table was set with the good tablecloth and silver, but no one looked very happy. His father brought out the Bible and had begun reading the Sunday scripture when someone knocked at the door. His mother looked at his father. When his shrug announced that he had no knowledge of a visitor, she went to the door.

"Why, good morning, Mrs. Gilley," they heard her say. "Won't you come in?"

Mrs. Gilley? What was she doing at his house? Jonnie-Boy swung around in his seat but was stopped by his father. "Practice your Bible verse," he said, "your mother will tend to Mrs. Gilley." As soon as he spoke, Mrs. Gilley followed Jonnie's mother into the kitchen.

"I have come to see Douglas," she said, addressing all of them. "I have something for his trip." She wasted no more words and turned immediately to Doug. "I am not certain you are right, but I think my grandfather would have liked for you to have this. My grandfather," she paused. "My grandfather was a man of his time. I think he would have respected you as a man of your time."

She placed in Doug's hand a small box, carefully wrapped in brown grocery bag paper. "Take care with it." Then as if she had completed a very formal ceremony, Mrs. Gilley turned to leave. "I can find my way to the door," she said, "please do continue your breakfast." Before his mother even remembered the crustless bread, Mrs. Gilley had issued her order and walked to the hall.

Jonnie-Boy's mother looked puzzled. "What on earth?" she asked.

"Probably a list of grandfather's relatives. Doug will have countless invitations to tea."

His mother ignored her husband's sarcasm, waiting for Doug to untie the string. He pulled off the paper and there was the same fading box that had been in the clock drawer. Jonnie-Boy must have been seeing things, but no, there it was on the kitchen table. Mrs. Gilley had given Doug her grandfather's watch.

"Must be quite valuable, by now," his father said, "a real antique." He passed the box to his wife. "She can't afford to give her valuables away."

"I think she can," his mother answered. "Knowing the watch is with Doug is more important to her." His mother stirred her coffee and looked at the watch. She handed it to

Doug to wind and they listened to the steady ticking until the meal had ended.

Without him even asking, Doug let Jonnie-Boy hold the watch. He clipped the clasp to his pocket and let the chain dangle almost down to his knees. His mother looked down and started to say something but was quiet. Finally she turned to her husband, her eyes steady. "If your son cannot have your good will, I think you might give him your respect."

"My son has not grown up," he said, and turned to look out of the kitchen window.

So, there would be more talking until Doug was on the bus and actually riding away from this house. Jonnie-Boy felt sad without being able to tell himself why. He wondered for a minute what his parents would talk about when his brother no longer came home. Now at least their voices were softened, knowing that in a few hours, Doug would be gone.

He did not want to listen, and unlatching the screen door, Jonnie-Boy walked straight to the backyard swing, clutching the watch that would go with Doug. He settled himself in the swing and with a big push he was up in the air looking over the whole neighborhood.

He held out his hand with the chain encircling his wrist and the watch swung with him, making silver arcs in the air. From the swing he could see everything—Doug's suitcase was set on the side porch, sunlight shining on the deep leather scratches. Mrs. Gilley's house looked as it always did. The dogs were lying still in the cleared-off spot under the tree and although the clock was gone from her porch, there was the mahogany footstool. He could even see Mrs. Gilley, sitting on her rocker, slowly moving with the wind.

TRAFFIC JAM

Mrs. Nelson had been to the kitchen to check on her or the screen door would have been latched when Libby arrived. She put her wallet on the windowsill, tied an apron around her short skirt, and took out the bowl she used to mix biscuit dough. She worked quickly, her fingers measuring and stirring from habit, her ears barely listening to the Nelsons' voices in the front room.

She put the biscuits in the oven and was bringing the breakfast dishes from the cabinet to the dining nook when Mrs. Nelson came in to say good morning. Although the curlers had been taken from her hair, she had not yet covered the dry-flakes-of-oatmeal skin with make-up. Mrs. Nelson always seemed to stand in the middle of a busy room, and after a year, Libby had become skilled in working around her.

"Libby," Mrs. Nelson turned her pale body toward the stove, "today's my club meeting day. Don't forget we have three tables this time. Mrs. Henderson has two ladies staying with her and I've invited another guest."

Libby nodded her head and set the timer for the eggs. As Mrs. Nelson breathed heavily behind her back, Libby's features assumed the mask of pretend-listening.

"Is Wicker over his cough yet?" Mrs. Nelson leaned over and pinched a piece of biscuit dough that had fallen on the enamel top of the stove. "It's too bad he's not going to be healthy like Hal," she said. "That's one good thing I can say about Hal, he was healthy enough to stir up devilment."

She dropped the dough into the step-on garbage can beside the stove. "Libby, let's have the watermelon pickle with the biscuits. I want to use up this jar before it spoils."

Libby nodded and walked toward the pantry. Sometimes she hated having to take things Mrs. Nelson gave her. Ever since she'd given Wicker that old blanket to keep him warmer when he had the flu, she thought she owned him. She always said she was taking care of him, hoping he didn't turn out like his father.

Mrs. Nelson continued to talk as she walked to the other side of the kitchen. "I told his aunt he was going to be no good," she said, leaning inside the refrigerator, "spending all that time fooling around with Papa's old car. You'd think if he wanted to be a mechanic he'd stay around here and learn the trade. He could still be working at the Esso station, but no, he decides to change jobs. You know," she turned toward Libby, "I still wonder why he didn't marry that little Thompson girl, they were two of a kind."

Mrs. Nelson looked distastefully at her fingers that were sticky from the biscuit dough. "Hurry up," she said, wiping her hand on a towel, "Mr. Nelson has to leave early."

Libby ignored her. Mrs. Nelson was always saying mean things about Hal and Libby had the hardest time holding her temper. Every time Libby thought about the woman pumping her friend Sally about things that did not concern her she got plain angry. Just because Sally worked for Mrs. Henderson, Mrs. Nelson thought she could poke her nose into Libby's business.

Libby didn't understand why Mrs. Nelson didn't come right out and ask if she were married. She could understand how the woman might be curious about where Hal was living. But that gave her no reason for spreading lies, going around making people think all Libby's five children were bastards.

"God, you can't trust none of them," she said, poking extra hard inside the pickle jar with the spatula. According to Sally, Mrs. Nelson had asked about the identity of the father of Libby's baby. She hinted, Sally said, that Libby bought herself a wedding band instead of Hal giving her the ring.

Libby took the biscuits out of the oven and began buttering the insides. The funny thing was she honestly thought Mrs. Nelson had believed her when she said her husband was up north working. She hadn't lied really. The last postcard she had from Hal said he was working in a canning factory upstate. She saw no reason to say that card had been written almost a year ago.

During her working hours she tried to avoid thinking about her husband. Calvin had been nothing but a baby when he left. At first she figured he only had left them for the summer. Lots of fellows she knew up and took off for a couple of months, but they usually came back in the fall. Not Hal. He didn't ever do anything according to a set pattern. One day he was working in the drug store and coming home and loving her at night, and the next thing she knew he was off and gone again. Some people just have a wandering bug in them.

She looked around her at the sunlit kitchen, comparing it to the narrow kitchen in her own home. Sometimes Meetrie didn't believe her when she told the children about the food the Nelsons had for breakfast. Talking about bacon and waffles made Meetrie's eyes shine. "For real?" she would ask, pulling her top pigtail. "For real?"

And sometimes when she was pouring those cornflakes into the four cups and stretching the powdered milk with more water than the welfare lady ever intended, she didn't believe herself. This morning when she had tied a dish towel around Wicker's neck and sat down to spoon-feed him his cornflakes, Meetrie made a regular nuisance of herself waiting for his leftover cereal, asking every five seconds if he had finished eating.

Every day this week she had come walking into Mrs. Nelson's house exactly on time, and every day Mrs. Nelson came into the kitchen to see if she possibly could come a little earlier. She put the eggs into the caddies and picked up the butter to carry to the table. She had left her own house in a mess as usual. Yesterday was so rainy the doors stayed shut all day and the odor of urine from the children's room invaded the whole house. But she was not at home now. She was working in another house. Nudging the swinging door with her elbow, she pushed her way into the dining room.

As Libby washed the breakfast dishes, the kitchen seemed to become uncomfortably hot. Mrs. Nelson cleared the table and brought the last dishes to the sink.

"Did you take Wicker back to the doctor?"

She took the cups from Mrs. Nelson. "When I took him

the first time the doctor said it was hay fever and he'd probably outgrow it." It seemed to Libby that if Mrs. Nelson were so concerned about Wicker she would suggest bringing all the children to play in her backyard during the day. That way Libby could keep an eye on them herself. Libby let the dishwater drain and rinsed her hands and face in cold water to cool off.

If Mrs. Dickens didn't soon move Calvin from the laundry basket on her porch the sun would be shining right into his face. Every morning when she put him and the clean diapers into the basket, she found herself wishing her mother were well enough to look after the baby. Although, with that last sickness coming back off and on she didn't feel right saddling her mother with her own problems.

She had asked Mrs. Dickens if she could leave Calvin inside the house, but according to Mrs. Dickens, six-thirty was too early to be fooling with a baby. "Besides," she'd said, "everybody around here's got too many babies to have to steal one off my front porch."

In the middle of the day, right when Libby was glazing the ham, Mrs. Nelson insisted on having a hot lunch. What upset her most about the woman was the way she could come up with more work when Libby was busiest. Mrs. Nelson was good for thinking up foolishness, especially if it meant working overtime. Usually, Libby didn't mind staying late without notice. Except once. She stopped puncturing the ham with cloves to count back. It must have been two Christmases ago, and she wished she had that three dollars now.

She saved for months to buy Hal a new fishing rod and had managed to put one in layaway. Then, on the last day she could make a payment before the store put the rod back into stock, Mrs. Nelson made her stay late to help with the church baking sale. All the while she was icing those simple Santa Claus faces she was watching the clock hands pass the store's closing hours. Then, when she was ready to go home, Mrs. Nelson gave her a small bag full of broken pieces and cookies that were too brown to sell.

She put the ham into the oven and opened a can of tomato soup for Mrs. Nelson's lunch. At home, about now, Meetrie was scavenging around the neighbors' fruit trees for apples. Since Libby never knew what fruit would be there for the picking, she always left out cold boiled potatoes for the children to eat. Sometimes there was enough food to make a sandwich for them to share.

During the afternoon when Mrs. Nelson was safely away taking minutes of the bridge club meeting in the living room, Libby pulled out a bundle of rough-dried clothes from a shelf in the pantry. Once a week, usually when Mrs. Nelson was spending the morning away from home, she did her wash and some of her mother's clothes in the electric machine.

Hers was such a paltry weekly wash. She smoothed the iron over a long piece of embroidered ribbon—Meetrie's favorite possession. Here and there the colored threads were becoming unwoven, but Meetrie would rather wear that ribbon than anything in the world. Hal had brought it home for her to wear to Sunday school and there had been enough left over to make a bracelet for Meetrie's slender arm. Now the folded ribbon that she tucked into a blouse pocket looked as if it might disintegrate into shreds.

At five o'clock, Libby folded up the ironing board, tucked the clothes behind the cake boxes on the bottom shelf, and began counting out plates for the cold buffet. She was soaping a heavy mixing bowl in which she'd made potato salad when she heard a noise in the backyard. Noises that time of evening never disturbed her. She imagined one of the neighborhood dogs was loose, although Mrs. Nelson swore up and down she would get rid of the next animal that dug up her chrysanthemum bed.

She had begun rinsing the silver when she thought she heard footsteps approaching the house. For no reason at all, she felt chilled; but then the footsteps stopped and she knew she was being silly. This time of year she had seen lots of people wandering through the neighborhood looking for odd jobs or something to eat. Besides, the kitchen had become too steamy and warm to do anything but settle into the quiet routine of cleaning.

When Mrs. Nelson came through the swinging door carrying the last of the dessert plates, she involuntarily jumped.

"Why, Libby, what on earth is wrong with you? You jumped like a scared rabbit cat."

"Nothing, ma'am. I guess I'm tired, from this heat." With the inside of her arm she wiped the perspiration from her forehead.

"That husband of yours should get himself home," Mrs. Nelson said, intently watching her face and sliding the dishes into the sink.

"Goodness girl," she popped her fingers again into the dishwater, "this water is ice cold." Then, as if she had not interrupted herself, she turned toward Libby. "With him home you wouldn't have to do both your work and his."

Libby nodded her head the way she always did, mumbled something that sounded like "yes, ma'am," and busied herself arranging the kitchen curtains until she was certain Mrs. Nelson had left the room.

She stored the silver in the chest, put away the company china, and went to see if Mrs. Nelson had anything else for her to do. The door to the downstairs bedroom was closed and, since Mr. Nelson usually ate Thursday dinner in town, she was finished for the day.

She returned to the kitchen and picked up two waxed-paper packages she had stuck behind the serving bowls in the cabinet. She dropped them into a paper bag and cautiously opened the refrigerator door. She counted the leftover salads, decided against taking any, and saw how much sliced ham was left. After slipping four large slices into her bag she checked the front and side doors to make sure Mrs. Nelson was shut in, and left by the back door.

Outside, she hardly could tell that the season had changed from summer to fall. The air was still and humid, hanging over the trees, preventing the green leaves from changing to red and yellow. The sleeveless blouse she wore felt surprisingly light after the heavy starched uniform she had worn all day. As she walked across the green lawn and toward the toolshed that bordered the summer vegetable garden, she could hear the quiet humming of the crickets.

Libby saw that the door was open, which was strange. The Nelsons had never locked the shed but kept the door closed to keep out the dogs. She was on her way to shut the door when she saw him standing by the wooden building.

"Hal?" Her lips silently formed the word. Still, she was not certain and her feet kept moving toward the wooden shed.

"Hal," she called softly, her voice was inaudible. She was almost upon him now, and from the way he reached into his pocket for a match she could tell he had been watching her all along. She wondered for a minute what she would say; she had imagined him coming home but not at a crazy time like this. Yet, she felt strangely sure of herself, certain that she was in no danger of making a fool of herself by crying. She kept walking toward him, and even this far away she could see the high cheekbones that marked all of their children as belonging to him.

"Hello Libby," he said, blocking the path in front of her and reaching for her. She knew he was kissing her and she was standing still kissing him back, but the whole moment seemed so unreal. All the while he held her she was wondering how he thought he could just come back as if he'd never left her before.

Finally she pulled away and his arms dropped to his sides; she watched his hands slip into his pants pockets.

"I didn't think you were never coming back," she said, still facing him and smelling the cheap aftershave lotion he always used, since before he started shaving.

"Where you been?" She looked past him at the hedge on the side of the yard, wondering why she should notice how he smelled. "After that last card I didn't have no way of knowing which way you were heading. And here you are coming back like there's not no reason for me to say I don't want you back."

The words came out in a rush, matching the tears that were falling on her cheeks. Hal stood quietly with the same solid unconcerned expression that always made her angry when she was upset. His arm reached out to her, but she pushed him away.

"Who do you think you are anyway?" she demanded, swallowing the sobs. "Who do you think you are going away for as long as you please?"

She was shouting now, and to her ears her voice seemed apart from the rest of her. Suddenly, she was pummeling his shoulders with her fists, and before she realized what she had done she felt the side of her cheek smarting from the pressure of his hand.

"Oh," she whispered, staring at him.

"Calm yourself down, girl," his voice was gruff, "you give me a chance to explain, you hear?" He took hold of her hand as if to keep her from striking him.

"I've been working, girl. I needed to get away. You think I'd write you those cards if I wasn't planning on coming back?"

She stared at him, her eyes following the green diagonal pattern in his shirt, on down to the cotton twill pants that were so new they still had a crease down the front.

"I just had to get away for a while. Seems like those children were making me crazy, always running around, not ever being still. Now don't you go saying I don't love you or those kids." He stopped talking and looked straight at her. "If I didn't I wouldn't be coming back here."

"The least you could have done was to tell me where you were." Her voice began to falter. "Wicker and Hamlet don't even ask about you no more. They ain't seen you in so long they forgot about you."

She was talking so fast her words seemed to pile up on each other. "People in town were all the time asking when you were coming back and I didn't have anything to tell them."

Hal stood quietly listening to her, he didn't even say anything when she stopped to catch her breath. "I got me a job. We were getting along without you." Suddenly she couldn't say anything else. There wasn't any sense in lying. Lots of times she wished Hal was at home to help her decide things about the children. This morning, like every other morning for the past month, she had to drag Wicker from under the kitchen table. He was all the time crawling under something, yelling his head off, and she didn't know what to do about him.

"How'd you know where I was?"

"I asked around," he answered. "One of the boys in the drug store said he thought you worked full-time out here."

She swallowed quickly, thinking that he couldn't even let her be the first person to know he was home.

"Well, I had to find you," he said, as if understanding her thoughts. "I stopped by the house but Meetrie wouldn't talk to me and wouldn't let the others even get close. Took the candy I brought them though. Don't you ever get them anything sweet to eat?"

"Reckon they knew who you were?" She waited for him to understand the meaning of her words. "What you doing buying candy, anyway? They can't wear candy on their feet."

Hal ignored her. "I got them some other things outside. They didn't seem to have too many toys to play with."

"How'd you get out here?" He looked too freshly pressed to have walked from town on the dusty road.

"I got me a car," he said, pointing across a field. "Parked it over there near the path." He was grinning like he expected her to be pleased.

"A car." Her voice dull. "A car?" Libby stood unbelieving. They wouldn't have any use for it, except to go to town on weekends. They didn't have money to be buying gas. Besides, all their friends and even the church were right in their neighborhood.

"It's not a new one, but it's all paid for. I got it to get me home. I even made enough money to get brand-new seat covers," Hal said proudly. "Bet you thought we wouldn't never have a car."

She nodded her head dully.

"Heh, honey, remember before we were married we talked about getting one of those little Fords. You know, with the two seats in front, one like we were going to get to drive up north." His voice sounded wistful, and he waited to see if she remembered. Seeing no bit of recognition in her eyes, he kept talking.

"I could have gotten me one of those dirt cheap, but at the last minute I sort of changed my mind."

She stood as if in a spell, listening to his voice, and wondering how he could be so excited over a car. He didn't even act like he had just slapped her.

"Come on," he grabbed her hand, "let's go look. I got it painted blue just like you always wanted."

Libby felt tears washing her eyes. Blue was her favorite color, yet she couldn't for the life of her understand him. Here they were needing to get the house fixed up so the chimney didn't smoke when the cold came. She still hadn't paid the doctor his money from the last time Calvin was in the hospital, and he decided to bring home a car.

She turned toward him. "Now that you're here, you going to sell it?"

He looked in the direction where the car was parked and again at her.

"No," he said, not meeting her eyes, "I'm going to keep it. Bet Meetrie would like riding in a car, and the little fellows too." Suddenly, he smiled. "It's got brand new pipes, the man up north put them on special for me. Libby, you should hear this baby when I take off."

He kept on talking about the car, forcing her to listen.

She couldn't even understand why he was so excited about exhaust pipes. Where they lived there weren't that many other people who could listen out for Hal's car.

She remained quiet as he finished smoking and dropped the cigarette butt on the ground, crushing the tiny red light with the heel of his shoe. He still held her by the hand, almost pulling her along as they began walking across the field.

"What you going to do for a job?" she asked, hurrying to keep up with him. She always forgot how tall he was until she had to try and walk beside him. He had a certain rhythm to his walk and she listened to their footsteps hitting the brittle grass.

"Still too fast for you?" He smiled down at her, matching his long strides with her fast, short steps.

"Oh, I'll get my old job back," he said, his brown eyes were smiling. "Webber'll be glad to get me back after fooling with those slow niggers."

Libby knew he was right. Every time she went to the drug store Mr. Webber made a special point of asking when she was expecting Hal home.

Hal was talking, but not particularly to her. "Haven't seen this old town in so long, just about forgotten what everything looks like." His eyes came to rest on the brown bag she still clutched in her hand.

"What's that?"

"Leftovers for the children," she answered, "I don't like for them to go to bed without anything in their stomachs."

"Mrs. Nelson give it to you?"

"No. I guess she knows I take what's left. Where're you planning to get money to buy gas? The Esso man won't give you no credit unless you been working steady around here."

He ignored her, his voice insistent. "She know you took this food?"

"Mrs. Nelson never gives away anything unless it's spoiled."

He did not say another word until they reached the car, and she was too tired to talk. Her whole body felt drained. She only wanted to see the car up close, touch it and see it at the same time, to end the moment she was dreading, and hope she didn't start crying.

As she stood looking at the old Ford, she felt her tongue almost stick to her throat. She walked to the front of the car and the headlights seemed to make a face at her. In the dusky twilight she could see the fresh paint, and the chromium parts were shining. Even seeing it parked there, just a few steps away, she still could not believe he had brought home a car when they needed everything else.

Then Hal was standing quietly beside her, his arms around her shoulder, pressing her close to him.

"Get in," he said, opening the door. He pressed the button to lock in and strode around to the driver's side. She watched while he pushed in the key, seeing past the dusty tint of the front windows, past the flat countryside.

She looked out at the window-darkened cotton fields and at the scrawny trees in the distance. The trees were stuck to the edge of the fields as if the men who cleared the ground had been too lazy to finish their work. She looked at the road she had walked this morning, seeing how it seemed to blend into the sameness of the surrounding land.

The starting motor interrupted her thoughts and then Hal was talking.

"I said did you want to stop by your mama's before we go home?"

She did not answer. He seemed to have a knack for making her do things she never planned on doing, but if she wanted him she had to want the car. There wasn't any sense in even thinking about fixing up the house. Now all their extra money would go for gas. But at least he had come back to her, and somehow nothing else was very important. She settled back into the seat, her eyes drawn to the profile of his head—the hair closely cut, his eyes so intent on the road that if she had not known better, she would have expected traffic miraculously to appear.

"No," she said, putting the paper bag on the seat between them, "the children are going to want you to play with them before they go to bed. We might as well pick up the baby and go home."

"NO BROWN SUGAR IN ANYBODY'S MILK"

Essie T-e-e-e. Essie T. Where is that girl? Essie T., hurry up and come in here and fasten the back of this dress. Honestly girl, are you always so slow?

A big clumsy-looking girl pushed herself across the room. She walked as if she were afraid that putting one foot down on the floor too hard would make the boards crack.

"I'm coming, ma'am."

"Well, hurry up, you move like dead leaves are falling off of you."

"Yes ma'am." She reached down near the older woman's belt and began pulling the zipper tab, watching the blue flowered cloth slowly come together and cover the whole of the woman's back. She joined the top snap.

"Well, don't just stand there. Go, get my coat. And don't forget chicken soup for Margaret and oatmeal for Doris. And tell Doris she may not have brown sugar in both her oatmeal and her milk. Absolutely not. Are you listening to me?" The woman put the lipstick down and walked to the edge of the room. "Essie T., are you in there?" Really, she was about to reach her breaking point with this girl. "Essie?"

"Yes ma'am," the voice reached her from the depths of the living room closet.

Mrs. Conrad Pierson Gordon III adjusted her hat in the mirror. Essie T. didn't like this hat, and Mrs. Gordon had to agree those Greta Garbo clothes didn't do a thing for her. But, as she told Conrad, in a proud duty-weary tone of voice, her position demanded that she keep up with the latest styles. She looked at her watch. Five of. Where was that girl with her coat? She was just about to call when Essie T. came out of the living room with the coat clenched tightly under her arms. Silently, she handed it to her mistress.

"Essie T.," Mrs. Gordon was disgusted, "what did I tell you last time? You help with my coat. Well, don't just stand there." The girl took the coat and held up one sleeve at a time until the woman was finally wrapped into the coat. She turned to Essie T. with a slight hint of approval showing in her face. "You're improving," she said, walking towards the door, "and by all means don't forget. No brown sugar in anybody's milk. Dr. Jones wouldn't approve." The door slammed and Essie T. began to think of the day's work.

She liked these mornings when Mrs. Gordon wasn't at home. She could do everything that she had to do whenever she pleased. Somehow she sensed that Mrs. Gordon thought she was stupid, and she was more comfortable being all by herself. First she would feed the dog. She put her two fingers in her mouth and let out the kind of soft shrill whistle her brother Chuck taught her. Carter, a magenta poodle with a rhinestone collar circling his neck, wandered into the living room and began to thump his tail rhythmically on the carpet, leaning beside Essie T. Poor little dog. Essie T. pulled the vacuum cleaner out of the closet and plugged in the cord. She began to stroke Carter's fur with the smallest vacuum cleaner brush. The dog, happy to have anyone pay him some attention, rolled around on the floor barking with the whiny sound of the cleaner's motor. She pushed up his fur with the brush and a few stray white hairs appeared. Poor pink dog. Mrs. Gordon was supposed to model in the charity fashion show Friday night. She had carried Carter all the way to Winston-Salem to have him dyed the color of her new spring coat. Essie T. had been in the kitchen when Mrs. Gordon returned from the pet beauty shop.

"Now Essie T.," she said, "don't you think Carter and I will look absolutely stunning together?" Carter slinked over to the icebox and let out what sounded like a moan. Essie T. wasn't too sure she knew what stunning meant, but she nodded and said yes ma'am and went right on ironing.

No, she wouldn't feed Carter now. He would probably like her better if he could have the oatmeal left over from the little girls' lunch. Ma never would've let a dog in her house but Carter and the two little girls liked to eat together. Margaret told Essie T. that her daddy had gotten really mad at Carter one time. He'd sneaked up and bitten their Aunt Grace on the leg. She had to go to the hospital and get a shot. And you could still see where the stitches had been on her ankle. Essie T. was looking forward to the Fourth of July, when Aunt Grace was coming and she could see those stitches. One of her brothers, the oldest one probably, had gotten into a fight one night and been cut real bad. Ma said the doctor took fourteen stitches on his head. But Essie T. never got to see the holes the stitches made. Somehow or other the head had become infected and her brother died. Finally, she'd get to see some stitches.

Essie T.'s hand shook as she measured the oatmeal into an aluminum cooking pan. She didn't mean to ever think of her brother again because thinking about him always made her remember Ma. She never exactly loved Ma, but she had gotten used to her and she was really sorry when she died. She'd come home from church one Sunday and noticed that the shades were all pulled down. Ma didn't go to church very often. Always said she figured when she needed saving, she'd save herself real quick. Poor Ma. Essie T. tried to make her go hear the new preacher that Sunday. But no, Ma was tired and wanted to sleep.

So, after church when Ma was still asleep, she stood out front and talked to the boys who came out of Charlie's Grill. She didn't stay as long as she usually did. She waited around until somebody bought her a soda, and she drank it real fast and went back across the street.

She went in through the front door and left it open, because being in the dark was kind of scary. She was going into the kitchen for a glass of water to get the sweet taste out of her mouth when she stumbled over a blob in front of the icebox. She gave it a kick and watched it roll over. It was Ma, laying there. Essie T. flew out of the house and across the street for Mrs. Graham, who promptly called a doctor.

"More than likely a heart attack," he said. "Don't be upset, some people survive them, some don't. Just keep your mother in a nice cool place until we call Joe." They carried Ma to bed and Essie T. sat in the rocking chair near the bed. Nobody was there but her and Ma. Every now and then she reached out to hold Ma's hand and make it warm again, but it was still cold. She couldn't figure out where those brothers were. One of them was supposed to have called Mr. Joseph. She left Ma sometimes to get something to eat. They were running out of food. So she took a dollar from the old alligator purse on the dresser and bought a quart of banana ice cream and ate it all by herself. A day and a half later, Mr. Joseph finally came. They put Ma in a nice blue casket and the services were at the funeral home. It was all very nice, and she could still see herself crying . . . She took a box of raisins and dropped a handful into the oatmeal. It was too bad about Ma. The oatmeal was growing into big cloudy bubbles which she burst with the spoon. The oatmeal was cooked and she took the pan off to cool. When the little girls came home from school, she'd heat it up again.

She walked from the kitchen to the bedroom and back again with big long strides. She remembered the first day she'd come to work here. The house looked so large compared to the apartment she lived in. She kept getting all turned around until finally Mrs. Gordon had just decided to take her on a tour like they did in magazines. Now that she'd been here three months she knew exactly where everything was. Ah, there it was. She stopped directly in front of the big red clock right above the stove. The little hand was on eleven, the big hand was on seven. That meant the little girls would be home from school in just a little while. She could hardly wait. Margaret and Doris. She said the names aloud and then again as if they were words in a very secret song. She learned who the little girls were the first day she'd worked here. Doris was the fat one. She always drank the last of Margaret's chocolate milk. Well, she'd fix that. She dragged a stool from across the room and propped it against the cabinet. She climbed up and opened the cabinet above the stove. Yes, there it was right where she'd put it when she first came in—a Big 10 chocolate bar. The man in the store said it had four whole almonds in it. Quickly she looked around, stuck the candy in an ice tea glass, and closed the cabinet door. Margaret liked candy bars. She'd be so happy she might give Essie T. a bite.

She wondered what the little girls would bring her home from school. She was glad Mrs. Gordon didn't have a baby she had to take care of. All you did was change diapers and fix bottles all day. All of her brothers and sisters were older than she but she knew what a baby was like. She'd had a baby once, when she was in ninth grade. Ma made her give it away and she didn't even have anything to keep after missing school all that time. She didn't ever get to go back to school. Ma said it wasn't any use in her going back so she found her a job.

Essie T. climbed down from the red stool and shuffled out the door to the living room. The vacuum cleaner was in the middle of the floor as she had left it. She sent Carter into another room, and switched on the machine. She just loved this living room. The carpet was so thick that whenever she was cleaning this part of the house, she walked around barefoot. She fitted a big brush on the hose while the vacuum cleaner made a nice humming sound. Slowly she dragged the hose up and down the carpet. After she'd done the room twice, she stopped the cleaner and put on her shoes. She looked around for something else to do. The stuffed pillows on the white sofa needed plumping. She should tidy the sofa before she put that vacuum cleaner in the closet.

Essie T. sat down on the sofa enjoying the feeling of disappearing into the pillows. Finally, she stretched out and propped her feet on the left arm of the white satin covering. She wished she had a bell. Now would be a good time for the maid to bring her that big Coke. Or should she call down to Robert Hall's and ask them to send her that beige coat with the black, dyed rabbit, imitation mink collar they kept talking about over WCOY. In a few seconds she would get up, have the girl put a leash on Carter and go riding in the Buick. But it was so nice lying here now. She did hope that girl remembered to dust off the car seat. White cashmere coats get so dirty so quickly.

The rest of the family would be home soon. It was a good thing she remembered to have that girl fix lunch. She really didn't feel like moving. Honestly, that girl was so loud, she must have dropped all of the pans into the sink. Probably burnt something too. Oh well, a few drops of the green perfume on the dresser would clear the air. Money was no problem. They could buy some more pork chops. She lay there a few minutes more, reluctantly stood, and began adjusting the pillows. She was tucking the satin cover around the edges when she saw the marks on the left end of the sofa. With her fingers she tried to brush out the dirt, not realizing she was merely grinding the grime deeper. She took her apron hem and began swatting the sofa. Still the marks stayed there. What was she going to do? The marks from her shoes on the pretty white cover wouldn't come off. She must have stood there for five minutes looking at the sofa, and brushing away her tears.

Suddenly she knew what she would do. She ran to the closet and got out the old black coat that belonged to Ma. She had buttoned the top button when she heard the little girls at the back door. Oh no, they were home from school. She'd have to hurry and go out the front way. She was tying her scarf, edging toward the front door when she heard Mrs. Gordon's car approach the walk. Quickly she shut the door. The little girls were yelling in the kitchen, "Where is lunch? Why isn't the oatmeal done?" She had to shut them up, shut them up quick. She turned around and ran for the back door. She ran through the hall to the bedroom and back through the hall to the kitchen. The little girls were standing by the stove pointing to the cold lumpy oatmeal. Margaret was crying. They ignored Essie T. but by the time she stumbled to the kitchen door, Mrs. Gordon had come through the living room and spied the shoe marks on the sofa. "Get her," she cried. "Catch that girl who ruined my sofa and make her pay." Essie T. tried to open the back door. It was locked but she pulled and pulled. She could hear voices calling her and she pulled harder. A windowpane fell to the floor and rolled under the table. She had just decided to climb through the paneless window when she felt somebody shaking her hard.

"Essie T., Essie T., what's wrong with you? How come you making all that noise? Wake up girl."

Essie T. fumbled among the blankets burying her head between the layers of cover. Meanwhile the woman with the rough voice walked to the window and jerked the shade cord. The light from the room's single window shone on the dull green walk. The dust particles from the window shade scattered through the room. It was impossible to tell the sex of the child crying in the brown crib. The baby had kicked off the covers and was beating its feet on the crib's barred sides. A rather rusty-looking dog lay out of the confusion in another corner of the room.

"Essie T., get up."

"Huh, what, what you say, Ma?"

"I said get up now. It's not my baby in here making all that noise. Heaven knows, I had too many of my own to have to fool with yours. Get up and change that baby. You haven't done nothing these last two months anyway. Least you can do is stop that child from yelling or let him start after I leave for work."

Slowly the big-boned girl came from under the worn army blanket and up from the bed. She lifted the baby out of his crib and patted his back while she hunted around for a clean diaper. From out of the window, she could see Ma, dressed in a faded black coat, standing at the bus stop. In a few minutes the bus would come to take Ma to work, the baby would be quiet, and she could stand by the window and watch the other kids walking to school.

FROZEN VOICES

Wanna dance, Jenny? Spring and soft rain. 1961. A Hamm's "Land of Sky Blue Waters" sign. O'Hara's, Ann Arbor. They all meet in O'Hara's. Nathan paints nudes and Jenny studies art history and Lloyd lives inside law books and Gabe constructs wild paper buildings for an architect's degree. Come on, Jenny. The dartboard on the wall, three darts in the bullseye. You don't love me enough. And Nathan with roses, but never enough roses. As graceful as a dancer, his touch an oriental brushstroke. Paint and color, dark colors. Sadness in games of pleasure, but such a beautiful man, such a soft, gentle weight between her breasts. Wanna dance, Jenny? A jar of Polish sausages packed in vinegar. Wieners stabbed on a spiked axle that revolves inside a small rotisserie. You don't love me enough. Now crossing over to the bar and sipping from a glass of foaming beer while fighting through red-swirling smoke. A girl in a small cage wrestling with an unseen monster. Couples on the dance floor. Artificial thunder from the glass-eyed god. Jesus and the Spoilers in the background. Electric organ and steel guitar. Come on, Jenny. You don't understand, Gabe. The truth is I'm as free as any man here. More free in fact because they all want me. There isn't one man here who wouldn't jump at the chance to take me home and screw. Wanna dance, Jenny? Jagged chunks of sound. Splashes of laughter. Wanna dance, Jenny? Soft as April rain, smooth as a quiet mountain lake, as mysterious as an ocean, as dangerous as white water in deep rivers, she drops from a white cloud and falls to green, a raindrop on a leaf. You don't love me enough. Dark, bloody drops of beer and wafer chips of flesh, a communion of human love. You don't love me enough.

And then she was dead. Summer and the sun. June, 1964. On a Delta jet bound for Europe. The roar of engines in crescendo. Pleasant terror of the rigid fury. I never said goodbye. Gabe's wife just died in a traffic accident in which his wife's lover escaped untouched, and now Gabe wants to lose himself in distance, but Nathan takes the same plane. And then she was dead. Inside the man-made world. The taste of brutal engines inside the privacy of self. Scotch and the Spanish hostess. Upholstered seats and reading lights. I never said goodbye. And Nathan with too many words. An actor with a hundred faces. An entertainer with a Janus smile. A sportsman preying for women. And then she was dead. Slow motion of nausea, then lift-off the entrance into woman, the enchantment of transitory loss. I never said goodbye. Waiting in the noise that reflects the loss, listening to the loudspeaker voice echoing off the walls, muffled in by closeness. I never said goodbye. The earth a huge balloon now small and smaller until the shock of silence, the alien suspension of the sun. And then she was dead. But the old idea of love made the woman a goddess. The man's life was completely centered around her. He worshipped her purity and he acted like a slave before his master. And then she was dead. The self in search of self, now high above the endless water. Thin wings slicing through fleecy clouds. The death of time and the shadow of the cross on the shimmer of waves. I never said goodbye. At first he's like a pile of wet rags hidden in the corner of a dark attic, and the rags begin to rot. Silence except for the chatter of passengers. The Spanish hostess with the dimples and the scotch. And then she was dead. Now closer to the sun but caught in the suffocation of escape. I never said goodbye.

I can't live like this. Autumn and the smell of earth. September, 1965. First the idea: a mansion with an elm-shaded driveway. Symmetrical lawns and gardens. An old tire swing in the backyard. I refuse to play the fool. Lloyd has been happily married to Jenny for the last three years. Little Stephan is fifteen months old. Gabe comes over to the house almost every night. Nathan sends occasional letters from Spain. I can't live like this. And the blueprint: in a high-class neighborhood, near Detroit. No prefabrication, no cheap materials, but modern, with a garbage disposal. I refuse to play the fool. And Jenny. A beautiful, once crazy girl now housewife, mother, and perfect wife. A good cook. A fine hostess. Her laugh like the sound of money. Her body somewhere between a model and a movie star. The right wife for a corporation lawyer. I refuse to play the fool. And then the building: a seventy-thousand-dollar house in Grosse Pointe, Michigan. Four floors, including cellar. Five bathrooms. A three-car garage. Rooms scooped out of solid stone. I can't live like this. Writing out letters, attending conferences, and filling out briefs, then driving home on the freeway, struggling through congestion but rising, fighting through the noise, alone in the bleaching sun. I refuse to play the fool, Jenny. The sense of wealth and power, prestige and self-respect. The comfort of a solid building, the safety of a stone foundation. I can't live like this. Where did you ever get that idea? You slept with Gabe once, didn't you? Now wait a minute . . . that part of my life is finished, remember? You promised that we'd never talk about that again. I refuse to play the fool. But too much empty space. Too much silence, too many echoes of the past. Then Stephan to fill the house with sound. But the bills and the mortgage. The gardeners for the gigantic lawn. I can't live like this, Jenny. Wrenched out of solid rock by a giant hand, he tumbles into daylight, and then they carry him away. I refuse to play the fool. The exhaustion of appearance tied around his neck, but Jenny here to comfort him, Stephan to play with, Gabe here as a friend. I refuse to play the fool.

There was nothing I could do. Winter. A cold wind. December, 1965. Snow, slush, and ice. An old man on a street corner, the white steam of his breath. I could do nothing. Nathan hears news of them two months later. As soon as possible he leaves Spain and flies back to Detroit. Before he visits the graves, he goes back to Ann Arbor, but O'Hara's has been torn down to make room for a parking lot. There was nothing I could do. The church a warm and private place. Saints that glitter from stained-glass windows. Silence and the sense of holiness. I could do nothing. And Lloyd the private loser. The public victor, the public hero, the public saint. Sympathy for Lloyd, the defender of morality. From the neighbors, from the newspapers, from the pulpits. An old woman on her knees before an altar, but no sound of church bells in the graveyard. I could do nothing. Not believing at first. Suspending the shock and the hollow laughter of regret, but saving the reactions, building up the memories. There was nothing I could do. And the voices like gusts of snow. The wind and the voices and the trees. The stunted evergreens. I could do nothing. And it looks like you lose, Lloyd. I warned you about her. I told you never to marry her, remember? The monuments and small gravestones. The whispers of the dead. The unbroken cover of snow. A bare maple tree, its branches in a pose of supplication. Small icicles on the thin crust of snow. There was nothing I could do. Light as air, as careless as a sudden breeze, he flows through space, alone in air. I could do nothing. But the voices. The strong, cold wind near the graves. And the taste of death. The frozen tears. The steps backward. The wind-chilled voices. I could do nothing.

You don't love me enough. They all meet in O'Hara's. Nathan paints nudes and Jenny studies art history, and Lloyd lives inside law books and Gabe constructs wild paper buildings for an architect's degree. Come on, Jenny. But nervous inside her. Nathan like a child's terror in the nights of sin. Afraid of light, intolerant of yellow sun and open love. Content with damp cellars and stagnant water, blind fish and water snakes. You don't love me enough. Jenny poses for Nathan. Always moving from Nathan to Lloyd. For two months Nathan and Jenny sleep together, and then he picks up another girl, so Jenny cries on Lloyd's shoulder while she waits for Nathan to come back, and whenever Nathan fails to show up, Lloyd walks her home. Wanna dance, Jenny? Precisely, that's exactly what I'm talking about. Each man here in some way controls your actions. You're twisting it around, that's not what I mean, can't you see? I control every man here because of sex. But you don't love me enough. They laugh away her pain, and Jenny sleeps with Lloyd, but Lloyd has to study law. Wanna dance, Jenny? And then she falls to earth and filters down through sand to bedrock. But you don't love me enough. So when she meets Gabe the night Lloyd leaves O'Hara's to study for a law exam, Jenny talks with Gabe all night. Come on, Jenny. The dartboard on the wall, three darts in the bullseye. You don't love me enough. And when Nathan, who's in O'Hara's with another girl, laughs at Jenny, she smiles, and after O'Hara's closes, Gabe staggers home with Jenny; and they talk for a while, climb into bed, make love, and then Gabe falls asleep. Wanna dance, Jenny?

I never said goodbye. Gabe's wife just died in a traffic accident in which his wife's lover escaped untouched, and now Gabe wants to lose himself in distance, but Nathan takes the same plane. And then she was dead. The outside of Nathan a prism of roles affecting friendship and compassion; but the inside of him a block of ice revealing mockery and cynicism, the con man on the make. So they sit together and talk of love and women. Gabe never mentions his wife, so Nathan tells Gabe how a middle-aged woman in Florida took care of him until she died, leaving him almost a quarter million dollars. I never said goodbye. Riding high above the pain, the momentary pleasure of meeting Nathan engulfed by the memory of his wife. Talking, listening to cover the emptiness. And then she was dead. Nathan laughs and tells Gabe about Jenny. She married Lloyd two years ago. They live in a mansion in Grosse Pointe, Michigan. I never said goodbye. That might be so, but the woman has no power. Exactly. By giving woman the exalted position, the man takes away her freedom. By treating her like a goddess, he forces her to act like a goddess . . . but the man is then free to act like a human being. And then she was dead. Nathan visited them last week, and when Lloyd went to the office, Nathan and Jenny made love for old time's sake. And then she was dead. Still the same old Jenny. And then she was dead. But his decomposition builds up incredible pressure, and suddenly the old rags explode into fire, and flames burst through the dark. I never saw her again. Gabe suffocates in pain. Choked into silence, his outrage cries for a release. Inside the man-made world. The taste of brutal engines inside the privacy of self. Scotch and the Spanish hostess. Upholstered tilt-back seats and reading lights. And then she was dead. He starts fighting with Nathan. Six passengers struggle to restrain him. When the plane lands, the police arrest Gabe, but when Nathan hears about Gabe's wife, the charge is dropped. And then she was dead.

I refuse to play the fool. Lloyd has been happily married to Jenny for the last three years. Little Stephan is fifteen months old. Gabe comes over to the house almost every night. Nathan sends an occasional letter from Spain. I can't live like this. But Jenny sometimes weak. Like jelly without him around to give her shape; like a plastic doll without him around to give her guts. I refuse to play the fool. Lloyd suspects nothing until he begins to receive anonymous letters saying that his wife is unfaithful, but Lloyd ignores them. I refuse to play the fool. And loving

Jenny. The soothing quiet of her yielding sense of peace. And laughing away the world at night. Welcoming Gabe at first, remembering O'Hara's, Nathan. I can't live like this. Then the mysterious writer suggests that Stephan is not his child. He shows the letters to Gabe, and Gabe expresses anger, then outrage. The next letter suggests that Gabe is sleeping with his wife. I can't live like this. But you seem to enjoy it when Gabe comes over. But he's an old friend, Lloyd . . . My God, you can't possibly be serious, can you? I refuse to play the fool, Jenny. Lloyd continues to work as if nothing is wrong, but the planted seed begins to grow. Finally he confronts Jenny, and she professes her innocence. Her explanations soothe his jealousy for two days, but the next letter blossoms the plant into flower. I can't live like this. And they push him inside a huge machine that pulverizes rock to dust, and they dump the dust into a huge container. I refuse to play the fool. He returns early from work, parks his car a block away from the house, steals into the back kitchen, walks into the den, takes the loaded pistol out of the desk drawer, walks quietly into the living room, and discovers them on the sofa. And the blueprint: in a high-class neighborhood, near Detroit. No prefabrication, no cheap materials, but modern. I can't live like this. Gabe smiles, Jenny frowns, and knowing that Gabe wrote the letters, Lloyd kills him first. Then he kills Jenny. And then he kills himself. I can't live this way.

I could do nothing. Nathan hears news of them two months later. As soon as possible, he leaves Spain and flies back to Detroit. Before he visits the graves, he goes back to Ann Arbor, but O'Hara's has been torn down to make room for a parking lot. There was nothing I could do. But the private fool, the little child playing king of the hill and losing to a woman. I could do nothing. Then he takes a plane to South Dakota, and for three days he searches for Lloyd's parents. Finally, he discovers that they moved to California. Searching back, remembering old faces, lost seasons, but shivering in the winter, the echoing fragments of time now frozen solid in the earth. I could do nothing. After a week he discovers Lloyd's parents, and finally he meets his son Stephan, but Lloyd's parents distrust him, and he flies back to Detroit. There was nothing I could do. One man was not enough for Jenny. She was a queen bee gathering drones, a spider engulfing flies. That was your wife, Lloyd. I could do nothing. Before he visits the graves, he drives past the house, and he decides to stop and see who lives there now. Jenny opens the door, but then he discovers that the young girl is not Jenny. Apologizing, he backs away. There was nothing I could do. Always there, always changing, always disappearing, reappearing, but Nathan is doomed to air. He buys three wreaths at a florist's shop. Then he goes into a church and kneels before an altar but no prayers can be said. He walks into the graveyard. They rest side by side. I could do nothing. The church a warm and private place. Saints that glitter from stained-glass windows. Silence and the sense of holiness. There was nothing I could do. Carefully, he places a wreath on each headstone. For half an hour he stands before the graves, and then he walks away. Three hours later he flies back to Spain—back to the Spanish hostess with the dimples and the scotch. There was nothing I could do.

You don't love me enough. And Nathan with roses, but never enough roses. As graceful as a dancer, his touch an oriental brushstroke. Paint and color, dark colors. Sadness in games of pleasure, but such a beautiful man, such a soft, gentle weight between her breasts. Wanna dance, Jenny? Pushing back into the exploding noise and the snapping hips, back to the giggling pinball machines, not trying to smile, but trying to glide above confusion. Come on, Jenny. But nervous inside her. Nathan like a child's terror in the nights of sin. Afraid of light, intolerant of yellow sun and open love. Content with damp cellars and stagnant water, blind fish and water snakes. You don't love me enough. But that's because we allow you to control us; but without a man you're nothing, Jenny. You're a puppet, and all these eyes are strings that jerk you back and forth, in and out. Do you want to sleep with me tonight? What's that supposed to mean? That I make the decision, not you. But without me, there wouldn't be any decision to make, so I'm controlling you already. Wanna dance, Jenny? But Lloyd with an open smile and laughter, white teeth and blond hair. Solid, dependable, and energetic. Concrete and glass, steel bridges, an advertising sign. Black and white like a family photograph. Cigars and big cars, money and power and self-respect. Come on, Jenny. Then she rushes under earth, is gathered in a cavern, a deep cave where she rests in dark silence until the river pulls her into daylight. You don't love me enough. But Lloyd the touch of smooth, brittle glass. No tears when he comes inside her; just artificial lights and electronic love. Jackhammer, steam shovel, flat-bottom truck. A noisy machine inside Brooks Brothers suits. Wanna dance, Jenny? A jar of Polish sausages packed in vinegar. Wieners stabbed on a spiked axle that revolves inside a small rotisserie. Wanna dance, Jenny? And Gabe. Not loud or quiet, but both and none. Explosions far away, sparks dying in a black sky. Not the past or the future, but twisted in the present like an accident of flesh. You don't love me enough. For two months Nathan and Jenny sleep together, and then Nathan picks up another girl, so Jenny cries on Lloyd's shoulder while she waits for Nathan to come back, and whenever Nathan fails to show up, Lloyd walks her home. Come on, Jenny. And Gabe a dancing stillness. Inside her a shiver of sunlight breaking through a black shroud. Rainbows. Like snow in summer, a rose in winter. Wanna dance, Jenny?

I never said goodbye. And Nathan with too many words. An actor with a hundred faces, an entertainer with a Janus smile. A sportsman preying for women. And then she was dead. Wanting to soar higher, hoping to leap into the whispering sun, but resting quietly in the words, trying not to move. The outside of him a prism of roles affecting friendship and compassion; but the inside of him a block of ice concealing mockery and cynicism, the con man on the make. So what you're saying is, the master is bound and the slave is free. That's it exactly. That's why I exalt women and treat them like queens while I act like a drone. Let them think they're the center of the universe. That's the only way you can be free. And then she was dead. And Lloyd too good-natured. The hairy, folksy, nonintellectual, crude-joking animal pretending to be human. I never said goodbye. He breaks out of confinement, blazes into light, and then he rages down through the house, gutting everything he touches. And then she was dead. Beneath Lloyd's tough-muscled exterior is a bloodless heart punched full of sentimental holes. Good old stupid Lloyd with his money and power and self-respect. Slow motion of nausea, then lift-off the entrance into woman, the enchantment of transitory loss. I never said goodbye. And Jenny with the long black hair. Cold-blooded, her marriage to Lloyd a flirtation with death. Hungry for power, and Lloyd the stepping stone. And then she was dead. Nathan laughs and tells Gabe about Jenny. Lloyd married her two years ago. They live in a mansion in Grosse Pointe, Michigan. I never saw her again. The outside of her a soft, tender, yielding woman, but inside of her the ocean, the strange monsters of the sea. And then she was dead.

I can't live this way. And Jenny a beautiful, once crazy girl now housewife, mother, and perfect wife. A good cook, a fine hostess. Her laugh like the sound of money. Her body somewhere between a model and a movie star. The right wife for a corporation lawyer. I refuse to play the fool. But then the drifting sense of helplessness, the sense of losing time. And the revealing letters, but laughing at his own suspicions, joking to himself, then hoping that the lie is true. I can't live like this. But Jenny weak sometimes. Like jelly without him around to give her shape; like a plastic doll without him around to give her guts. I refuse to play the fool. When Nathan was here . . . Were you fucking around with him? I'm not going to listen to another word. You better listen, Jenny. I'll be goddammed if I'll let you screw around when I'm not here. I can't live this way. But

Nathan irrelevant, powerless, nothing but a simple lecher, a helpless little parasite trying to suck warm love from cold tits. I refuse to play the fool. And they dump him into a huge vat, and the vat pours him into cleansing fire, and the fire petrifies him into steel. And Nathan the spineless little child. Amusing. Harmless. Sometimes nice to have around. I can't live like this. And the building. A seventy-thousand-dollar house in Grosse Pointe, Michigan. Four floors, including the cellar. Five bathrooms. A three-car garage. Rooms scooped out of solid stone. I refuse to play the fool. But Gabe a lousy fucking prick. No sense of humor, the cool hatred in his eyes. Then the mysterious writer suggests that Stephan is not his child. He shows the letter to Gabe, and Gabe expresses anger, then outrage. I can't live like this. Then the next letter suggests that Paul is sleeping with his wife. I can't live this way. No sense of respect. No pride. Just a bastard hatred underneath his silence. I refuse to play the fool.

But there was nothing I could do. And Lloyd the private loser. The public victor, the public hero, the public saint. Sympathy for Lloyd, the defender of morality. From the neighbors, from the newspapers, from the pulpits. But the exasperating need to resurrect the dead. Not the bleeding of a lonely heart. Not the ending of a morbid fascination. Not the sense of guilt. There was nothing I could do. And Lloyd the private fool, the little child playing king of the hill and losing to a woman. I could do nothing. Jenny had to prove that men needed her, that she didn't need a man; and Gabe had to prove that women needed him, that he didn't need a woman. They succeeded quite well, wouldn't you say so,

Lloyd? I could do nothing. Yet Gabe a different kind of fool. The need for revenge. The desire to crush the kind of life he couldn't have. So ridiculous, his passion for evil. But there was nothing I could do. The heat of the sun, the movement of water, the growing earth—these are the forces that cause him to react, and without them he drifts alone. Motionless. Nothing. I could do nothing. From the ideal to the demonic, Gabe's hatred a strange test of death, as if death were a woman. An old woman on her knees before an altar, but no sound of church bells in the graveyard. There was nothing I could do. But why Jenny? Such a simple woman. Not the power of mind or the energy of spirit, but the power of sex. No mysteries in Jenny. No secrets hidden below the surface. But there was nothing I could do. After a week he discovers Lloyd's parents, and finally he meets his son Stephan; but Lloyd's parents distrust him, so he flies back to Detroit. I could do nothing. And Jenny. Not a housewife or a mother or a mistress; not a wife or a hostess or a whore. A woman. Elemental. Simple. I could do nothing.

Come on, Jenny. Now crossing over to the bar and sipping from a glass of foaming beer while fighting through red-swirling smoke. You don't love me enough. But what would Lloyd say? What the hell do I care. Would you tell him? Of course not, it's none of his business what I do. But if you told him, he'd never look at you again. Wanna dance, Jenny? Now watching couples bowing to the jukebox, now wandering, always moving from Nathan to Lloyd to Gabe. Come on, Jenny. And she goes dancing down to sea. Through mountain gorges, across the jagged rocks, around the deep, smooth bends she slides with liquid grace. You don't love me enough. Pushing back into the exploding noise and the snapping hips, back to the giggling pinball machines, not trying to smile, but trying to glide above confusion. A girl in a small cage wrestling with an unseen monster. Couples on the dance floor. Artificial thunder from the glass-eyed god. Jesus and the Spoilers in the background. Electric organ and steel guitar. Now riding high on screaming stillness, now walking in the silent rain and now running zigzag down the alley and now skipping across the wet street and splashing down the gutter, now dancing up the stairs. Come on, Jenny. And they laughed away her pain, and Jenny slept with Lloyd, but Lloyd had to study law. Come on, Jenny. And bouncing on the bed, soft bed, and holding Gabe and slipping off her clothes, wet clothes, then yawning open like a cloud, still screaming rain, shattering in the fall. You don't love me enough. But Lloyd the touch of smooth, brittle glass. No tears when he comes inside her; just artificial lights and electronic love. Jackhammer, steam shovel, flat-bottom truck. A clumsy machine inside Brooks Brothers suits. You don't love me enough. But sighing into sunshine, raining golden rainbows down wet, slipping skin. Come on, Jenny.

I never saw her again. But waiting in the noise that reflects the loss, listening to the loudspeaker voice echoing off the walls, muffled in by closeness. I never said goodbye. But what happens when the woman puts the man on a pedestal? Ah yes. Then the woman takes away the man's freedom. You see, by worshipping his penis, she forces the man to be faithful, thus allowing herself freedom to be unfaithful. And then she was dead. I never saw her again.

But riding high above the pain, the momentary pleasure of meeting Nathan engulfed by the memory of his wife. Talking, listening to cover the emptiness. And then she was dead. But beyond forgiveness, beyond control, he gulps down air and fills his lungs with flame, and the walls begin to disappear. Wanting to soar higher, hoping to leap into the whispering sun, but resting quietly in the words, trying not to move. The earth a huge balloon now small and smaller until the shock of silence, the alien suspension of the sun. And then she was dead. Forcing himself to listen, smoking a cigarette, moving his legs, wiping away the sweat that seems to be blood, forcing himself to dream, now praying for an end of pain. I never saw her again. Nathan visited them last week, and when Lloyd went to the office, Nathan and Jenny made love for old time's sake. Still the same old Jenny. And then she was dead. Talking and laughing and listening to hide the suffocation, but the memories snapping back like an elastic band, the pain coming back to fill the inside of the plane. The hypnotic churning of the waves. I never said goodbye. And beneath Lloyd's tough-muscled exterior, a bloodless heart punched full of sentimental holes. Good old stupid Lloyd with his money and power and self-respect. I never saw her again. Now hanging just above the desperation, floating just above the terror, sinking now smashing, screaming, cursing, flailing in the fire like a drowning man. I never said goodbye. I never saw her again.

But I can't live like this. Writing letters and attending conferences and filling out briefs, then driving through congestion, but always rising, fighting through the noise, alone in the bleaching sun. I refuse to play the fool. But where did you get these crazy ideas? Listen, Lloyd . . . Gabe bores me to death but I keep inviting him back because he's lonely. He still can't get over his wife's death . . . and Nathan was here for just one day. But I can't live like this. And loving Jenny. The soothing quiet of her yielding sense of peace. And laughing away the world at night. Welcoming Gabe at first, remembering O'Hara's, Nathan. But I refuse to be a fool. They pour him into a mold and leave him to cool and harden. Then the mold is cracked apart, and they pound him into shape, and then they roll him off the production line, a finished product. But I can't live like this. The drifting sense of helplessness, the sense of losing time. And the revealing letters, but laughing at his own suspicions, joking to himself, then hoping that the lie is true. I am not a fool. The sense of wealth and power, prestige and self-respect. The comfort of a solid building. The safety of a stone foundation. Working through the tedium, driving through the doubt, but reaching the deeper fear. Suffering the child, trying to bleed away the truth, but dreaming of revenge. Sinking into earth and crawling among snakes and worms. Lloyd continues to work as if nothing is wrong, but the planted seed begins to grow. Finally he confronts Jenny, and Jenny professes her innocence. Her explanations soothe his jealousy for two days, but the next letter blossoms the plant into flower. I am not a fool. Pretending a love, but echoing the laughter of despair. The trembling lacerations of the self, but the last letter bringing peace. Plotting the discovery, walking into the house, holding the gun, enjoying the silence, watching them, listening. The sudden memory of Nathan, the spineless little child. Amusing. Harmless. Sometimes nice to have around. I will not live this way. And smiling, pulling the trigger again and again, now feeling the weight of iron, the touch of steel, the distant sound now disappearing. I will not be a fool.

But I could do nothing. Not believing at first, suspending the shock and the hollow laughter of regret, but saving the reactions, building up the memories. There was nothing I could do. But I pity your stupidity, Lloyd. You should have known, but Gabe had to write letters and tell you what was going on. Couldn't you see that he wanted to die? And couldn't you see that she wanted to kill him? But I could do nothing. Searching back, remembering old faces, lost seasons, but shivering in the winter, the echoing fragments of time now frozen solid in the earth. And when the earth turns to dust, when the water runs dry, when the sun burns out, he is lost in empty space, just gliding through eternities of air. I could do nothing. But the exasperating need to resurrect the dead. Not the bleeding of a lonely heart, not the ending of a morbid fascination, not the sense of guilt. There was nothing I could do. The voices like gusts of snow. The wind and the voices and the trees. The stunted evergreens. But wanting to affirm the denial, linking their death to men, commemorating time and redeeming memory, the exasperating need to resurrect the dead. But struggling through air, fighting through the mind. I could do nothing. Before he visits the graves, Nathan drives past the house, and he decides to stop and see who lives there now. Jenny opens the door, but then he discovers that the young girl is not Jenny. Apologizing, he backs away. There was nothing I could do. Now disappearing in the labyrinth of reconstructed passion, winding down corridors that spiral upwards, climbing up steps that twist downwards, now emerging inside a graveyard, conversing with a ghost. I could do nothing else. From the ideal to the demonic, Gabe's hatred a strange test of death, as if death were a woman. Kneeling down, lips against snow. Wanting to scream for a return. But now shivering. The freezing voices. There was nothing I could do.

Come on, Jenny. You don't understand, Gabe. The truth is, I'm as free as any man here, more free in fact, because they all want me. There isn't one man here who wouldn't jump at the chance to take me home and screw. You don't love me enough. And she reaches long plains of peace that slowly bring her down, down to the rushing lowlands, pushing her out to sea. Come on, Jenny. Home. But that's what I'm talking about. Each man here in some way controls your actions. You're twisting it around, that's not what I mean, can't you see? I control every man here because of sex. Wanna dance, Jenny? Jagged chunks of sound. Splash of laughter. Wanna dance, Jenny? Come on, Jenny. But that's because we allow you to control us; but without a man you're nothing, Jenny. Nothing. You're a puppet, and all these eyes are strings that jerk you back and forth, in and out. Do you want to sleep with me tonight? What's that supposed to mean? That I make the decision, not you. But without me there wouldn't be any decision to make, so I'm controlling you already. You don't love me enough. So when she meets Gabe the night Lloyd leaves O'Hara's to study for a law exam, Jenny talks with Gabe all night.

Come on, Jenny. But what would Lloyd say? What the hell do I care. Would you tell him? Of course not, it's none of his business what I do. But if you told him, he'd never look at you again. You don't love me enough. And Gabe. Not loud or quiet, but both and none. Explosions far away, sparks dying in a black sky. Not the past or the future, but twisted in the present like an accident of flesh. Wanna dance, Jenny? Come on, Jenny. But you'd like Nathan to know, wouldn't you? Look, it's none of their business, Gabe. But you're still controlled. You can't do anything without a man. Come on, Jenny. And bouncing on the bed, soft bed, and holding Gabe and slipping off her clothes, wet clothes, then yawning open like a cloud, still screaming rain, shattering in the fall. You don't love me enough. You think you're indispensable, don't you? But I'm just a man, Jenny, just a man. Shall we make love, Jenny? Come on, Jenny. Show me how much I need you. Teach me how to be obsessed. Come on, Jenny.

And then she was dead. But the old idea of love made the woman a goddess. The man's life was completely centered around her. He worshipped her purity and he acted like a slave before his master. I never saw her again. And windows melt, metal breaks, stone turns black, and the victims scald in flame. Consuming the air, he refuses to retreat. And then she was dead. That might be true, but the woman had no power. Exactly. By giving woman the exalted position, the man takes away her freedom. By treating her like a goddess, he forces her to act like a goddess . . . but the man is then free to act like a human being. And then she was dead. The self in search of self, now high above the endless water. Thin wings slicing through monster clouds. The death of time and the shadow of the cross on the shimmer of waves. I never said goodbye. So what you're saying is, the master is bound and the slave is free. That's it exactly. That's why I exalt women and treat them like queens while I act like a drone. That's the only way you can be free. Let them think they're the center of the universe. And then she was dead. Gabe suffocates in pain. Choked into silence, his outrage cries for a release. I never saw her again. But what happens when a woman puts a man on a pedestal. Ah yes. Then the woman takes away the man's freedom. By worshipping the man, she forces the man to be faithful, thus allowing herself freedom to be unfaithful. And then she was dead. And Jenny with the long black hair. Cold-blooded, her marriage to Lloyd a flirtation with death. Hungry for power, and Lloyd the stepping stone. She can screw around all she wants to because she's human and the man is God. That's what Jenny learned when she married Lloyd. Talking and laughing and listening to hide the suffocation, but the memories snapping back like an elastic band, the pain coming back to fill the plane. The hypnotic churning of the waves. I never saw her again. She worships Lloyd, but she's free. Last week we slept together, just for the hell of it . . . Is something wrong, Gabe? I never saw her again.

But I can't live like this. Where did you ever get that idea? You slept with Gabe once, didn't you? Now wait a minute . . . that part of my life is finished, remember? You promised that we'd never talk about that again. I will not be a fool. And the motor works, the machine can move, can duplicate itself, can function like a human being until the driver has an accident. But you seem to enjoy it when Gabe comes over. But he's an old friend, Lloyd. My God, you can't be serious, can you? I can't live this way. But too much empty space, too much silence, too many echoes of the past. Then Stephan to fill the house with sound. But the bills and the mortgage, the gardeners for the gigantic lawn. I will not be a fool. When Nathan was here . . . Were you fucking around with him when I wasn't here? I'm not going to listen to another word. You better listen, Jenny. I'll be goddammed if I'll let you screw around when I'm not here. I refuse to be a fool. He returns early from work, parks his car a block away from the house, steals into the back kitchen, walks into the den, takes the loaded revolver out of the desk drawer, walks quietly into the living room, and discovers them on the sofa. But where did you get these crazy ideas? Listen Lloyd, Gabe bores me to death, but I keep inviting him back because he's lonely. He still can't get over his wife's death . . . and Nathan was here for just one day. I refuse to be a fool. And Gabe a lousy fucking prick. No sense of humor, the cool hatred in his eyes. Christ, you must be insane. Do you actually believe that as soon as you go to work, I hop into bed with the nearest man? What the hell do you think I am? I'm your wife, Lloyd, not the local whore. Then what about the letters? I can't live like this. Pretending a love, but echoing the laughter of despair. The trembling lacerations of the self, now sudden peace. Plotting the discovery, walking into the house, holding the gun, enjoying the silence, watching them, listening. What letters? Here, read them. I'm sorry about the questions, but I just had to be sure. Do you actually believe . . . ? Here, give them back. I'll burn them. I'm sorry, honey. Forgive me. I will not be a fool.

But there was nothing I could do. Looks like you lose, Lloyd. I warned you about her. I told you never to marry her, remember? Wanting to burn in fire, wanting to drown in water, wanting to bury himself in earth, he tries to reach down. But I could do nothing. One man was not enough for Jenny. She was a queen bee gathering drones, a spider engulfing flies. That was your wife, Lloyd. The monuments and small gravestones. The whispers of the dead. The unbroken cover of snow. A bare maple tree, its branches in a pose of supplication. Small icicles on the thin crust of snow. Jenny had to prove that men needed her, that she didn't need a man; and Gabe had to prove that women needed him, that he didn't need a woman. They succeeded quite well, wouldn't you say so, Lloyd? I could do nothing. He buys three wreaths at a florist's shop. Then he goes into church and kneels before an altar, but no prayers can be said. He walks into the graveyard. They rest side by side. But I pity your stupidity, Lloyd. You should have known, but Gabe had to write the letters and tell you what was going on. Couldn't you see that he wanted to die? And couldn't you see that she wanted you to kill him? But there was nothing I could do. But why Jenny? Such a simple woman. Not the power of mind or the energy of spirit, but the strength of sex. No mysteries in Jenny. No secrets hidden below the surface. But I could do nothing. Not one damned thing. But I was the guilty one. You should have known that, Lloyd. You married my creation, and my creation destroyed you, but Gabe ruined my creation, so we both lose Lloyd, do you understand? I could do nothing. Now disappearing in the labyrinth of reconstructed passion, winding down corridors that spiral upwards, climbing up steps that lead downwards, now emerging inside a graveyard, conversing with a ghost. There is nothing I can do. So we all lose, right Lloyd? Only Stephan remains. My son. I don't think I'll ever tell him. Does that satisfy you? Is that enough? I can do nothing.

Come on, Jenny, wanna dance? Soft as April rain, smooth as a quiet mountain lake, as mysterious as an ocean, as dangerous as white water in deep rivers, she drops from a white cloud and falls to green, a raindrop on a leaf. Dark, bloody drops of beer and wafer chips of flesh, a communion of human love. Come on, Jenny. And then she falls to earth and filters down through sand to bedrock. When Nathan, who's in O'Hara's with another girl, laughs at Jenny, she smiles; and after O'Hara's closes, Gabe staggers home with Jenny; they talk for a while, climb into bed, make love, and then Gabe falls asleep. Then she rushes underneath the earth, is gathered in a cavern, a deep cave where she rests in dark silence until the river pulls her into daylight. Come on, Jenny. Inside her a shiver of sunlight breaking through a black shroud. Rainbows. Like snow in summer. A rose in winter. And she goes dancing down to sea. Through mountain gorges, across the jagged rocks, around the deep, smooth bends she slides with liquid grace. Sighing in sunshine, raining golden rainbows down wet, slipping skin. And she reaches long plains of peace that slowly pull her down, down to the rushing lowlands, pushing her out to sea. Come on, Jenny. You think you're indispensable, don't you? But I'm just a man, Jenny, just a man. Shall we make love, Jenny? Come on, Jenny. Show me how much I need you. Teach me how to be obsessed. But lost in the billowy pounding of the waves, she drowns in the scorching sun, and she goes back to clouds.

And then she was dead. And he's like a pile of wet rags hidden in a dark corner of the attic, and the rags begin to rot. Silence except for the chatter of passengers. The Spanish hostess with the dimples and the scotch. Now closer to the sun, but caught in the suffocation of escape. And the decomposition builds up incredible pressure, and suddenly the rags explode into fire, and flames burst into the dark. He starts fighting with Nathan. Six passengers struggle to restrain him. When the plane lands, the police arrest him, but when Nathan hears about his wife, the charge against Gabe is dropped. But he breaks out of confinement, blazes into light, and then he rages down through the house, gutting everything he touches. And then she was dead. The outside of her a soft, tender, yielding woman; but inside of her the ocean, the strange monsters of the sea. But now beyond control, beyond forgiveness. He gulps down air and fills his lungs with flame, and the walls begin to disappear. Now hanging just above the desperation, floating just above the terror, sinking, now smashing, screaming, cursing, flailing in the fire like a drowning man. And then she was dead. Windows melt, metal breaks, stones turn black, and the victims scald in flame. Consuming air, he refuses to retreat. I never saw her again. She worships Lloyd, but she's free. Last week we slept together, just for the hell of it . . . Is something wrong? There is not enough water, there is not enough earth. And consuming the air, he devours himself, and he turns into smoke and ashes.

But I refuse to play the fool. Wrenched out of solid rock by a giant hand, he tumbles into daylight, and they carry him away. The exhaustion of appearance tied around his neck, but Jenny here to comfort him, Stephan to play with, Gabe here as a friend. And they push him inside a huge machine that pulverizes rock to dust, and they dump the dust into a large container. Gabe smiles and Jenny frowns, and knowing that Gabe wrote the letters, Lloyd kills him first. Then he kills Jenny. And then he kills himself. They dump him into a huge vat, and the vat pours him into cleansing fire, and the fire petrifies him into steel. I will not be a fool. No sense of respect. No pride. Just bastard hate underneath his silence. They pour him into a mold, and then the mold is cracked apart, and they pound him into shape, and then they roll him off the production line, a finished product. Smiling, now pulling the trigger again and again, now feeling the weight of iron, the touch of steel, the distant noise now disappearing. And the motor works, the machine can move, can duplicate itself, can function like a human being until the driver has an accident. I will not be a fool. What letters? Here, read them. I'm sorry about the questions, but I just had to be sure. Do you actually believe . . . ? Here, give them back, I'll burn them. I'm sorry, honey. Forgive me. I can't live this way. But now standing in the rain, a mangled piece of steel, his strength is sucked away by water, fire, and air, and he crumples into rust.

And I could do nothing. Light as air, as careless as a sudden breeze, he flows through space, alone in air. The strong, cold wind near the graves. The taste of death. The frozen tears. The steps backward. The wind-chilled voices. Always there, always changing, always disappearing, reappearing, but he is always doomed to air. Carefully he places a wreath on each headstone. For half an hour he stands before the graves, and then he walks away. Three hours later he flies back to Spain—back to the Spanish hostess with the dimples and the scotch. But the heat of the sun, the movement of water, the growing earth—these are the forces that cause him to react, and without them he drifts alone. Motionless. There was nothing I could do. A woman. Not a housewife or a mother or a mistress; not a wife or a hostess or a whore. A woman. Elemental. Simple. But when the earth turns to dust, when the water runs dry, when the sun burns out, he is lost in empty space, just gliding through eternities of air, just floating through timeless air. Kneeling down, lips against snow, wanting to scream for a return, but now shivering. The freezing voice. Wind. Wanting to drown in water, wanting to burn in fire, wanting to bury himself in earth, he tries to reach down. But I guess we all lose, right Lloyd? Only Stephan remains. My son. I don't think I'll ever tell him. Does that satisfy you? Is that enough? But there is no way down to death; there is no way up to life; just random gusts of wind, these voices, these echoes through an empty mind.

OUR TRIP TO THE NATURE MUSEUM

Latonya scrambled through the door, knees rusty, pigtails glazed with Royal Crown hair dressing, and probably all of her smelling unclean. Miss Spears watched her hop on the black tiles, straight to the coatroom. Lord help the people at the nature museum—Latonya would be one of thirty-five. What a horrible experience for anyone to face on a Monday morning. Not too many of them would smell today though, most of them took the week's bath sometime over the weekend. After six years of odors, she had confirmed her major hypothesis about these children. The more they smelled, the earlier they came to school.

Latonya's dress was still torn, the seam split a little more each time she wore it. If Miss Spears had a needle and thread she would sew the sleeve before Latonya unraveled at the nature museum. At first when they came with sleeves and belts half on or off she had been afraid to sew the children into their clothes. These people out here were sensitive and if there was anything she didn't want, it was some mother coming to the classroom and cussing her out. You never could tell with these people. One minute they were smiling at her and saying, "You're right ma'am. She should have a bath every day." And then they just might whip out a knife and stick it in her throat.

One thing was for sure, nobody could force her to make night visits. Some man would never grab her and drag her God knows where. Her own people she shouldn't talk about but she preferred to think of herself as separate from them. Going to this school day in and day out was her own special misery. Six years of odors. Nothing seemed to improve, but then things never got worse. She only saw more of what she did not want to see. Each fall she told herself if she could survive the winter, spring would be different.

Even these children had to grow with color, become warm when light was everywhere. April came and in the green outdoors their minds burrowed deeper underground.

"What do you like best about spring, boys and girls?"

As usual there were no answers, the row of faces poised ready to nod "yes ma'am."

"Hey Miss Spears," Latonya had said. "My mama say spring don't mean nothing to her. Only means summer's going to come and we ain't got no air conditioning, just flies." She giggled and ducked her head beneath the desk.

Each spring Miss Spears signed up for a bus and she and the children rode to the nature museum. This afternoon they would return to the room and talk about "Our Trip." Everybody would contribute an idea for the chart on the wall, and everybody would make a construction paper scrapbook to take home to the family. She would see the scrapbooks sometimes, the ragged pages under a table or chair, when she visited the home. Night visits never. In broad daylight people tried to steal her hubcaps. Then when the car doors were locked she had to step over

Latonya or some child like her begging for a nickel to buy a snowball. At night the encounter would not lead to begging, he would take.

Safely across the street she would climb the steps and peer through the patches of cotton stuck on the screen to keep out flies. The door would be open, the screen door latched, and nobody at home but a grandmother or an aunt. The old woman would shuffle to the door and stand stupidly in red sneakers until Miss Spears asked if she could come inside. Within the cluttered room the smell the child carried to school would be intensified.

"Have a seat, Miss Spears."

She sat down, gingerly feeling for the wet spot, wondering if this was the sofa Latonya or her baby sister had wet the night before. The Budweiser calendar looked so strange tacked up on the wall. Instead of the usual "God Bless This Home," or "Jesus Saves," there was a beer can. Her eyes roamed past the armchair and suddenly she felt her stomach well up. Good Lord, why didn't they keep him outdoors. The puppy was drinking from the baby potty near the door. The room wasn't big enough for people, certainly not a dog. The old aunt caught up with her eyes.

"How Latonya doing in school?"

The words slid from her mouth, slow, the tone flat. Miss Spears knew she waited for an answer but her eyes were fixed on the television that almost engulfed the room. In a glass on the mahogany surface a set of teeth floated, covered with murky water. She dared not draw her eyes from the glass—they would travel to the puppy on the other side of the room. And in her nervousness she had to hold her hands to make sure she didn't reach over and begin stuffing cotton back into the sofa pillows.

What could she say about Latonya that she hadn't tried to explain before?

"She's a quick learner and one of the brightest children in class, but I don't think she gets enough sleep. She drops off at rest time and sometimes I have a hard time waking her. Latonya is always telling me what she saw on the late show. Don't you think that's a bit late for her to be staying up?"

"Lord child, I try to make sure she goes to sleep but as soon as I get one down and into his night clothes, another one is up again. See Latonya, she's next to the youngest and she and the baby sleep on the sofa. Where you're sitting at. And Latonya's mama when she comes home she's tired and wants to relax so she tells Latonya to turn her head to the wall and she watches the television. Reckon that's how the child hears all those things."

"Is there any chance you could fix up a cot for Latonya somewhere else?"

The aunt smiled vacantly. "Not enough room nowhere else. The other ones they sleep in there." She pointed backwards, in the distance. "And Latonya's mama and daddy got to have someplace to stay. Won't always be like this honey. Latonya's mama going to send the oldest boy up to New York to stay with my son. That'll make this place a little less tight. Honey I'm sorry I can't offer you nothing to eat, but would you like a little tea. I was just on the way to fixing me some when you knocked."

"No thank you, but you go right ahead." Miss Spears could feel the tea creeping through her bloodstream, contaminating her insides.

"You say Latonya real smart? She must of took after her daddy. She begs him to help her some with her homework but he don't have much time. She does that homework though if nothing else gets done." The woman chuckled, a whispering wheezy sound.

Miss Spears glanced at the teeth, the wires of the television antennae making ears spring up behind the glass. The tumbler had turned into a smiling bunny. The puppy came over and began licking her ankles.

"Shoo, dog." The aunt reached over and pulled it by the neck. "Don't you go bothering Latonya's teacher. This here's Latonya's dog. Said he followed her home but if I know that child she drug him here. Seems we got enough to feed without adding an animal, but Latonya's daddy said she could keep him. You wouldn't want a dog, would you? She might not mind losing him so bad if somebody like you kept him."

Miss Spears looked at the matted fur, the bones woven into the skin. "There's a rule where we live," she said, "no pets. He seems to be a good dog though."

Latonya's aunt looked down disenchanted. "If you like dogs," she said.

They sat quietly for a few minutes looking at the dog stretched out on the cement floor.

"Please tell Latonya's parents that I'm sorry to have missed them but I have a few more runs to make." Miss Spears stood. Some of the cotton stuffing from the sofa rose with her and she felt her blood freeze. If she reached down and wiped it off she would be acknowledging the family's poverty. She couldn't walk to the car wearing a cotton bunny tail. Maybe it would drop off. She would have to think of something to say. Drawings? Collages? What had they done in art yesterday? Oh yes. "Latonya learned her primary colors very quickly. Yesterday she cut out more pictures of purple than any other child in the class." Suddenly she was overtaken by the urge to giggle.

"Here honey," the woman reached out and brushed her backside, "some of this sofa done stuck to you." And that was how she left the apartment, the old woman swatting her behind.

"Hey Miss Spears."

"Good morning Latonya."

"We still going on that trip today?" Latonya's chin rested on the desk; her head looked as if it might roll across the surface and land flat down, like a paperweight. "I saw you yesterday, didn't I Miss Spears? How come you wouldn't give me no nickel for a snowball."

"Now Latonya, if I gave you a nickel I'd have to give one to all the other boys and girls."

"No you wouldn't, I wouldn't say nothing."

"Latonya, Miss Spears has some work to do. You go play in the kitchen area until someone else comes."

"I'll be quiet."

Miss Spears continued writing, conscious of the head resting on her desk. The eyes were peering past her hand, past the bright pink sweater—"Wear colorful clothes," the supervisor had said, "these children need to be surrounded by cheerful things"—the eyes went straight to her heart. Her hand was beginning to shake, but this was ridiculous and she refused to put down the pen.

"Miss Spears?" The child seemed actually amused and the teacher looked up.

"You been drinking Miss Spears? My aunt's hand goes just like that when she's been drinking and she can't pick up nothing. My mama say I got a cloudy brain because my aunt dropped me a whole lot of times. But that's when I was a baby. Miss Spears you shouldn't take a whole lot of drinks."

Miss Spears was peeved. "Latonya, I'm not drunk."

Latonya giggled. Miss Spears had the sudden urge to reach out and twist the head so that the fuzzy pigtails were facing her instead of the eyes.

"Now Latonya, you're disturbing Miss Spears. Go over to the reading corner and see how much you can read by yourself. Maybe you can tell the other boys and girls what you've read."

Latonya had not brought back a signed permission slip to go to the nature museum. At first Miss Spears planned to leave her behind. Every other child had remembered, why should she cater to Latonya. She came home from church slightly relieved and disappointed too. Suspended over these mixed emotions was the thought of saying goodbye to Latonya as the other children lined up to board the school bus. MacArthur hadn't come to church. Not that they had a date, nothing so formal as that but she was used to seeing him. Just somebody to say a few pleasant things, exchange professional ideas. There weren't too many younger people teaching first grade.

He had a really good recipe for play dough. She had meant to thank him this morning but he wasn't at the eleven o'clock service. After church he would stand by the oak tree, rocking back on his heels until she came down the steps. Barely breathing in his tightly buttoned gray suit, he would ask her what she thought of the sermon.

"Reverend Martin . . . a very fine minister . . . one of the finest I've heard . . ." Each week she planned to answer something different. Each Saturday night as she was washing her hair and filing her fingernails, she practiced something bright to say. Sunday morning in broad daylight, the words sounded too thought-out, as if she were lecturing to him. And he was half a head shorter than she, which shouldn't make any difference because it was the soul that counted, but it did.

After half an hour, everyone would have gone home, and she would begin searching in her handbag for the car keys. MacArthur never changed.

"You ought to come to the Young Adult Discussion Club," he would say. "We're going to talk about a really good book. I can lend you my copy."

As usual she would decline, murmuring something about school reports. She couldn't think of him too seriously, he was too short to marry. This Sunday he had not showed up. Probably he was visiting another church, he did sometimes, and it was just as well he had not come today. She found herself thinking too much about MacArthur Gilmore and she couldn't even wear heels with him.

Sunday afternoons she finished up the week's library books. They had to be returned the next day. Not that they were due on Monday but she liked to have them back in the library by then and a fresh supply of books on the back seat of the car. She sat down on her bed to read, but every time she turned a page she caught a glimpse of Latonya's sad eyes as the bus rolled away. The child would never understand why she had to have permission to take a trip.

The family was out on the front steps when she drove up. Latonya recognized the car and was at her side begging for a ride. Another little boy, shorter and thinner if that were possible, followed her into the street. Latonya reached over and kicked him when he walked too close to Miss Spears. "George Thomas, you get away from her, she ain't your teacher." Latonya reached for Miss Spears's hand.

"Latonya, that's not nice, you should be friends with your brother."

"He's not really my brother Miss Spears. My daddy say nobody in our family got red hair but George Thomas. That's how he makes my mama mad."

The little boy seemed oblivious to everything. Impulsively Miss Spears reached for his hand. Latonya looked disappointed. "He ain't in your class Miss Spears." The three of them had reached the sidewalk. "My teacher came to see me." Latonya made the announcement to whomever would listen. She halted on a crack in the sidewalk. "You came to see me, didn't you, Miss Spears?"

"I came to see you and your parents, Latonya."

The child's mother sat on the top step. A girl slightly

bigger than Latonya with bowed legs even when she was sitting, half squatted on the next step. Latonya's mother was dipping two fingers into a big jar of Royal Crown hair dressing and depositing a glob on the child's scalp. The girl clutched a big black comb which she kept reaching out to her mother. Latonya's mother began braiding the hair and looked up at Miss Spears. Her thighs seemed to ooze out of the red shorts.

Her husband sat beside her, fingering the stocking cap he wore to mat his hair flat to the scalp. Miss Spears understood the stocking cap, she just had difficulty imagining men being so concerned about their hair. There was a barbershop near the school that straightened men's hair. When rain came she would see the men standing outside with scarves wrapped around their heads. In sunlight they all wore stocking caps.

"Hello." Her voice was lost in her throat. "I'm Brenda Spears, Latonya's teacher. Latonya's teacher hasn't brought her permission slip . . . I mean Latonya didn't bring a note for the trip to the nature museum. I thought I'd stop by and remind you to sign it. We'd hate to have her miss the trip." She fished in her handbag for the slip of paper.

Mr. Davis leaned over. "We're glad to meet you," he said. He moved closer to his wife as if expecting her to sit on the step beside the two of them. And in her good suit too. She was strangely conscious of his legs draping past the steps to the sidewalk. He was so tall. She did not like the way he looked at her.

"Here's a pen," she said and immediately dropped it. She felt her skirt inch up as she bent to retrieve it. He didn't offer to help, but continued looking down at her. She held the pen in midair wondering to which parent she should offer it and the permission slip.

Mrs. Davis reached up and jerked the paper from her, reading as she reached for the pen. "I already signed this one time," she said. "Latonya, what you done with that paper I signed?"

The child shrugged her shoulder.

"You tell me what you done with it." The mother leaned over and for an instant Miss Spears was afraid Latonya was going to get a big glob of Royal Crown between the eyes.

"It's not that impor . . ." She started to speak but the woman glared, making herself more ferocious, and Miss Spears was quiet.

"I guess I lost it Mama."

"You guess, you should know. You been losing enough things. Go get that strap, I'll teach you to keep up with things." Latonya's eyes had become rounder and deeper; they seemed to overshadow the folds of her cheeks. Miss Spears had to come to the rescue.

"It's not important," she said, braving the woman's cold-weather stare, "we can use this one. A lot of the little people just misplace things. I'm sure Latonya didn't mean to lose it."

Latonya did not answer but scuffed her sneakered toes on the crack in the sidewalk.

"You stop that girl, you wear out your shoes that way." Her mother glared at Latonya and slapped the paper on the step, bending over to sign her name. Her father all this time had not taken his eyes from Miss Spears. She felt herself burning and tried looking around her at the other apartments. She flicked her eyes toward Latonya but she could feel his gaze circle and tie a knot around her neck. Mrs. Davis handed her the signed paper and the pen. She had one final word for Latonya. "Next time don't you lose nothing else, making the lady come all this way out here just so you can go on some half-assed trip."

Miss Spears felt herself shrink.

Latonya was triumphant. "See there Miss Spears, I told you Mama was always saying that."

Friday when the class was finger painting, she had given each child one color. Latonya had balked at the splotch of green on her paper. "I don't want no half-assed green," she said, "I want yellow." Miss Spears had explained to her that little ladies didn't use impolite words. "But my mama does," she answered.

Now her mother took the comb and made another part in Latonya's sister's hair.

"Thank you." Miss Spears involuntarily waved bye-bye.

Mrs. Davis nodded. She wasn't sure, but almost certain Mr. Davis winked.

"Hey Miss Spears." Latonya brought her book and plopped it on the desk before placing her chin on the cover. "Miss Spears my daddy said you were pretty. He made my mama ma-a-d. She got so mad she was gonna put him out of the house but he left anyway." Latonya's eyes were focused directly on her. "Know something Miss Spears, he may come home tonight but my aunt says he might not ever come back. He was awfully mad. My aunt says my mama called him some names something awful. Said she don't know where she got them names from. She ain't never heard names like that before."

Latonya had assumed a different stance, one hand on her hip, the other hand shaking a finger at something invisible in the distance. "My aunt said to me: 'Girl, you get on back there in the bedroom before you get yourself hurt.' Me and George Thomas and James Charles went. My baby sister, she was already asleep. Miss Spears, they were yelling something awful in there. George Thomas was laughing and laughing and then when my daddy hit my mama upside the head and made her fall on the television he started crying until my aunt stuck part of the pillowcase in his mouth. He stopped crying all right. He didn't do nothing else but lay on the floor rolling his eyes around in his head. I wasn't scared though. My daddy don't hit me."

"Latonya?" Miss Spears leaned over the desk. "Don't you think you'd better get off the floor before your nice clean dress gets dirty?" Before she completed her sentence Latonya had bounced up to the desk.

"Miss Spears, when am I gonna learn how to read?"

"You're learning now, Latonya. You know more words than anyone else in the class."

"Good." Latonya's grin was self-possessed. "My daddy said he was going to take me to the bookmobile all by myself soon as I learn to read good. He's not going to take nobody else, just me."

"That's nice Latonya. Please move your finger, you're getting Miss Spears's papers all dirty. These are important papers Miss Spears has to turn in to the office."

"Miss Spears your pen sure does go fast. Can I come watch you write? I promise I won't mess up nothing." Even as she spoke the child had darted around the desk. She eased into the slight space between the desk and the chair, breathing deeply. "Miss Spears you sure do smell good. Your mama make you take lots of baths?" She did not really expect an answer and her eyes dropped to the paper, caught in the rhythmic sweep of pen and hand.

Her eyes fastened to the slightly bent knuckles that left line after line of loops and half-curved letters. Impulsively she reached out, her thin palm resting on the hand that guided the pen.

"Latonya!" The other hand came down with a hard smack on the child's wrist. "Latonya, look what you did." Miss Spears gazed down at the nearly completed form, the smeared ink clotted the lettering.

The child stood paralyzed, her hands rigid across her face, the fingers pressed against her eyes. She stood perfectly still waiting for the blows to fall. Miss Spears put down the pen.

"I'm sorry," she said, putting her arm around the thin shoulders. "Miss Spears didn't mean to hurt you."

Latonya did not move, the blood flowed inside her, but she was frozen.

SPIDERS CRY WITHOUT TEARS

"Here comes Meg now." Sally waved to the woman shaking her umbrella in front of the shop's glass door. Meg passed the refrigerated case of variously colored gladioli and smiled her greeting to the manager.

"Aren't you disgusting!" Sally said, circling Meg with a swoop of her hand. "Here everybody else is soaked to the skin. Do you always have to look so good?" Sally playfully made a face at her. "You know, honey, I just don't feel like the day has started until you come."

"I'm honored." Meg smiled and hung up her raincoat.

"Gee, that's a pretty blouse," Sally said as they walked toward the worktable. "You're lucky you can wear almost anything. My neck would be engulfed by all those ruffles. Say, did you have a good time last night?"

Sally turned to scrutinize her friend's face and seemed relieved when Meg nodded. "He's a good guy, honey. Warren thinks the world of him and you should be thinking of settling down. I know. I know." Sally raised her hand to her eye. "Enough is enough, shut me up quick. Besides, here comes one of your regulars."

Meg turned on her warmest smile. "Good morning, Mrs. Davis. May I help you?"

The day had begun. Two days down and four more to go, days of blending ribbon with flower color, selecting the right container for the occasion, packing the delicate blossoms into the boxes. She really tried to be helpful when the customer asked "What do you think?" Talking to people and helping them make up their minds suited her. Even at church socials she always found herself hostessing the women's teas for foreign missions.

At first she had taken this job just to have something to do. Talking with strange people, day after day, at least kept her from thinking about Harry. Then Jay was in boarding school the whole winter long. All she did was wake up—the second cup of coffee lifting the heavy sleep that bandaged her mind—and think about Harry. Money was a problem but an unimportant one since Harry kept Jay in school. He seemed to think that sending his son to a military academy would turn Jay into a junior Harold.

And there were small sums of money from home—aunts dying here and there leaving her a few dollars to be banked. Primarily she remembered those days as a series of letters to her son. Letters written when she had nothing else to do. I miss you. I will be glad when Thanksgiving comes, or Christmas, or Easter. And there was really nothing else to tell him. Not even news of a dog because they had no pets. How do you tell an eight-year-old that each year fingernails become more brittle and strange men whistle from buses?

Thank God thinking about Harry had lasted for only a year. To be truthful, a little more than a year. Then she had taken hold of herself and marched down to the Women's Shop to fill out an application blank. She had always gotten along well with people. Except, she thought wryly, the ones she married. Her father had been horrified when he received news of her job.

"Come home," he said. "Bring the boy, I don't like the idea of your living there, with no family." He had come to visit once—"Nashville's too big"—and returned home after a week.

The tinkle of the little brass bell hanging over the door heralded the arrival of a customer. He was not the usual kind of customer and that was what disturbed her. There was something about him at first, something she just did not like. Her feelings must have showed as she carefully snipped the dead leaves from a pot of mums. He wanted "something very special"—all right—she would give him so many choices, he'd be nervous before he made up his mind. She opened and closed display cases so rapidly that he barely had a chance to glance at one flower before another was brought to his attention.

All of her actions he took very calmly until finally he spoke. "With a chance to look at one, I might be able to decide."

The words were spoken without emotion, and before she could control herself she blushed. For a moment her dislike was intense; and even now she still could not be certain he was colored. As long as those gray eyes watched her she was uncomfortable. And a lot of them had such straight hair. They were like human chameleons disguised as normal people. Finally he decided on a dozen red roses in an exquisite cut-glass vase.

Each week he appeared on schedule. A bunch of violets, a dish garden, a pot of daisies, a single beribboned dahlia.

Always the gift card was signed simply "Walt"—no last name. He didn't need one. He was a commission—nothing more!

Business was light during the morning. Hour after hour, in between the few shoppers, she watched a transparent stream of rain drip down the awnings that sheltered the shop windows. At ten of twelve Meg tidied the worktable, preparing to leave for lunch, and looked up at him. The navy raincoat was slick with water and glistened as he bent to place his umbrella in a corner near the door. She waited until he walked to her end of the counter.

"Please watch your umbrella," she said. "Somebody might accidentally walk off with it."

"Oh you people don't steal." For a moment she was not certain whether he was serious.

"Do you?" This time the mockery was evident.

"What'll it be today?" she asked icily.

"Oh just let me look around a bit—maybe I'll be inspired." He gestured toward a bespectacled youth. "Go on and wait on the young man." He casually examined several potted plants and moved toward her with a gloxinia as she smiled at her customer from the counter.

"I won't need a card this time." He glanced at his watch. "It's your lunchtime."

"Yes, but I'm not in that big a hurry."

"You usually eat with a group of talking females. Why don't you have lunch with me?"

Almost instinctively she turned to see if anyone was listening.

"I can't go to lunch with you."

"Somebody might see us?"

"No, I can't go—you know that."

He waited until she picked up her purse and then he walked beside her to the door. She could feel the customers staring, but then it could have been her imagination. And he could be a foreigner, some of them were even darker.

"Please have lunch with me, I promise to act just like a kind old friend of your family." And assuming that she would follow, he raised his umbrella. She felt like a fool. In her haste to avoid him she had left her own umbrella behind the counter.

"Come on," he said. "I can at least keep you from getting wet." There was nothing to do but follow him through the glass door. She walked with him to his car, and even as they were driving across town she wondered how she came to be sitting there. He parked behind the grill near the garbage cans, and she had to crawl behind the steering wheel to leave the car. The driveway was pockmarked with mud puddles and inside the walls were blotched with blue paint. The ceiling, patched in places, was whitewashed.

As she walked through the door, the air rushed around them and conversations were silenced quickly until Walt found a table. Then the noise resumed.

"How you doing, Doc?"

"Hello, Doc." The greetings were muffled and once or twice someone started to speak and hesitated, making her feel uncomfortable. Her eyes scanned the room. "REAL SOUL FOOD," the sign over the jukebox was silver glitter sprayed on blue cardboard.

"Well, what will you have?" She looked around for a menu.

"It really doesn't make any difference," he said.

She felt herself tighten. "What do you mean?"

"What I asked you. There's no menu. If they have what you want they'll bring it out. If not, they bring what they think you should have." He laughed, expecting her to join in. As he spoke she watched the waitress plod toward them. She wore no hairnet, but each strand of hair looked frozen into place.

"You want the special?" she asked. "Barbecued chicken and lima beans?"

"Two, and iced tea to drink."

"That'll cost you extra."

"Now, Glendora, as long as I been eating here you know I know that." The mask slipped and her eyes smiled. "Just want to make sure." Carefully she studied Meg. "Your taste improving."

He laughed aloud and pinched her arm. "Get moving girl, the lady and I have to go back to work." She had not noticed until the waitress left that the talking in the room had quieted. Then with each step the waitress made toward the kitchen, the volume was turned up. No one bothered them until they were ready to leave. Then Glendora reappeared with a small paper bag.

"For the dog," she said. "If you still let him eat bones." He took the grease-spotted bag and winked.

"Glendora's like everybody else around here. Sees that simple pup one time and likes him better than me. Hodge Podge and I thank you," he said. Meg could tell from watching the lines deepen around Glendora's face that the dialogue was part of a frequently played game. And although she knew he would never say, secretly Walt was pleased.

He might as well have been a widower he told her, although legally he could not call himself that. She could move around the house and occasionally venture outside, but most of the time Marian was confined to her bed. There were no children. At first they had not wanted any, then it was too late, maybe all for the good. Now neither one of them could have cared for children. He did not have time and the disease that crippled Marian solved the problem for them.

He obviously had thought a great deal before telling Meg even that much and then he was silent, talking about his patients or telling her how quickly their new house was being constructed. At night when she was safe in her own duplex, surrounded by normal neighbors, she would look at her son's picture and wonder, aloud sometimes, what he would think of his mother. Probably nothing, she decided, as long as she never cut his supply of butterscotch cookies.

Involving Jay was silly and as long as his picture was on her dresser Walt would never come to the house. Not that he would want to come anyway, he still met her for lunch, sometimes for dinner. She never before dated a married man, always trying to be certain Jay grew up without scandal. Having to live with a divorced mother was uncomfortable enough for a child.

She and Walt talked—oh about everything, things neither one of them could discuss with anyone else. Theirs was the kind of relationship where neither one of them was in danger of quoting something said by the other. Talking to him, even knowing that today he might enter the shop, she was unaware of the months passing.

When she had not seen him for weeks, not even in the shop, she would tell herself it was a good thing she had not become involved. Besides, there was always someone who wanted to take her out—one of Sally's friends or a friend of someone in her bridge club.

"You know, it's a good thing you're not married," Pattie Grier told her the other night. "You're the only person we know who fits in with everybody."

"I feel like a television commercial," Meg answered, and the whole table laughed. Now, thinking about her bridge partner's words, she was vaguely disturbed.

"You're still young," Sally was always saying. "You really should settle down. Warren and I will send Jim to pick you up at eight." She heard Sally's speech so often she was amused at her friend's seriousness.

On Sunday evenings she could count on being invited to the movies and to Sally's house for supper. The new discovery would always call and suggest another date, and she would go because she enjoyed being with other people. Through the years she lived in Nashville there had been a steady succession of men—there was somebody named Stan something and for a while she dated Warren's cousin, Joe. Sally's latest discovery was Mike, who worked out of town during the week, coming home for the weekend. Since she did like Mike, Meg had a good excuse not to be free when Walt called. She knew that sooner or later she was bound to lose the distance between them, and knowing this she became determined to put Walt out of her mind. Just when she had succeeded concerning herself with Mike, he would come in at noon the next day to buy Marian's flowers and Meg's lunch.

Her life at home and at the shop were completely separated. Jay came home only on vacations and now he went around with his college crowd. Once, teasingly, he told her about one of the neighbors declaring his mother hid away a new boyfriend. For a horrible moment she dared wonder how her neighbors discovered Walt. Then she saw he was smiling and remembered bumping into Wanda Hardy when Warren's Mike escorted her home from a party.

At the Blossom Shop new orders came in weekly and so did Walt unless he called to meet her for dinner. In spite of herself she saved every hope for the weekend when he could put away the prescriptions and leave a nurse to wait on his wife. Sometimes even the weekends did not belong to her, but Mike was always there with the endless supply of tickets. And so she convinced herself that she did not miss Walt when Marian rallied and actually seemed to be improving. Then there was a relapse. At these times she never questioned Walt but was thankful she had him for as often as she did.

This funny relationship—sometimes weeks would pass before she even heard from him. Sometimes too, there would be a note about his wife in the news. Of course not on the society page, but she was active enough to be mentioned in the local news columns. From her bed, Marian still managed to speak up for charity groups, and to serve on community boards, even to have neighborhood meetings at her home.

Whether she would sleep with Walt had not been a
question for Meg. After a while he just assumed that she
would. That first time she had awakened before light began
slipping through the venetian blinds, feeling that some bit
of uneasiness should have come. But in the half-light there
was nothing to disturb her. When the sun had been up for
hours and she had to face herself—comb her hair and brush
her teeth—perhaps she would be ashamed. Maybe for her
grandmother's sake even disgraced. She was probably the
first Kelham to spend the night at a colored motel. And
the thought made her smile. Then there was nothing, no
emotion, only sleep returning. She had become accustomed
to having him beside her.

Gradually as the years passed she gave up the idea of
remarrying, as if she had ever seriously considered another
marriage. Oh, she could have brought Mike around to
proposing—once, playfully, half seriously he had asked if
she would like an engagement ring. But the first go-round
on those godforsaken army posts had been enough, and
now Harry was a part of her life that no longer existed. On
common-sense, practical grounds her life with Walt was
nonexistent. Mike was a good thing to have around. He was
like herself, permanently unattached.

Whether she wanted to or not she found herself comparing
Walt with Harry. She often thought it was too bad she had
not waited around for someone like Mike in the first place.
He would have been the kind of boy her parents liked—never
questioning anything, just accepting and expecting a pleasant, minor-problemed life. He fitted in so neatly with their
way of living. They told her at home she was too headstrong,

especially to be a girl. "Nutmeg," as she was called then, often thought that the discontent felt by generations of Kelham women had built up and culminated in her.

She did not want to spend the rest of her life being a Kelham lady. All the girls in her family marched in the annual Daughters of the Confederacy Parade, smiling at the groups of Negro children who waved them to the cemetery. There was never any question about a new white dress until she was eighteen. Then her mother nearly had heart failure before Meg agreed to take part in the Memorial festivities. Her family did not understand where she got these crazy ideas. And, looking back at a childhood filled with piano lessons and Twinkle, Tweener, and Teener parties in that age order, neither did she.

Her father packed her off to the Episcopalian junior college to make sure she learned some sense. The college was located near an army base and although there was no written rule, everybody understood that Saint Mary's girls did not associate with soldiers. Harry was a soldier then, neat—not good-looking in his uniform.

He seemed to know about everything. He too did not want to live in his hometown with people constantly gluing their eyes down his throat, expecting things of him he was never certain he wanted. Late one Thursday when everybody was leaving campus to begin an early weekend, her dorm roommate showered her with rice behind their locked door. She signed out for home and in November of her freshman year, she and Harry were married.

The excitement wore off too soon, but since she was an only child, her parents could not disown their baby. Her father even offered to help Harry find a job in the real estate business, but Harry was a soldier by profession. Her parents sent them money, enough to buy things for the baby and clothes for herself. She was never exceedingly happy or unhappy, although during the first year she supposed she thought in terms of contentment.

Harry's desertion when Jay was eight was not really a surprise. She went home, enrolled Jay in school, and helped her father in the office until the school year ended. Then, looking around her house, at the relatives lined up on the mantel and the living ones lined up in towns throughout the state, she was determined not ever to be stuck in South Carolina. So, packing all of their belongings—nothing was much of a keepsake—she and the child came to Nashville.

"One daughter and only one grandchild." Her mother felt cheated having reared only one child. Now Meg had betrayed her by limiting her number of grandchildren. Meg went home only occasionally, usually to attend funerals. First her mother and a favorite uncle brought her back to Sumpter in the same year. Then another uncle, and a cousin who cheerfully steeped her tea with whiskey, and finally her own father. Although the aunts urged her to come home again, she rented the house and returned to Nashville. And to Walt.

Somehow, even consciously being careful, the years made her careless. Thinking in terms of "Walt and I" was natural. One afternoon, just before closing, Sally asked if he were Portuguese.

"I mean how on earth did a Portuguese get this far south. Listen Meg, I don't mean to get mixed up in your business but everybody is talking. They say he looks like he's trying, well you know, to pass."

She had become quiet waiting for Meg to deny the accusation. "I told everybody they were just being silly, that he was only your customer. And even if he did look White you wouldn't be mixed up with colored people. Besides, I told them you were going with one of Warren's friends."

The pencil shook as Meg tried to set it down without Sally guessing the frequency of her trembling. "I usually take care of myself," she answered.

Sally looked hurt. "All right, I didn't mean anything. I should've kept quiet, but you know Mr. Morgan wouldn't like what you're doing behind his back." She quickly turned around. "Oh honey, I wouldn't say nothing to him about your private life for anything in the world, but some of these people just might. I didn't want to say anything," her voice was pleading, "but the other girls wanted me to tell you they knew."

"Well, you tell them we both know." She was amazed at herself even daring to answer Sally. She did not understand from where the bravery came. She liked the other girls and thought they were friends of hers. They seemed genuinely happy for her when she was chosen assistant manager. But Sally never would have spoken unless she was really worried. And with her honest do-good nature, Sally was better off uninvolved in controversy. So, with the same quiet approach with which she once sought Sally's friendship, she now widened the distance between them.

Meg was not aware of the slights at first. Everything seemed to happen at once; only later did she realize that the incidents had been building. At lunch, sitting at the Woolworth's counter she and the girls talked about the usual things. At Thanksgiving they did not ask for her contribution to the shop's needy family. She just happened to see one of the girls collecting money and gave her the dollar bill.

The Thanksgiving basket she did not even think about. What really bothered her was being ignored when the group planned a party for Christmas weekend. She would not have known about the party if Sally had not mentioned Warren's buying a new suit for the occasion.

"But honey, I thought you knew all the details. The committee's been planning for weeks. Emily called everybody personally to make certain they got the time down pat." Then she stopped. "That ass, she purposely didn't call you. We wondered why Mike didn't act as if you had invited him." Sally was quiet again.

"Never mind," Meg turned away, "I couldn't go anyway."

For some reason they did not try to take away her job. She was not certain whether the other girls lacked nerve to complain to Mr. Morgan. But he did not act as if anything strange was occurring. After thinking of all of her coworkers, she rather thought the management did not know.

A long time passed since Sally had invited her out. Meg sat at the kitchen table, manicuring her nails. Sally was still friendly at the shop but they no longer spoke of personal matters. She could never keep anything from Warren, and he definitely would not approve of Walt. One of Warren's major quests in life was to find restaurants that Negroes had not yet integrated. Then when his stronghold was invaded, he went in search of another one. She and Sally used to laugh at Warren's great stalk. Now that she was contaminated, Warren probably had Sally strike her name from the list of people to be invited places.

Then, as if Sally had heard, the telephone rang with an invitation to Sunday supper.

"Jay is home for the holidays and leaving Sunday."

"Oh honey, pack him off in the afternoon."

She explained that she wanted to spend the last day with him because he was visiting his roommate for spring break and would not return home until June. Besides, she had told Mike she could not go to a movie that evening because of Jay. "What about a rain check?"

Her voice was much brighter than it should have been. Sally was silent for a second.

"Sure thing, honey."

Immediately after Jay's plane slipped off the ground, she rushed home to wait for Walt's call. The telephone rang once when Jay phoned to assure her of his safe arrival. She still did not regret refusing Sally's invitation—even after several months when she realized there was never another one.

Mike kept calling though. She could not decide whether he never saw Sally or Warren, or if he was just curious about her. He never asked about her life during the week, but then she did not question him closely at all. The last time she was out with him he asked why she was not wearing lipstick. With a shock Meg realized she was absorbing so much of Walt. He disliked lipstick, teasing her so much about wearing the protective coloration—that finally she acquiesced, returning to bare lips. In trying to please him she was turning into a little girl, incapable of rebelling.

She talked to Walt on Friday. He was in a hurry, speaking quickly, and in her mind's eye she could see him doing something else, probably completing a form while he talked to her. She would not see him until later, next week, because Marian again was ill.

Tuesday during her lunch hour she and Sally were sitting in Woolworth's coffee shop reading the newspaper before the waitress brought their soup. Just by accident her eyes skimmed the obituary column. She must have let out a soft cry because Sally put down the comics.

"What is it honey?"

"Nothing," Meg answered, burrowing behind the paper, trying to keep her hands from trembling while she read. ". . . SURVIVORS include her husband, Dr. Walter Carter of the home; a sister, Mrs. Bernadine Cleveland of New Orleans . . ." Five minutes must have passed before she realized the waitress had come and left. The peculiar thing was that if anyone had asked she could not have said how she felt.

There was nothing to be happy about; they would always have to be careful. The way her friends acted at the shop only meant they would have to be more cautious in the future. Oh, she supposed for a minute the possibility of marriage was a conscious thought. But she was not completely crazy or so much in love that she would subject herself to the solitude his marriage would impose. Putting the paper under the counter, she carefully lifted the spoon and watched the soup shake in her hand.

Every time the phone rang she jumped, and when he did call, he assumed that she knew. Just like that, as if she pored over the obituary columns waiting for news of his wife's death. She never would ask why he had delayed calling. That would be admitting something and at the time she admitted "nothing to no one," not even to herself. Walt saw her once in June and that was to tell her he had decided to take a vacation.

"A long one." His eyes looked tired. "Marian's sister is going to get the house in order and I could do with an airing out."

They were sitting in the same grill, at the table under the largest patch on the ceiling. The waitress had taken the order on her grimy pad and they sat waiting for Glendora to bring their plates. Now when she followed Walt through the door, the men tipped their hats and the waitress acted as if she was not an eyesore, or a museum piece from another world.

"I've got to straighten out things and now's as good a time as any."

She was sitting by the window and as he spoke, her eyes circled first the room, then the scene planted outside the window. The boards of the house next door were gray where the paint had peeled, exposing the colorless wood. Next door was a beauty parlor and they were close enough to hear the whirring of the electric fan in the window.

"Why don't you come to Atlantic City for the weekend? You could fly down on Friday and be back by Sunday night."

For a moment she was covered with excitement, actually going somewhere, a place where neither of them had to care what anybody thought. Even that was impossible. A lot of Jay's classmates worked in the resort area during the summer. He had just graduated from the university in May; she would not take the risk of encountering his friends, and shaming him. He was still too young not to care what people thought.

"Well?" He leaned over toward her. "What do you say? No? Don't you want to come?"

"Of course, but I can't. I just cannot go." She hoped he was not angry. He did not mention the trip again and when he stopped the car a few yards from where her car was parked, she jumped out before he could say goodbye. Both of them would be much better off if the night were a permanent goodbye.

He did not write from Atlantic City, not even a postcard. They never exchanged letters, yet every afternoon, hoping perhaps—she was never certain—she quickly shuffled the mail. There was nothing, just the bills and letters from Jay, who had a government job in Baltimore.

Saturday she came home thankful for the promise of a day of rest. She had told Mike she could not possibly have dinner with him. He had sounded hurt but she knew him well enough to know that he would call again. He was funny about her, telling her that no other woman he dated would dare be so unpredictable. "I'm just partial to pretty women," he said, kissing her good night. Not that she was hard to decipher—one minute particle of Southern womanhood gone to hell. She would like to see his face if he knew about Walt. Warren probably had told him something, but Mike thought she was incapable of lying. He would call again, next weekend, curly hair slicked down, asking what she wanted to do that evening. She would go out with him, having nothing constructive to do, except not to think about Walt, to keep him out of her mind.

Meg recognized the car when she pulled into the driveway. Then she was slamming the door and running around the back of the house. He had never come here before and he would not have come now unless he wanted to say something final. She slowed her steps until she again was in control and there were his long legs straddled on the porch, his coat unbuttoned, his clothes looking positively thrown on him. A delivery man once, the girl who had stayed with Jay when he had chicken pox and she could not take leave from work—these were the only colored people who had set foot in her house. And now him. Immediately she was ashamed; even after these six years, she thought of him in terms of color.

She had to think a long time before she agreed to marry him. Then she realized there was nothing to think about. She had succumbed so long ago, the time did not matter. Jay came home one weekend for part of a weeklong vacation. She tried to act like a normal mother, asking if he was getting enough rest and eating his green vegetables. But since he had finished school, she really no longer controlled his actions. She waited until Sunday for him to get settled, then announced that she had thought of marriage.

"To who?" he asked, his head stuck in the refrigerator.

"Dr. Carter. Walter Davidson Carter to be exact."

"A rich and wealthy surgeon. Hah! Mama, you're coming up in the world."

He chuckled and came over to kiss her on the cheek. "I'm glad Mama. Is he from around here?"

She watched him drink the Coke, counted to five, and said that the doctor was a Negro. He put down the bottle and stared.

"Mama, if you want to play games, come up with something else."

She did not move and seeing her stand so still, he knew. "Mama, why?"

"He's a good person, Jay." Good indeed, she reminded herself of a soap opera heroine. "We have been together so long . . ." She stopped abruptly. No, not even that sounded right to say aloud. The words belonged to her own ears.

"Mama, you know I have nothing against them. They went to school with us but they didn't bother anybody. My God, Mama you're going to be one of them." As if that thought was too horrible to utter aloud, Jay turned and left the kitchen.

Jay did not come home that night. Neither did he come home the next day. On Tuesday afternoon when she had almost given up talking with him again, he came to pick up his luggage.

"I'm sorry for you," he said. "I only hope he's too old to have children." And then her ears stopped listening. In his eyes there was pity for her and unless she did not know him well after twenty-two years, pity for himself.

In February she resigned; in February she was married again—a simple transition. There was no need to move anything, none of her furniture would fit into his house. And so she had under the bed in the guest room, in a locked suitcase, Jay's baby pictures, a few letters she had saved to remember something good about Harry, and a pair of shoes. They were the same shoes she had worn every other day for four months when she first met Walt. She supposed she should have pitched them out, or had the heels slimmed, but she preferred having them shut away. Knowing that they were there was important, knowing something in this house belonged to her.

For a long while she did not hear from Jay. Then a letter came, full of formal phrases. She could not expect to see him at home. Anytime she wanted to come upstate to visit she was welcome, alone. The letters came regularly, twice a month. On those days when the mailman brought the letters or even when the wrinkled blue envelope was overdue she found herself in the guest room, pulling the suitcase from under the bed.

She avoided looking at the box beside her simple piece of luggage. The same elegant lettering engraved on the cardboard box was etched on the label of her stole.

"Happy birthday, baby. You'll look good in this."

The box was conspicuous on the sofa when she came home from driving. She did not even have time to comb her hair before he, warm and antiseptic, was bending over her and the package. Funny she had never noticed he had such a distinct smell, like his office. Her fingers untied the knot and the cord, dividing into quarters the words "Dillon Furriers," fell to the floor. She picked up the stole and, rubbing the fur against the nap, did not know what to say.

"I'm glad you like it." He did not ask but assumed that she was pleased. Not until after supper when they were sitting in front of the television watching some medical drama that absorbed him did she remember.

He had talked once of having picked out a stole for his wife. The furrier held it in reserve as a spring surprise for Marian. With warm weather she would go outdoors again. That spring had passed. Now another autumn was almost ending and Marian's stole had come home from the furriers. She looked at Hodge Podge stretched across Walt's knees, making a rug of blond ringlets on his pants leg. The tears went down her throat and to the cushion inside. He could have picked out another kind of fur—at least a different style in which to wrap his wife.

During the Thanksgiving holidays at the one dance Walt decided to attend, Helen and Pete Harbison greeted them in front of the hatcheck counter. Helen had been one of Marian's childhood friends.

"Marvelous," Helen said, covering her with a glance while the men checked their wraps. "Marian would have loved it."

"Loved what?" Peter asked. "Who would have loved what?"

"Let's go inside," Helen answered, "you two come along."

Since Thanksgiving the stole had remained underneath the bed.

For the length of time she stayed, Meg might as well have not gone to college. All of her neighbors were graduates. She knew nothing about sororities except to comment on the college girls who occasionally came to the shop, but after a while there was nothing else to say about them. And the stiff little brunches and bridge meetings in her honor to show Walt they accepted his wife. She always felt the party began after she left.

Some of the women were friendly. They always told her how nice she looked. They asked her to join the medical auxiliary, and included her in plans for neighborhood barbecues; but at the end of these get-togethers, she received no individual invitations. Always she was invited only with the group and she had to wait for them to make the first gesture. Of course she called them for lunch and to play bridge, but again they came and left in a group. After a few months she stopped entertaining altogether.

So seldom did the doorbell ring that she found herself nervous when answering the door. Yesterday she was almost speechless when she saw Debbie Gabriel standing on the other side of the screen. Debbie, who had been Marian's college roommate, did not seem to notice the strain. Hodge Podge yelped so furiously with happiness at seeing her that both of them were embarrassed.

"He remembers," she murmured, half apologetically.

"I wish he'd be half as affectionate toward me." Meg meant the half-serious words as a joke.

"No, he's Marian's dog." Debbie picked up Hodge Podge before she cut short her words.

Even when Walt was home the dog ignored her—maybe she should say especially when Walt was home. Hodge Podge had been a gift to Marian from Walt, but Marian was not able to feed the puppy or take him for walks and in a few weeks the dog belonged to Walt.

Debbie and she talked about the Christmas holidays and a new fruit cake recipe she planned to try. Meg had learned

259

to cook as a child and ordinarily she would have enjoyed exchanging recipes. But both of them were trying to leave Marian's name out of the conversation and after several embarrassing silences, Debbie left, explaining that she had to pick up her son from band practice. Debbie was the only woman who had come to visit without her husband.

Walt's house was like a mural on a funeral home calendar. She could always mark the days, blot out each number, and then rip the month away, making visible the next allotment of time. No matter how many days passed she still woke up in the morning, washed the breakfast dishes, and if it was the maid's day to clean, made herself busy in her own room or car. In either space the windows were always open and she did not know whether she was letting something in or trying to keep inside something she could not describe.

After Debbie left, she sat in the living room trying to decide when she finally had adjusted to the routine of this house. She had adjusted quietly, exactly as she had to every other phase of her life. There was a sun deck over her head, and French provincial in the bedroom. Lots of women would envy her in this position, and as she walked through the house, straightening the books, finding odd jobs ignored by the maid, she admitted to herself that she was past caring.

Tomorrow morning at eight o'clock she would get up in time to make coffee for Walt and herself. Since he had to watch his weight, breakfast was always the same—a boiled egg and orange juice. At least his simple breakfast gave her a chance to dress, to take her time in smoothing liquid make-up over each tiny imperfection of her complexion.

One of those weekday mornings when she had come out of a heavy sleep and sat down at the kitchen table, her face merely licked with a damp washcloth, she saw what had not occurred to her. She looked down at her hands, even nail polish did not camouflage the wrinkles and she was shocked not having before seen her age. A natural process, of course, but to discover that now she was completely dependent on Walt. She no longer had a choice of going or staying. Since she had become a part of this world she could never completely return to what she had left. Who else would want her? She tried to think, to come up with an honest answer, and at the end of her thoughts there was only an abrupt "no one."

Walt could have someone else. Someone to him as she had been during Marian's illness. Only she was not incurably ill. He owned her exactly as he did the house, the cars, and those poor people who thought their hearts would collapse if her husband retreated from medicine.

Just then Walt strode through the door, bringing the morning paper. Hodge Podge, scuttling along behind him, stopped to sniff at her before hopping into a chair. Instead of moving the dog, Walt sat at the other end of the table. Although he smiled as he cheerfully said good morning, she saw herself as he saw her, aging, even under make-up. Since then she had busied herself not thinking, filling her mind with whatever she saw, or heard, or read. And read and read.

Tomorrow morning she would awaken at seven-thirty and by eight she would be dressed—not exactly as she was today, because tomorrow was not a shopping day. One of the ground rules of her routine was that no two consecutive days would be devoted to shopping. She had been downtown all morning, making a few purchases, but spending a great deal of time looking, waiting until lunchtime.

Out of habit she found herself standing in front of Woolworth's revolving door. She entered the dime store and walked past the hair-care counter and notions to the snack bar. Lord, there had been so many lunch counters in her life. She probably could turn into a Woolworth's counter if she tried hard enough. Putting her packages under the counter, she looked at herself in the mirror. Her brown eyes reflected absolutely nothing.

The waitress was slow, but no matter, there was no place to go but home. Soup here or soup at home made no difference. In her kitchen the people she talked to usually were characters from the Literary Guild book selection. Here at least the people moved, swiveling themselves on stacked-pancake stools to face the countertop.

"You'd think those people would be satisfied by now."

The words slurring together came from her right, the woman's face appeared from behind the newspaper. "All those demonstrations, really they've run things into the ground."

Meg looked past the woman to the article on the front page and read the dateline from some small Georgia town, one she had not before heard of.

"I don't know," she said, trying hard to be polite.

"Well, it seems to me," and the woman tugged at the scarf covering her hair, "seems they'd be satisfied and try to use what they got now."

"I don't know," she said again and turned to watch the waitress bring her soup.

She did not know—and by now she should know what to think. Even a year before her opinion would have been no problem; she did not have to think at all. Now she found herself trying to hurry the day, waiting for the next morning when all of the hours until tomorrow would have passed. Then there would be one less newspaper headline to remember, to associate with her own life.

Tomorrow she would get up and unpack all of the bags and boxes that had been purchased last week and today. Then, up to the attic to bring down the luggage stored away since their last vacation.

This year Walt was taking off for a month to travel in New England. She would need unlimited changes of clothes, and packing would take a great deal of time. If she worked slowly she could stretch the job into two mornings. Lord, she could remember the days when there was not enough time to finish anything. After lunch, by the time she could drive home from downtown, the kennel manager would be expecting Hodge Podge. The dog was growing old and Walt did not feel travel would be healthy for him.

Taking the spaniel to the kennel would be her afternoon excursion. Imagine that. Nothing to do but take a simple dog to a kennel or spend the afternoon watching soup grow colder.

Meg turned to look again at the headline, but the woman with the newspaper was gone. Everybody at her end of the counter had gone. In a few minutes she would be sitting alone. Suddenly Meg could not wait for the waitress to return, and reaching into her purse, she pushed a dollar bill on the counter. Strangely conscious of no longer carefully counting her change, she picked up her packages and slid off the stool.

She did not run through the store; her heart was beating so quickly she only felt as if she ran. She stumbled past the door marked PUSH and walked blindly to a display window. Staring down at the case filled with beach toys she tried to keep her eyelashes from becoming wet. "Dear God. Dear God." Over and over again. She stood by the thick glass not knowing the words could be so deep within her. Finally, the sound of her own voice comforted her, the words pushing her home and toward Hodge Podge's kennel.

They

by Kay Dick

With a new foreword by Carmen Maria Machado

This is Britain: but not as we know it. THEY begin with a dead dog, shadowy footsteps, confiscated books. Soon, the National Gallery is purged; dissidents are captured in military sweeps; violent mobs stalk the countryside destroying artworks – and those who resist. Survivors gather together as cultural refugees, preserving their crafts, creating, loving and remembering. But THEY make it easier to forget . . .

'Creepily prescient . . . Insidiously horrifying.' Margaret Atwood

'A masterpiece of creeping dread.' Emily St. John Mandel

'The signature of an enchantress.' Edna O'Brien

'Delicious and sexy and downright chilling. Read it!' Rumaan Alam

'A masterwork of English pastoral horror: eerie and bewitching.' Claire-Louise Bennett

FABER

EDITIONS

FABER

Maud Martha

by Gwendolyn Brooks

With a new foreword by Margo Jefferson

Maud Martha Brown is a little girl growing up on the South Side of 1940s Chicago, where she dreams: of New York, romance, her future. Soon, she falls in love, decorates her kitchenette, gives birth. But her lighter-skinned husband has dreams too: of the Foxy Cats Club, other women, war. And the 'scraps of baffled hate' – a certain word from a saleswoman; that visit to the cinema; the cruelty of a department store Santa Claus – are always there . . .

'I loved it and want everyone to read this lost literary treasure.' Bernardine Evaristo

'An exquisite portraiture of black womanhood by one of America's most foundational writers.' Claudia Rankine

'Reveals the poetry, power and splendor of an ordinary life.' Tayari Jones

'One of the most spatially poetic novels ever . . . Awesome.' Eileen Myles

'Alive, reaching, and very much of today.' Langston Hughes

EDITIONS

The Glass Pearls

by Emeric Pressburger

With a new foreword by Anthony Quinn

London, June 1965. Karl Braun arrives as a lodger in Pimlico: hatless, with a bow tie, greying hair, slight in build. His new neighbours are intrigued by this German piano tuner; many are fellow émigrés, who assume that he, like them, came to England to flee Hitler. That summer, Braun courts a woman, attends classical concerts, dances the twist. But as the newspapers fill with reports of the hunt for Nazi war criminals, his nightmares worsen . . .

'A tremendous rediscovery . . . A wonderfully compelling noir thriller.' William Boyd

'This extraordinary novel had me hooked from start to finish.' Sarah Waters

'A remarkable novel, as startlingly original as any of Pressburger's films.' Nicola Upson

'Stunning: incredibly good, thought-provoking and tense.' Ian Rankin

FABER

EDITIONS

FABER

The Shutter of Snow

by Emily Holmes Coleman

With a new foreword by Claire-Louise Bennett

Some days, Marthe Gail believes she is God; others, Jesus Christ. Her baby, she thinks, is dead. The red light is shining. There are bars on the window. And the voices keep talking. Time blurs; snow falls. The doctors say it is a breakdown; that this is Gorestown State Hospital. Her husband visits and shows her a lock of her baby's hair, but she doesn't remember, yet . . .

'In this extraordinary novel, Coleman rebelliously shows how women might write if we were free.' Lucy Ellmann

'Haunting and evocative, this is a timeless portrayal of madness.' Catherine Cho

'Startling, luminous and magnetic.' Yiyun Li

'With its deep musicality, Coleman's unique voice was years ahead of its time.' Sinéad Gleeson

EDITIONS

Palace of the Peacock

by Wilson Harris

With a new foreword by Jamaica Kincaid

A crew of men are voyaging up a turbulent river through the rainforests of Guyana, led by a domineering captain. But their expedition is plagued by tragedies and haunted by drowned ghosts. As their journey into the interior – their own hearts of darkness – deepens, it assumes a spiritual dimension, leading them towards a new destination: the Palace of the Peacock . . .

'A magnificent, breathtaking and terrifying novel.' Tsitsi Dangarembga

'The Guyanese William Blake.' Angela Carter

'A masterpiece.' Monique Roffey

'One of the great originals . . . Visionary.' *Guardian*

'Staggering . . . Brilliant and terrifying.' *The Times*

FABER

EDITIONS

Termush

by Sven Holm

With a new foreword by Jeff VanderMeer

Welcome to Termush: a luxury coastal resort like no other. All the wealthy guests are survivors who reserved rooms long before the nuclear disaster – but their problems are only just beginning. The Management begins censoring news; disruptive guests are sedated; generosity towards Strangers ceases as fears of contamination grow. Soon, they must decide what it means to forge a new moral code at the end (or beginning?) of the world . . .

'Like someone from the future screaming to us in the past.' Salena Godden

'A chilling and prescient tale.' Andrew Hunter Murray

'Mesmerising . . . Mischievously surreal and terrifyingly real.' Sandra Newman

'Compulsive, elemental and true.' Kiran Millwood Hargrave

The Mountain Lion

by Jean Stafford

With a new foreword by Hilton Als

Ralph and Molly are inseparable siblings: united against the stupidity of daily routines, their prim mother and prissy older sisters, the world of adult authority. One summer, they are sent from their childhood home in suburban Los Angeles to their uncle's Colorado mountain ranch. But this untamed wilderness soon becomes tainted by dark stirrings of sexual desire – and as the pressures of growing up drive a rift between them, their childhoods hurtle towards a devastating end . . .

'One of the strangest and angriest novels of the twentieth century.' Lauren Groff

'An extraordinary, savage novel.' Olivia Laing

'Breathtakingly original.' Tessa Hadley

'One of the best novels about adolescence in American literature.' *New York Times*

'A brilliant achievement to set beside Carson McCullers's masterwork *The Member of the Wedding*.' Joyce Carol Oates

Hackenfeller's Ape

by Brigid Brophy

With a new foreword by Sarah Hall

In London Zoo, Professor Darrelhyde is singing to the apes again. Outside their cage, he watches the two animals, longing to observe their mating rituals. But Percy, inhibited by confinement and melancholy, is repulsing Edwina's desirous advances. Soon, the Professor's connection increases – so when a scientist arrives on a secret governmental mission to launch Percy into space, he vows to secure his freedom. But when met by society's indifference, he takes matters into his own hands . . .

'So refreshing and interesting.' Hilary Mantel

'Pitch-perfect.' Ali Smith

'By turns mischievous, outrageous and exacting in its artfulfulness – a satire revealing Brophy at her beastly, risky best.' Eley Williams

'There is nobody like her, no one who sees the world quite in her original way.' A. S. Byatt

'If animal welfare, space rockets and baroque-but-on-point novels do it for you, read *Hackenfeller's Ape* . . . Stunning.' Isabel Waidner